Praise for C.F. Lindsey

"*Old Field Pines* is a propulsive work of historical fiction. C.F. Lindsey writes Prohibition-era Stone County, Arkansas with such honesty and intimacy. He knows every nook and cranny of this landscape, as well as the hearts and minds of those who call it home. This engrossing tale of a moonshiner fighting for his family and a sheriff fighting for the soul of a town will keep you in suspense until the very end."

-Caleb Johnson, author of *Treeborne*

"A harrowing story of a war-haunted moonshiner trying to save his family in prohibition-era Arkansas. Brutal as bathtub gin and swollen with heart. Like a 1920s Arkansas *Breaking Bad*."

-Dr. Micah Dean Hicks, author of *Break the Body, Haunt the Bones*

"*Old Field Pines* is a pure delight for the heart and the mind and the senses. Gorgeously narrated, it is a sensitive portrayal of family life—the legacy of loss, the necessity for forgiveness, and, most of all, the sacrifices one makes for love. At the same time, the novel is an exciting, hard-bitten story of admirable lawbreakers and corrupt cops. It all works in flawless harmony in this astonishing debut work. With a single memorable stroke, C. F. Lindsey has established himself not only as one of today's premier southern novelists, but as one of the best storytellers our whole country has to offer."

-John Vanderslice, author of *The Last Days of Oscar Wilde*

OLD FIELD PINES

BY C.F. LINDSEY

APRIL GLOAMING

Edited by Lance Umenhofer

©2021 by C.F. Lindsey
Cover ©2021 by Drew Holden

-First Edition

Publisher's Cataloguing-in-Publication Data

Lindsey, C.F.
  Old field pines / written by C.F. Lindsey
ISBN: 978-1-953932-00-6

1. Fiction - General 2. Fiction - Southern I. Title II. Author

Library of Congress Control Number: 2020948915

For my loving wife.

Thank you for always supporting me in everything I do.
Your love gives me the strength to continue striving to be the best that I can be.

All that I do, I do for you.
I love you.

And to my father.

This dream of writing would not have come to pass if not for your encouragement and support throughout a lifetime of cherished wisdom, guidance, and friendship.

PART ONE

PART ONE

The Stone County Democrat

26 September 1924

Decorated Veteran Faces Criminal Charges

Stone County Sheriff Harroll Dibbs arrested Mountain View local William Henderson late Wednesday, September 24th. Henderson was taken into custody for the possession of illegal bootlegged liquor. Sheriff Dibbs spotted Henderson driving and pursued after noticing erratic maneuvers as Henderson proceeded through Mountain View township.

"Look like he's trying to take up the whole road, way he was driving," Sheriff Dibbs commented on Thursday. "Figured I'd see what all the issue was, so I decided it best to stop him before he hurt himself."

Dibbs stopped the vehicle to discover Henderson intoxicated. What would have been a simple few nights in the tank and a small fine, escalated when Dibbs searched the vehicle.

"Ain't never seen that much shine," Dibbs commented. "Tarp in the back of the pickup covered up a pallet of several full jars. Didn't seem like much recreational drinking was going on. Had no choice but to take him in."

Henderson is being held at the Stone County Sheriff's Department. Investigations of the Henderson homestead are being conducted for further evidence of any liquor operation.

"Really hate making arrests like these," Dibbs commented further. "Especially against a veteran. Folks around here are just trying to make a living best they can, and things like this happen out of desperation. Never much agreed with that prohibition thing myself, but the law's the..."

The Stone County Democrat

30 September 1924

Bootlegging Charges Lead to Possession

Circuit Court Judge Derre H. Coleman ordered the convening of the trial against William Henderson on Monday, September 29th for the charges of production and distribution of illegal liquor. A lack of evidence of a moonshine operation on Henderson's property led to Judge Coleman reducing charges from production to possession with intent to distribute. This saved Henderson from a charge of up to 5 years in a state institution.

"After the evidence was brought forth, it didn't seem like there was any real choice but to drop the production charges," Judge Coleman stated after the trial. "With the lack of a still site, the case against Henderson being the production source went out the window. I feel the jury made the best decision for the situation."

L.W. Copeland, Mayor of Mountain View, County Seat of Stone County, said the trial was a wake-up call for the activity of the town. He addressed the citizens of Mountain View after conclusion of the trial.

"There will be changes," Mayor Copeland said during his address to the township. "I, as your civil servant, will not allow for such reckless lawbreaking to become the norm for this fine city. As mayor of this fine town, I promise to you that there will be swift and just action against those who would see our town become a lawless pit of debauchery due to the influence of illegal substances."

William Henderson was sentenced to 1 year at the Cummins Unit in...

The Stone County Democrat

3 November 1924

Sheriff Dibbs to Run Opposed

Stone County Sheriff Harroll Dibbs to run opposed for the first time since his inaugural term in 1919. Former Sheriff of Searcy County, Michael Baker, has announced his candidacy for Sheriff of Stone County.

In an address to the town, Michael Baker said, "The good people of Stone County have been made to settle for far too long. With the rise of bootlegging, I believe now, more than ever, it is time to bring swift justice to those offenders of this federal law."

Baker continued by calling fault to Sheriff Dibbs' attempts at stopping the rise of illegal liquor sales in Stone County.

"Sheriff Dibbs, while seeming to address the issue of moonshining in Stone County, has continuously let perpetrators walk free without so much as a slap on the wrist. Shouldn't more care be taken for our wonderful citizens, for our children, when enforcing the laws of our country? I know that you all, as good, Christian folk, want to stop this horrible blight from spreading further through this community. I will not allow for such transgressions to go unpunished, like your current Sheriff. If you elect me to the position, I promise that there will be more than just a slap on the wrist for the sale of temptation that endangers lives and the wholesomeness of our community and families."

Mayor Copeland publicly announced his support of Baker's candidacy during the rally. "I promised you change. I feel that Michael Baker, with his reputation of squelching the moonshining industry in Searcy County, is the answer that we have been praying for. I am confident that the citizens of this fine town, and the county at large, will make the right decision when they cast their vote on..."

The Stone County Democrat

23 January 1925

New Sheriff Begins Hunt for Local Bootleggers

CHAPTER I

THE SQUEAL OF THE METAL WHEELS braking on the tracks awakens Willie Henderson from his first good sleep in months. It wasn't his straw bed in his cabin with a fire in the stove and Mabel nestling beside him, but it was quiet, and he was undisturbed when he began to nod off. Sunlight streams in from the train windows. He blinks from its brilliance and rubs at the crust caking shut the corners of his tired, gray eyes. Some of the flakes fall into his mass of a black beard with the beginnings of gray fleckings peeking from below his chin where the hair hides a scar on the lower left jawline. He'd been gifted that while plowing up a plot for his Mama's flower garden with his Daddy and their stubborn mule, Delilah. That back leg coming back to kiss his chin knocked him cold for two days and a night. Damn near killed him. He'd recovered well enough, though. He was big, even then, and it took a lot more than the hoof of some angry farm animal to take him down. Folks had been trying for most of his life.

As he grew from boy to man, the tall, gangly look about his limbs began to pack on muscle from hours behind the plow and the axe, tossing hay bales and other farm tasks to keep the homestead in working order. Sitting now in the train car, he looks almost comical in a you'll-only-laugh-once sort of way. His large frame is hunkered over with the stiffness of the wooden rest behind him. He leans over to allow his thick, hairy arms a perch on the bench in front of him. The knees of his patched trousers rub uncomfortably against the seat in front of him as if the sitting area wasn't quite made for someone his size. He's able to splay his legs out a bit, though, with the sparsity of passengers on the train. He has fifteen rows of benches to the front and back of him all to himself, and he'd been able to sleep lying down with half his torso hanging off the edge of the bench.

Leslie's small station rolls into view as the cart gradually slows to a stop. From here it will be a thirty-some-odd-mile trip to the Stone County seat

OLD FIELD PINES

of Mountain View, Arkansas. Home. Willie can almost see it now: slogging through the mud of Main Street past the service station with young Kebel Hinkle running to and fro to fill up the autos as they pull through. A little ways further on, the Lackey Store standing on the corner with groups of men seated out front smoking cigars while reminiscing about the war and bitching about the rising price of gasoline from eighteen to twenty cents a gallon. Cliff Jennings will be out front listening into the conversation while pretending to sweep the store's porch under the careful watch of Mrs. Jennings behind the counter at the register. The Rosa Drug Store door will be open, wafting the smell of fresh coffee from behind the soda shop counter with grumbling men gathering around smoking cigarettes and waiting on any parcels that might have come in from the post. More toward the town center, the Case Hotel stands with the Lackey House, which cost George Lackey a pretty penny to build, dwarfed only by the colossal stone structure of the courthouse with the county jail a small distance to the east. Willie could pass on the last two if given the opportunity.

Beyond the station, Willie eyes the forested peaks and grassy hillocks that encompass the outskirts of Leslie; the familiar sight of farmland stretches over the plateaus lined with dirt roads leading back into the trees where small homesteads wait with wood smoke coming from the chimneys and the smell of breakfast on the stove. Willie closes his eyes, wishing the fixed windows could be opened so to take a whiff of the cool mountain air. He is tired of being confined to the moving can with its rows of seats empty, save two other travelers he doesn't recognize but knows from the station close to the Cummins Unit. They'd avoided him since he sat down, taking seats toward the back and the front of the train car and leaving him the fifteen or so wooden benches in the middle. His clothes are normal: old overalls and shirt with work boots tattered from use and labor. It must be something they could smell on him that triggered their want to stay as far away as the passenger car would allow. Willie doesn't mind. He likes silence. He hasn't gotten enough of it lately.

The train makes a full stop and the door of the passenger car opens to admit the conductor in his crisp uniform. He slides open the door to the outside of the train and places a wooden step stool on the platform. "Leslie Station!"

he yells into the morning air. Willie wonders at why he would yell this. They can hear him just fine.

The man sitting behind Willie rushes past him in a blur and is off the train and high-stepping toward a woman and child waiting for him by the station entrance. Willie rises, the hair on his head nearly brushing the roof of the car, and makes his way toward the exit. As he nears, the woman sitting close to the front sinks into her chair and busies herself with the activity of counting the buttons on her coat.

"What's the quickest way to get to Mountain View?" Willie asks the conductor, who is craning his neck to eye him from the platform with his hand waiting to help Willie down.

The conductor looks at him questioningly. "Ain't got no kin waitin'?"

"Don't reckon I do."

The conductor twiddles his thin mustache and scratches at the stubble on his cheeks. "Welp, I'd bet the mail truck could give ya a ride thataways. Be a long trip, though." Seeing Willie occupied, the button woman pushes past and jumps out of the door. She stumbles a bit on impact but continues walking toward town. The conductor, surprised, watches her go. "Thanks for riding the Doodlebug!" he calls after her before turning back to Willie.

Willie watches the lady disappear, hocks some phlegm out the door and nods. "All right."

"Don't be forgettin' any belongin's up in storage."

"No need," Willie says with his foot on the wooden step. "Ain't got none." He exits the train car and looks around at the scenery. He takes a deep breath and exhales the cool steam from his lungs through his nostrils, tickling the hair of his mustache. He turns back to the conductor waiting by the car entrance, who spits into a tin can held in his right hand. "Got any baccy?"

The conductor reaches into the pocket of his jacket and pulls out a plug of chewing tobacco from a rolled-up pouch. He rips off a large chunk and gnaws down with his front teeth, throwing Willie the remainder. "Good luck to ya, son." With that, he grabs the stool, steps into the car, and disappears with the sliding door slamming shut behind him.

Willie turns and starts toward town. He takes it slow, though his naturally-long gait eats up the distance from the station to town quickly. Leslie is relatively quiet at this time of morning, as either people haven't started their day, or, in the case of the loggers and farmers of the area, have already long been to work. A few people mill about town square as Willie makes his way to the brick building reading Post Office on the outside in faded, white paint. Some of the residents stare at the bearded stranger. Willie ignores their glances and whispered comments back and forth.

A bell tinkles with the pushing of the door as Willie enters the empty post office. The floor is made of tile scuffed here and there. His boots tap as he walks toward the desk that blocks the lobby from the mailroom with a wall of wooden mail slots from floor to ceiling. A small man pops his bald head from behind an opening in the wall.

"Be right with ya!" he calls to Willie and disappears once more. The sound of clicking feet comes scuttling from the back before the postmaster appears in the doorway. He walks to the counter, barely able to peer over the surface, before hopping on a stool that allows him a clear view of patrons. Sweat drips from his long nose and makes his bald head shine in the false light. He adjusts his glasses and picks up a pen, habitually opening a ledger in front of him on the counter. "What can I do ya for, stranger?"

"Conductor of the Doodlebug said I'd get ya to give me a ride on the mail truck."

The postmaster's wire-frame glasses slip down his nose and he readjusts them, smiling wearily across the counter. He checks the ledger and makes a few nondescript marks. "We can do that. Where ya headin'?"

"Mountain View."

"That'll be a long day fer ya, Mister. Gotta make stops in Alco, Timbo, and cut up t'wards Onia before doublin' back toward Mountain View. Be an all-day ride."

"Be a long walk, too."

The postmaster chuckles and nods nervously. "Yeppers. Reckon it'd be a long way on yer own two legs. I'll getcha set up with Billy Davis here quick. He'll be driving the truck along that route. Can I just get yer name right quick?"

"Henderson. Willie Henderson."

"Right," the man nods and scribbles down the name furiously. "And whereya headin' from?"

"Elsewhere."

The little man looks up from his writing and gives Willie an up-and-down look pityingly. "Now, come along, Mr. Henderson. Just protocol. I's just got to get the information fer the records here. No harm meant."

Willie lifts his mitt of a hand to run it through the pompadour-style hair that used to be his. His hand finds the rough shave job instead from when he'd caught a bad case of lice on the farm. He still forgets about it sometimes, though his hair is prickling back to the surface. "I's was workin' outside Little Rock fixin' railcar track." Willie doesn't like to lie. He'd become good at it, though. It was necessary, much easier most of the time.

"Thank ya, sir. Now, if you'll just wait right 'round here a minute, I'll go and let Billy know you'll be ridin' along."

The postmaster hops from his stool and vanishes behind the counter once more, his tapping feet fading from the room. Willie looks around the cavernous room and out the window of the front door where folks peer in as they pass and quickly look away when they realize that he can see them as well. He sighs and pulls the chewing tobacco from the front pocket of his overalls. He bites off a chunk and rolls it around in his mouth. He closes his eyes at the taste, savoring the tingle that runs through his gums as the juice accumulates. He looks around for a spittoon but can't find one in the tiled room. He eyes a brass umbrella stand by the door. Turning his head toward the counter to make sure the postmaster is still out of sight, he heads over and spits in the opening.

The clicking of small feet sounds behind him as the postmaster clears his throat. He stares at Willie in distaste. "Billy has already left for the day." With that, the man takes his place behind the counter and looks at his ledgers.

"What ya mean, gone?"

He doesn't look up from his scribbling. "Just that. Sorry we couldn't help ya."

"What the hell am I s'posed to do, then?"

The postmaster sighs and looks up. "Guess you'll have to go after 'im. He normally stops off at his Mama's down the road a bit for some coffee 'fore headin' out. You hurry, you can catch him there." He points with his pen to the wall on the left side of the building. "Just go down there past the station and keep on that road till you see his truck." To signal the end of the conversation, he resumes writing furiously in his ledgers.

"Any markers I need ta keep a lookout for?"

"Only place with a truck full a mail thataway."

Willie grunts and turns to the door and opens it. He thinks for a moment and then leans over and spits into the umbrella stand once more before exiting, letting the door hang open behind him.

THE WEASEL OF A POSTMAN was right; the mail truck wasn't hard to find, despite the dense foliage and shrubbery of the area. Willie stumbles upon it parked down a small dirt track off the main road a few miles down from Leslie. The pot-holed driveway has a fine dust along its path that kicks up in clouds with his steps. The property, like most of the country around it, is wooded and overgrown with brush and muscadine vines that seem to choke the light when entering the thickets dotting the hilly country. Fruit from the vines scatters the path with some having been crushed by the truck's tires to leave a blood-like stain in the dirt. The right side of the drive is lined with rotting fence post crudely attached with barbed wire in uneven lines connecting them. A docile cow watches from the other side of the fence, oblivious to the fact that a sneeze would knock the fencing down to let it run free. Its eyes follow Willie as he continues toward the house and lets out a groan for the intrusion.

The sight of the truck halts Willie mid-stride and he moves toward it for a closer look. Even with the green having been changed to a rich blue, the truck, a Model 16 GMC, was of the same model that had carried him across the fields of France. The metal frame of the passenger carriage was gone, a wooden crate container sitting in its place loaded with a few bulging brown bags along with a shovel and various other bits of miscellaneous junk. Small flecks of blue paint barely clinging to a few areas revealed the original paint underneath. Willie runs his hand along the surface for a moment and closes his eyes. He sees the wooded area below, a group of dirty men in a truck staring blankly with cigarettes hanging loosely from cracked, open lips. The stink from the surrounding waste—craters and shattered trees and barbed wire—mixes with blood. A pile of haphazardly-covered bodies litters the floorboard by their boots. A hand hangs limply from the tarp next to Willie's foot.

The faint click of a rifle's cocking action sends Willie reeling back to reality.

"I suggest ya step 'way from that there truck and come out where'n we can see ya."

Willie raises his hands above his head slowly and turns toward the porch. His eyes slowly go up the porch steps covered in vines and weeds to a pair of twiggy legs coming out of the bottom hem of a long nightgown patterned with blue flowers. The woman rocks back and forth on unsteady feet, her arms jiggling with the weight of the rifle that swings side to side and in loops in an unsteady manner. Her gray hair pulled up in curlers, she glares at him with eyes half-blinded from squinting and spits a stream of tobacco juice onto the wooden porch. Some hangs on the rifle butt to fall in spots that stain her gown.

"Ya from the guvment?" she asks, shuffling her feet as a gray tabby cat comes to nuzzle against her. "Ya look like a guvment man."

Willie inspects his ratty overalls, looking for the cause of the confusion. "No'm. Not from the government."

"Just what a guvment man'd say."

Willie steps forward, reaching out his hand to take the rifle. "Why don't ya just lower that there rifle for me?"

The woman squares her shoulders and the rifle narrows its circling to point at Willie's chest. "That'll be close 'nough."

He takes another step. "Come on, now. Give it here."

The shot rings through the woods, hitting the ground a few feet to Willie's left. Rocks and clods of dirt go flying through the air and spray Willie with their shrapnel as he barrels for cover behind the pickup.

"Shit, lady! Ya damn near shot me!"

The sound of the lever action shucking the spent casing and sliding a new bullet into the chamber reaches him behind the hood of the truck. "Think I made myself pretty clear. Now state yer business. Whatcha doin' slinking 'round my land?"

OLD FIELD PINES

Willie takes a few breaths to calm the rapidness of his heartbeat; after palpitating from the excitement, it slams in his chest in a vigorous rage. He presses his hands to his ears to stop the reverberating ring from the shot. "You Ms. Davis?"

"Who's askin'?"

"Mama?" a voice from inside the house calls. The tap of footfalls on squeaky hardwood floors echoes before the slamming of the screen door against the frame makes Willie jump where he crouches behind the tire. "Ya get 'im, Mama?"

"Nah. Missed 'im. He a squirrely bastard."

"Gimme that rifle. I'll go 'round and flush 'im out."

"Hold up," Willie hollers from his hiding spot. "You Billy Davis?"

"How's he know yer name?" asks the whispered voice of the woman. The sound of a hand slapping on flesh and the echoing yelp of surprise reaches Willie from the porch. "What the hell you do?"

"Nuttin', Mama," the man whimpers back. "I ain't done nuttin'. How's it you come by my name, stranger? What's yer business?"

"Postmaster sent me. Said you'd let me hitch a ride far as Mountain View."

Silence answers Willie for a moment. His head swivels from side to side, wondering from which direction the rifle barrel will appear. This is not the way he imagined leaving the world. Not like this, cowering behind a bald truck tire. And this close to home, to boot. After so long.

A deep laugh bellows through the silence, making Willie jump again with the suddenness. "Well, hell. Why din't ya just say so? Come on out from behind there. Ain't no one gonna shoot ya."

The old woman stomps her boot on the boards of the porch. "Whatcha mean ain't nobody gonna shoot? You give me that rifle, boy."

"Shut it, Mama. Go on inside and get this man somethin' ta drink. He needs it." The old lady mumbles curses directed at her son's stupidity as the screen door opens and slams shut. The cat lets out a disappointed meow. "Come on out. I got the rifle set here on the porch. Now's I gonna back 'way from it a bit."

Willie considers running, despite hearing the thunk of the rifle butt on the wood of the porch. That could just be some kind of trick, though. A trick to get him out in the open for a clear shot. The chances are pretty good he could make it into the trees before Billy could fire off a shot. He'd have to move quickly, though, through twenty yards or more of open terrain before reaching the shelter of the wooded area.

Boots thumping around on the porch reach Willie's ears. "s'all right. I'm steppin' 'way from the gun." More exaggerated footsteps follow.

Willie rises, slowly, from his crouched position to peek around the hood of the car. The rifle rests alone against some railing on the porch that leans haphazardly in a slant as if loose, or the person who'd fastened it had been drunk during construction. He stands, ready to spring back at the first sign of danger. A man, wiry of frame and tall of stature, stands a few feet away from the gun with his hands in the air, signaling truce.

"Billy Davis?" Willie asks, looking around for the older woman from before should she come up from behind him with more armaments.

"Yeppers. Who you?"

Willie steps out from behind the vehicle, fully exposed, and raises his hands to mimic Billy's gesture. "Willie Henderson. Just tryin' to get me a ride back home toward Mountain View."

Billy smiles, dropping his hands to his sides and coming down from the porch to meet Willie in the yard. He sticks out his hand for Willie to shake. "Folks 'round here call me Clyde." Willie shakes the offered hand. It's got a firm grip despite the malnourished look of its owner. The lines in Clyde's face show his skull hiding behind a thin layer of skin. His face is shaved clean and his large, hooked nose reaches out almost like one of them tropical birds that Willie had seen in pictures from foreign lands. "I'd be happy ta take ya. How 'bout we get ya some coffee first? Calm down ya nerves a bit from all the 'citement." He slaps Willie's back and uses the hand to steer him toward the porch steps. "Mama!" he yells through the door. "Where's that coffee fer our guest?"

Ms. Davis appears in the door with a steaming mug that shakes dangerously in her ancient hands curled into claws with age and arthritic pressure.

"Ima comin'. Ima comin'. Too damn impatient fer yer own good." She hands the mug over to Willie and sticks a bony finger in her son's face, smooshing his nose down with each thrust. "I can still be makin' ya cut a switch fer me."

Clyde rubs his nose where she'd poked him. "Ouch. Ya just go on back in the house, Mama. We's gotta get goin' if'n I ain't gonna be late with the mail 'gain." Willie just stares at the mug. Clyde smiles and takes the cup in his hand, healthily sipping the hot liquid. He smacks his lips, "Mmm. That's good coffee."

Willie takes the mug back and takes a sip. The burning sensation is unexpected, not from the heat, but from the other contents of the mug besides weak coffee. He coughs wildly as he swallows and doubles over. A hand pounds his back until he's through.

Willie looks up with watering eyes into Clyde's smiling face that waits expectantly for a verdict. "Well, pretty good stuff, ain't it?"

Willie coughs again. It's not. "Yep. That gin in there?"

The smile widens. "Ya know yer likker."

Willie shrugs. "Guess so." He takes another drink, more prepared, to be polite.

"Mama makes it in the tub. It's nice to have some when most're goin' without. We're real thankful. Good if'n ya have warts, too."

Willie coughs once more, trying to keep the rotgut liquor down. "I bet."

Clyde hops off the porch and claps his hands together, stretching his lanky body from side to side. "Welp, best be gettin' to it. I'm sure yer ready to be gettin' home after yer travellin' and all." He turns to the porch with a wave as he climbs into the cab of the truck. "See ya tonight, Mama."

The woman, sitting in a rocker on the front porch, waves off the comment. She smiles at Willie as he climbs into the cab, just as sweet as she can be. "'Twas nice mettin' ya, honey. Ya come on back anytime." The cat jumps into her lap and kneads a spot to lie on her nightgown.

Willie nods his head. She's a crazy old bird, but she seems all right with the gun out of the picture. She spits a stream of tobacco juice as the truck rolls to a start and heads down the road.

"Don't mind her none," Clyde says from the driver's seat. "Mind's been slippin' on her fer a few years now. She pulled that gun on me a few times gettin' home late when she don't recognize me." He laughs, looking over at Willie next to him on the bench seat. "Damn near shot my ear off one night."

Willie grunts politely to let Clyde know he's been heard. Looking back to see the trees covering the porch from view, Willie pours out the contents of his cup and settles in for the ride home.

CHAPTER II

WILLIE GRIPS THE SEAT TIGHTLY with both hands as the truck screeches onto the highway off of County Road 263. Clyde howls in excitement as the tires leave asphalt on the hill outside the small community of Timbo. They come down hard, losing a box of mail in the process, and careen around the sharp curves heading into the valley toward Mountain View.

"How 'bout that? Handles pretty good, don't she?"

Willie nods, gripping tighter as a curve nearly throws him from the open cab into the holler below. He looks down, an inadvisable viewing, to reflect on how many rocks his skull would bust against before he loses consciousness or his life while rolling the twenty feet to the bottom into the trees and briars below. The curves of the road lessen as they continue downward. Soon the trees become scarcer, fading behind them as the road straightens and fields of hay greet them hemmed with barbed wire fencing running along the highway.

"Here," Clyde shuffles in his seat, "take the wheel for me. I gots somethin' fer us." He releases the steering wheel without waiting for Willie, the truck swerving sharply toward the ditch and some fencing beyond.

"Shit," Willie grabs for the wheel, righting them before they jump the ditch and crash into the fields, decorating the vehicle with strings of sharp metal line. Clyde searches under the seat, pressing the gas pedal farther as he digs. On a side road ahead, Willie can make out the lights of a police cruiser waiting. "Clyde, we gotta Sheriff's car ahead."

"Almost got it."

The truck rockets past the cruiser. Willie waits for the impending scrape of gravel followed by the sirens coming after them. No sound comes, however, and Clyde straightens himself, retaking the wheel from Willie's trembling hand. He looks out the door and waves obscenely behind them. He laughs and unscrews the cap from a canteen and drinks deeply.

"Ah," he passes the canteen toward Willie. "That's some good stuff."

Willie decides that he'd have been safer hoofing the distance from Leslie to Mountain View. If he'd cut across country, it wouldn't have taken him as long as he'd thought. The smell of the gin from the canteen almost makes him sick. "You're 'bout mad, ya know that?"

Clyde laughs again, taking back the canteen for another swig. "They ain't gonna stop us. Nobody wants to piss off the postman." He offers the bottle again and Willie takes it this time, imbibing a large drink of the pop-skull liquor to calm his nerves a bit.

He swallows and closes his eyes against the burn. He can already feel the comings of a small headache from drinking bad liquor, but he doesn't much mind. Having gone without for months was tough enough, and you need some liquid courage when taking rides from a madman. "Ya ain't right in the head." Clyde cackles maniacally from his seat in reply, drinking from his canteen once more. The truck continues down the road, passing a sign that prounounces their arrival to Mountain View in two miles.

THE TRUCK SKIDS TO A HALT in front of the brick structure of the Rosa Drug Store. Entering town, people have to jump out of the way of the reck-lessness of the county employee. Unsightly gestures and curses are hurled in their direction before catching sight of Willie's familiarly large form unfold-ing from the truck's cab. Willie exits the vehicle on shaky legs, glad to have made it out of the ordeal with his life intact.

He helps Clyde unload the remainder of the parcels. People walking about and, in the store, folks he's known since childhood avert their gazes and refuse to acknowledge the presence of the bearded and scraggly figure they had once known and had been friendly with. Even John Mitchell, sitting in his usual spot on the porch of Rosa's smoking a hand-rolled cigarette, ignores them as they walk onto the wooden porch and enter the drug store. Franklin Hinkle, behind the counter in his apron, also busies himself with the menial task of sweeping the immaculate floor after instructing them where to place the bundles of mail.

People stare and whisper as they pass Willie waiting by the truck. Clyde climbs in, looking around confusedly at the people walking by. "Ain't never seen these folks so skittish. Normally a pretty friendly bunch. Like they think you's a ghost or something."

Willie nods, "Guess I am kinda. Been gone a good bit."

"Well, welcome home. Ima sure it'll be gettin' back to normal 'fore too long. What's the plan now?"

Willie takes out a plug of chewing tobacco, having purchased a fresh pouch from Franklin's stock. He rips off a chunk with his teeth. "Go home, I s'pose. See my wife and boy."

Clyde takes a drink from his flask resting between his legs. He smiles, leaning across the bench seat and sticking out his hand. Willie shakes it. "Well, I won't keep ya. Gotta be gettin' back myself." He sits back and shifts the truck into first. "You let me know if ya be needin' anything. You know where to find me."

The truck jerks forward, spitting a cloud of dust from the rear tires. Clyde makes to turn around and backs into a post, nearly knocking it from its setting. John Mitchell looks over angrily from the cloud of cigarette smoke surrounding his balding head. He scratches at his white whiskers and spits on the wood of the porch. Willie waves at the strange man behind the wheel as he rights the vehicle and heads back the way they had come, swerving to miss a few pedestrians crossing the street. They yell in outrage and Clyde beeps the horn in a return salutation as he disappears from sight of the town square.

The town sinks into a quiet with his companion gone. People seem to disappear as Willie's eyes scan the familiar sights of the town square. The courthouse steps loom before him with the tall oak tree beside it. The chair resting beneath sits empty. The sound of music playing on a Saturday night, couples dancing to the lively picking of the guitars, and the sawing of the fiddles is only a memory. A ghost of a memory. The lonely feeling that envelops Willie makes it seem as if the past had never happened, that he is lost—a stranger—in a foreign place where neither the people nor the landscape accept his sudden arrival that is disturbing the relative peace of the town. No one knows him. It's no longer the hometown that he had dreamed of returning to while staring at the ceiling from his prison bed during those lonely nights. It doesn't matter, though. Willie will not accept this refusal from this place. He is home. He closes his eyes and breathes in, swishing the tobacco juice against his gums. He opens his eyes, spits, and starts walking away from the courthouse and the stares of the people he'd once called friends.

As he passes the barber shop, two uniformed Deputies approach and cut off his path. Neither of them smiles, despite their familiarity.

"Jack," Willie addresses one to break the silence. "Tommy. How're ya doin', boys?"

"Howdy, Willie," Jacks says. Tommy looks uncomfortably at his feet as if the secret to ending world hunger lies in reach hidden beneath his shoelaces. "You're back, I see."

"Yep. Just pulled into town."

"Welcome home."

Willie smirks and looks around. People look at the gathering from the windows of Rosa's and the barber shop. "Yeah. Feels really welcomin'."

Tommy looks to Jack and clears his throat. "Listen, Willie..." his words catch in his throat.

"We's gonna need ya to come with us," Jack finishes for his partner.

"Why?"

Jack scratches at the back of his neck uncomfortably. There are several pimples threatening to burst on his nose and forehead. "Sheriff wants to see ya."

"Sheriff Dibbs'll have to wait. I'm goin' to see my family." He makes to step around the pair in front of him. They move to block his escape.

"Dibbs ain't the Sheriff no more," Jack says.

"Got a new man down from Searcy County," Tommy chimes in. "Sheriff Michael Baker."

"Here to help the...erm...*shine* problem we got."

"Well isn't he just a peach for such an effort." Willie sidesteps the officers and continues walking. "Tell Sheriff Baker that I wish 'im the best a' luck in his endeavors against the evil liquor."

Jack and Tommy scamper after him, moving into his path once more. They look nervously from each other to Willie. "Tell 'im yerself, Willie," Tommy squeaks. "We gotta take ya to see 'im."

Willie rests his closed fists on his hips. "How 'bout y'all step the hell out my way? I've been gone for too damn long. I ain't gonna have you two piss ants that used to buy up my liquor keep me from seeing my family any longer. What in t'hell happened to you boys?"

Jack gulps down a lump making its way up his throat. He eyes Willie nervously, knowing full well that the big man could snap them both like twigs. "'Pinions changed, Willie. New Sheriff got bootleggers left and right back in Marshall. He's gonna clean up Mountain View and keep the peace."

Tommy nods his consent. "We's all God-fearin' folk here. We's just want to be right by the law."

"You two means to tell me y'all gave up drinkin'? Just like that. On the word of some big-in-his-britches lawman?"

The two young Deputies look uncomfortably away.

Willie looks them up and down. He leans forward and spits a stream in front of their feet. He turns to face the town around him. People look on from open doors and windows all around. "Hypocrites," he whispers through his whiskers. "Y'all's a bunch of damn hypocrites!" he yells, turning back to the Deputies. He wags a finger toward each of them in turn. "You two's some of the worst. Don't go condemning me when I'd be selling to both of you if I hadn't been locked up. 'Sides, I'm done with shining. I served my time, learned myself a damn good lesson. I just want to make whatever honest livin' I can off my land." He starts forward again.

Jack reaches out and grabs hold of Willie's shirtsleeve. Willie stops and faces the young Deputy. "You sure you wanting to do that, son? I'm just tryin' to go home."

Tommy steps to Willie's other side. "That's all fine and good, Willie. But you're gonna come with us to see the Sheriff first."

Willie widens his stance into a fighter's pose, flexing his hands for the possibility of having to throw the two boys out of his path. "That a fact?" If he were to grab hold of Jack's hand, he could toss him into Tommy and make a break for it.

Jack keeps eye contact, pleading silently for the tension to die down. Willie can feel his hand shaking against his arm despite the hard grip on his shirt. "We'll cuff ya if we got to."

Willie considers trying for a clean break despite the threats. He's sure that he could take them both without causing any serious damage to them and make it to the woods before they could recover. He sighs, though, deciding against it, and lets his tense body relax gradually. "All right, boys." He spits into the dirt. "I'll come along with ya." Seeing him safely in custody, the townsfolk, who Willie had laughed, drank, and grown up with, breathe a sigh of relief and continue their daily tasks, grateful for the end of the disturbance in their day. Some continue to cast glances his way as the Deputies turn him toward the Sheriff's office on the other side of the town square behind the courthouse.

"Let's go see this Sheriff Baker."

HE WATCHES FROM THE WINDOW as the two gangly Deputies walk the large, bearded man past the courthouse and toward the entrance of the jail. Townsfolk look on with interest at the scene; this makes the man smile from behind the hand-rolled cigarette hanging unlit between his lips. He turns back to a small mirror hanging from a single nail on the wall of his office. There is a wash basin in front of him with soapy water in it that still steams from being heated. He picks brush and foam and lathers his bristled face, leaving the well-kempt mustache untouched. He shaves, scraping away at the stubble on his cheeks with care. He hears the door of the jailhouse open and the sound of conversation enter. He smiles again and continues his shaving. He'd already shaved once this morning, but he wants to look his best, requires it of himself. Impressions are everything in this line of work, and a shabby shave shows weakness. He wants to exemplify control.

He splashes warm water on his face and wipes the remaining soap away with a white towel next to the basin. He picks up a pair of scissors and grooms the voluptuous, gray mustache, nicking away at any scraggly hairs that refuse to fall into line with the rest. When finished, he brushes the hair with a small comb and applies wax to curl the ends in the fashion that he has always done. He checks his reflection in the mirror once more—looking satisfied—and lights his cigarette as he sits down at his desk. He taps the Pist-O-Liter on the wooden top absentmindedly as the door of the cell in the main room opens and is shut. He could go out there now, but it is better to wait. It lets Mr. Henderson know who is in charge around here.

OLD FIELD PINES

WILLIE IS PLACED IN A SMALL HOLDING CELL on arrival to the jail-house. He grimly remembers his first time in the cell around a year ago as he awaited his trial, his wife and small son standing and crying outside of the bars. His hands were too big to reach very far through the bars, and he was only able to grasp their hands through them. Fletchie, his boy, had cried. Willie hadn't the heart to tell him not to cry, that everything was going to be all right, because he didn't know that for sure and Willie'd felt like crying, too. Telling his son to do otherwise would be wrong and the reasoning would have been a lie, and he couldn't stand lying to his son anymore than he already had.

The Deputies sit a few feet away at their desks separated from his area by the thick bars that reach to a couple inches below the ceiling. The office is warm despite the pleasant temperature outside, and the efforts of a single fan shaking violently in its fixture go mostly unnoticed. Willie watches its rapid movements, staring up at the ceiling from the bed of his cell. He wonders what would happen if the fan were to fall and hit him. The Sheriff's office door was closed upon them arriving and remains that way. Willie'd thought he saw a shadow pass behind the frosted glass a few times and figured the new Sheriff to be inside making him wait. It was all a play of power.

"What's the time?" Willie asks, waiting for one of the Deputies to answer him. Neither respond. He leans closer to the bars toward the figure of Jack reclining in his swivel chair with his booted feet on his desk. His eyes are closed. "Jack." Nothing. Willie whistles loudly, the noise reverberating off the stone walls of the small room. Jack jumps in his seat and the wheels slide a bit, nearly spilling him into the floor.

"Dammit, Willie," he huffs, breathing deeply with his hand covering his thumping heart. "Ain't ya s'posed to let a sleepin' man lie?"

"When the Sheriff gonna get off his ass and get this over with?"

Jack looks to Tommy pacing nervously back and forth in front of his desk. He shakes his head in reply. "He'll be out shortly, Will... I mean, Mr. Henderson. Just go on and sit back and relax."

Willie huffs in frustration. "Well, could ya 'least give me back my 'baccy? Been goin' without for quite a while now, and I'd like to enjoy it."

Jack looks to his partner again who nods his head slightly. He rises from his chair and digs through the pile of belongings in a metal bucket on his desk. Willie rises and walks two steps to reach the bars. He sticks his hands as far through the openings as they will allow. Jack finds the pouch of tobacco and walks toward the cage in the middle of the room. As he hands the plug over, Willie grasps his wrist with his free hand and yanks. Jack surges forward, off balance, and slams his face into the bars, shaking the cage with the impact. Tommy falls into his seat laughing as his partner lies groaning on the wood floor. Blood seeps from an already-swollen lip and nose. Willie kneels down and leans against the bars next to the injured man.

He rips off a piece of chew and gnaws down for a moment. "Jack, you know I like ya."

The young Deputy looks up, his face a bloody, tear-soaked mess. "You sum bitch," he replies, his voice muffled and slurred from his hands clamping over the injured area. "I think ya broke my nose."

Willie shrugs. "Just asked a simple question. Coulda answered me."

Tommy slaps at his knees, still laughing at the misfortune of his partner from the comfort of his chair. Jack looks around accusingly at him. "You ass," Jack says glaring. "Why ain't you doin' nothing?"

Tommy continues his laughing for a minute but loses the grin after another bloody glare from Jack. He rises, approaching his injured partner. "All right, let me see it." Jack drops his hands to show the damage. "I don't know, Jack. Willie mighta done you a favor. Looks distinguished this—" he cuts off, falling into another fit of laughter.

Willie stands, spitting on the floor. He takes a seat back on the bed in the cell and reclines against the bars with his hands behind his head.

Jack looks toward his partner, standing before him and laughing. He yells out in anger and plants a swift punch to Tommy's groin. The laughing stops abruptly as Tommy drops to the floor next to Jack. Jack laughs this time, giving his face a wild appearance with the blood still gushing from his nose, dripping down his face to coat his uniform. "That's right, ya bastard. Don't like it so much when it's—" He stops with the crushing weight of Tommy pouncing on top of him, taking him back to the floor. Punches rain down from both sides as the cursing pair roll, entwined, across the wood flooring. Willie spits on the floor again and stares up at the ceiling fan rocking above him, largely ignoring the struggle a few feet beyond his bars.

OLD FIELD PINES

"Hey," a booming voice echoes through the small space, freezing the grappling Deputies mid-punch. Willie follows the Deputies' stares to the door of the Sheriff's private office. He is a tall, slender man wearing crisp blue jeans and pointed-toe cowboy boots. Shit-kickers, Willie's heard 'em called. His shirt is the same as the two Deputies', yet pressed and cleaned, with his shining badge of office pinned squarely on his left breast. His eyes, a hard, icy blue, stay fixed on the two Deputies as they remain frozen in their fighting positions on the floor. The tips of his boots stop a few inches from Tommy's and Jack's heads. "What in the Lord's name do you two ignorant mules think you're doin'?"

"Well—he—chew and—slamming," they stammer together.

The Sheriff runs a finger over his pristine mustache. "Looks like you two's gettin' mighty cozy together. That what y'all doing, boys? Y'all gettin' to know each other spiritually?" The pair look down at their awkward position. The toe of the Sheriff's boot connects sharply with Tommy's shoulder. "Get up. Incompetent shits. I won't go having my department acting fools in front of our guest."

Both men scramble quickly to their feet and stand rigidly at attention. The Sheriff looks both of them up and down for a moment with a grimace. "Go clean yourselves up." Tommy and Jack nearly barrel over each other in their haste to the nearest exit; both men rub at the various bumps and bruises inflicted by the other as they disappear from view.

The steely-blue eyes of the Sheriff turn for the first time to meet Willie's through the bars of the cage. His gaze refuses to falter as his cowboy boots click on the wooden floor before stopping a foot or so from cage door. He smiles. It isn't a pleasant thing. "William Henderson, I presume."

Willie spits on the floor to the edge of the cage door. Some spittle splashes the Sheriff's boots as Willie's eyes continue to give a harsh gaze without answering.

The Sheriff smiles wider, revealing straight, yet yellowing teeth. He ignores the spittle on his boot. "Well, thank you for bein' here, Mr. Henderson."

"Didn't have much a choice."

The Sheriff pulls a book of cigarette papers from one of the back pockets of his jeans. "Nope. I don't guess you really did, did you?" He loads a small patch of paper with tobacco from a pouch kept in his long-sleeve shirt pocket and rolls it gingerly in his fingers. "The effort is 'preciated, none the same."

"Well," Willie starts, leaning against the bars of the cage near the Sheriff, "ya got me here. What ya wanting to talk to me 'bout?"

The Sheriff lights his cigarette with a lighter he produces, a pretty pewter thing in similar shape of a pistol with delicate carvings along its smooth surface. He inhales deeply and looks around at the surrounding room for a moment as if contemplating whether redecorating was within the budget. He blows out a cloud of smoke as his eyes refocus on Willie. "Figured I'd like to meet ya is all."

Willie spits again. "Bullshit."

Sheriff Baker puts his hand over his heart in a gesture of good faith. "Honest, Mr. Henderson. I wanted to meet the legend everyone talks about. Your trial was simply fascinating to me. I've been over the paperwork countless times." He shakes his head in disbelief, smiling that same crooked smile. "An unprecedented technicality, if I'd ever saw one, saved your hide from a much longer sentence." He blows out another cloud of smoke. "Truly fascinatin'."

Willie shrugs against the bars. "The law knows what's right."

The Sheriff nods his head in agreement at such gospel. "Tell me. How'd you do it? How'd you convince a judge and jury that it weren't you making the liquor? Did you move the still, Mr. Henderson? Was it ever there?"

Willie shifts the wad of tobacco from one cheek to the other and crosses his arms over his massive chest. "Why's it matter? You awful obsessed with shinin' for a lawman. You lookin' at jumping ship and startin' in a new line of work?"

The man laughs, a throaty sound from deep in his chest, wiping away nonexistent tears from his eyes. "Not at all, Mr. Henderson. Moonshining, however, is my life. I am quite obsessed with the process and the ins and outs because I am good at my job. Which is why the fine folks of Stone County thought fit to elect me their Sheriff." He puts the dwindling cigarette in his teeth, brushing back his long mustache before depositing it and reaching out his hand. "Which reminds me of my manners. The name's Michael Baker."

Willie ignores the gesture. "Yep. Nice to meet ya. Now that we got all the pleasantries and acquaintances out the way, when do I get to go home? I haven't seen my family in some time now thanks to—"

"Thanks to you, Mr. Henderson," Baker interrupts, jabbing his finger through the bars toward Willie's chest. "You're the reason you haven't seen your family. Your choices of producing and distributing illegal—"

"I weren't guilty of producin'. Check the records."

"Bullshit," Baker yells, slamming himself into the bars and startling Willie into jumping back in surprise. The Sheriff recovers quickly, slicking back his thinning gray hair with a shaky hand and taking a last drag from his cigarette. "Splitting hairs, now, Mr. Henderson." He drops the nub to the floor where he stomps out the cherry with the toe of his boot. "I expected more out of such a decorated veteran. 153rd with the 39th, correct?"

Willie nods in affirmation.

"Then when the 39th was dissolved as a replacement division, you were sequestered by the 165th, are you of Irish descent?" Willie opens his mouth to reply but is cut off as Baker continues, "Made it to Belleau Wood. Injured there, recovered, and sent back into combat for a time before returning home. A Victory Medal, two Purple Hearts, and a Silver Star." He gets through listing these items like checking off an inventory in his head. He looks Willie up and down with his gray eyebrows raised. "Impressive."

Willie chews down on the wad in his mouth. It's gone dry. "How'd you know all that?"

As if sensing his thoughts, Baker pulls a handkerchief from his jeans and offers it to Willie through the bars. "I know you, Mr. Henderson." Willie takes the strip of cloth and spits the chew into it, staining the white surface. He offers it back. The Sheriff waves it off absentmindedly, so Willie pockets the handkerchief. "We both know that it was a miracle that you got back home alive after what you went through, and we know it was a miracle that you got off with such minor charges. I had you brought in here to tell you that your miracles have run their course. You won't be so lucky next time. Not with me."

"Ain't gonna be a next time. It's like I told Jack and Tommy, I'm done with shinin'. I just want to provide for my family best I can. I 'tend on really makin' something of that land I got there—"

Sheriff Baker cuts him short with a chortling laugh. "There's always a next time, Mr. Henderson. I'm just here to tell you that you won't be getting off so easy when I am the one to catch you."

The pair stare at each other for several moments. With lack of nothing better to say, Willie smiles. "I 'preciate the warnin', Sheriff."

A door opens and Tommy and Jack file in. Willie and Baker continue their staring match, unfazed by the disturbance. The Deputies stand at attention, waiting for orders with paper hanging from nostrils and handkerchiefs pressed to swollen lips.

Baker smiles, finally. "I'll be seein' you, Mr. Henderson." He breaks the stare and moves back toward the door of his office. "Officer Fowler." Jack stumbles forward and presents a clumsy salute, letting his handkerchief fall to the floor. Sheriff Baker watches this spectacle and sighs, shaking his head in disbelief. "Give Mr. Henderson a ride home. I'm sure he's missing his family."

"Yessir," Jack says, stomping his right foot for emphasis. He starts toward the cell, digging through the ring of keys he produces from a clip on his belt.

As Baker opens his office door, Willie calls out, "So where'd you serve, Sheriff?"

The Sheriff freezes in mid-step. He turns to Willie and stares for a moment before letting a smile cross his bony features. "My entire life is service, Mr. Henderson." He turns to head into his office and stops once more, turning back to Willie as if he's forgotten an important detail. "Your wife's Mabel Henderson, correct?"

Willie says nothing. A scowl covers his face at the bastard speaking his wife's name. He doesn't like the way it sounds slithering from Sheriff Baker's tongue.

The Sheriff's smile widens. "I figured. You have my deepest sympathies. I'll continue to keep her in my prayers." He slams the door of his office shut before Willie can come up with a response. There are too many questions now. By the time he regains his senses, Jack has the cell door open and the Deputies are shuffling him out the doors of the department.

CHAPTER III

TOMMY AND JACK WERE AFRAID they would have to shackle Willie as they half-carried him, hands already cuffed, to the waiting vehicle. No amount of pleading or asking him what folks might think if they saw him being dragged in chains could pierce the delirious state that had overtaken him. He'd been lividly demanding answers to the Sheriff's comment about his wife as they man-handled him down the stairs of the building to the waiting streets below. The ride out of town was no better with Willie thrashing about in the middle of the bench seat of Jack's truck, cursing both Deputies and their kin for not answering his questions. Both Jack and Tommy felt bad for their silence. They were given strict orders, though, to keep their mouths shut and to not speak to their former friend. For the lack of answers among the raging in the cab, Willie busted Tommy's nose open with a hard swing of his head as the Deputy made to calm him further.

The curving switch-backs of the dirt track don't help any. The bumping gravel of the road leading outside of Mountain View toward Willie's homestead has never seen a planer or leveler with its massive potholes and worn wagon ruts from the local farmers not yet switching to the conveniences of the automobile. Finally, Jack has enough of the caterwauling and jerks the truck to the shoulder, letting the dusty track of their quick stop envelop the open cab of the pickup.

He turns to Willie and plants a left hook to his jaw as hard as he can manage in the close confines of the car. It does more to his hand, dislocating his middle finger, than it does to Willie's face other than to anger him further, that anger turning on Jack.

"Shit," Jack says, shaking his throbbing left hand. He grasps it with his right hand and turns to Willie who sits fuming in the seat next to him, their shoulders touching uncomfortably. "Now, you know I don't wanna do this stuff, Willie."

Willie only stares as he strains against the restraints strapping him to the seat.

Tommy reaches below his seat with a sigh and pulls a jug from below. He unstoppers the cork and lugs it toward Willie's face. "Here. Drink up."

Jack reaches over and slaps at the jug, turning on his partner. "We ain't s'posed to have that."

"Well, hell. He sold it to us. What's it matter?" He brings the lip of the jug back to Willie's waiting lips and pushes it upward. Willie allows his head to be tilted back to drain the drink of liquor down his throat. He closes his eyes with the familiar burn and calms in his seat.

"Now," Jack continues, "you know we don't wanna do all this paradin' 'round."

Willie takes a deep breath, swallowing the last mouthful of booze and looks from Tommy to Jack. His gaze is pleading to the two boys whom he's known since they were rooting around knee-high to a grasshopper. "I just wanna know about my wife."

Jack and Tommy eye each other over Willie. Jack lets out a long breath and reaches for the jug, tilting it back on his forearm. His Adam's apple bobs up and down for a few seconds, liquor streaming thinly on both sides of his mouth, before he takes the bottle away and passes it back to Tommy.

"We don't rightly know, Willie."

"Whatcha mean you don't know?"

Tommy brings the bottle back into his lap from his drink. "No one rightly knows, Willie. She just hasn't been seen in town fer a while."

"Yeah," Jack pipes in. "And yer boy been comin' 'round going to school and such. Been kinda mopey."

Willie turns back and forth between the two. "Whatcha meanin'? Spit it out, boys."

Tommy scratches his pimply cheek. "Ya know. Fletchie's been comin' into town all sad and such since you been gone. Just thought it was sadness from ya bein' away and all. When Mabel stopped comin' with 'im, it just seemed to get worse."

"Then Doc Monroe got called out there to check 'er."

Willie turns toward Tommy, rattling the cuffs on his wrists. "Ulysses came out? What's he sayin' it is?"

Jack reaches and gently pushes Willie's torso to face Tommy. He unfastens the cuffs, gathering them in his hands and putting them on the dash. Willie rubs at his sore wrists. They hadn't been on him that long, but he'd put those chains to the test, for sure. He looks at both of the young men in turn. "Boys?"

Jack huffs once more. "We don't know, Willie."

"No one does," Tommy says. "Doc ain't gonna tell nobody 'bout his patients."

"'Cept maybe the Sheriff."

"Why'd he know anything?" Willie asks.

"Baker had us pick up the Doc when he got back to town. He brought 'im in his office and talked to him a while with the door closed."

"Then he told us ta take him home."

Tommy spits out the cab. "Doc never said a word t'us."

Willie stares through the windshield at the curving gravel road ahead. The trees have begun to change color to reds and oranges with some vibrant yellows mixed in among them, signaling the impending arrival of fall. It's Willie's favorite time of the year. Everyone will be going to harvest the last of the crops, canning and smoking would begin for the winter months, fires would be lit in the town square, the pickers and grinners of Mountain View unfazed by the changing weather. Folks still needed their music. He and Mabel'd gotten married in the latter days of October years ago with the colorful leaves falling around them in the courthouse square. She'd looked radiant as some of the leaves fell and caught in her long brown hair flowing down her shoulders in waves. They didn't make it all the way home that afternoon without stopping the buggy twice along this same stretch of road he was travelling now to tangle up in the beds of crunching leaves.

Willie, breaking from his reverie, sighs and reaches for the bottle resting in Tommy's lap. He takes a long pull and looks down the road once more. "Take me home, boys."

Tommy jumps out quickly to crank the truck up, and soon they barrel along the wooded highway toward Willie's home.

THE DEPUTIES DROP WILLIE OFF at the end of the long dirt drive—
rutted from tire and wagon alike—that switch-backs up the mountainous terrain toward the log cabin that he calls home. Willie stands for a few moments
outside the cab of the running pickup, staring at the vast expanse of wilderness that covers his land. He envisions some of the trees cleared toward the
house and on the backside of the mountain for planting various crops where
his still used to sit. Lester Thompson, his cousin, had gotten sober enough
to come help Mabel clear out any of the evidence when Willie was arrested.
Lester'd probably drank up the rest of his stock for the trouble, too. An owl
hoots to his left. Willie lets his eyes wander in the direction of the call, taking
in the scenery with misty eyes. Home.

Jack clears his throat over the rumbling of the engine. "You all right,
Willie?"

Before turning back to the car, Willie tries to nonchalantly brush at his
eyes. "Yeah," he croaks back and gives a half-hearted smile toward the pair
in the truck, Tommy leaning over Jack's lap to see out. They smile in return
with their swollen and bruised faces.

Jack's face grows serious after a moment. "He's gonna question us as
soon as we walk in."

Willie knows this and nods his head. "Whatcha gonna tell 'im?"

Jack looks to Tommy who smirks and nods his head. Jack turns back.
"Not a damn thing."

Willie nods again, giving a small smile.

"You need anything, Willie, you just come'n get us, ya hear?"

Willie nods a third time and turns back to the drive, takes a deep breath,
and begins his ascent. The truck rumbles as it is thrown into gear and turned
around on the narrow road toward town. Willie doesn't look back. Instead he
trudges along with his thoughts in the soft quiet of the Ozarks. The road is
overgrown more than he remembers. Brush encroaches the settled dust of the
path toward the fading tire ruts along both sides. Pine needles intertwine with
branches of black walnuts to create a shade of darkness more appropriate
for the twilight hours with the midday sun peeking sadly through the dense
overhanging. Willie lifts his hand to tickle his fingertips with the soft prickle
of the pine limbs and snatches a gumball from a branch. He looks down at

its spiked surface as he walks, fascinated by the bristly exterior of the spines. The impending encounter with a sick Mabel rips him from his wonder at the natural world he has been long-absent from, and he picks up his pace despite the want to slow down and put the bad news off for as long as possible. He doesn't want to think about such things at the moment, even though he knows that he is closer to facing it with each stride. Instead he imagines the smell of Mabel's hair, the way she sings when she works in the yard or hangs laundry from the line. Her voice had been the first thing that he'd remembered hearing that nearly caused him to faint from its allure. She'd stood on the steps of the courthouse one Saturday night many years ago when she was but a teenager singing along to the lively strumming of the old timer's guitar strings. He fell in love, then and there. No question in his mind. His hand drops the gumball on the dirt floor of the drive where it rolls into a pothole holding water, floating along the surface, unable to escape.

Near the top of the drive, the denseness of the trees and brush clears a bit to reveal a more open field area on a slight incline—like much of the land in the region—with long-stemmed grass growing in patches where the rocky soil allows. The cabin he'd built by hand stands under the same two pine trees. Pine needles and leaves litter the wood-shingled roof as if a natural blanket of insulation is trying to help fight back the cold radiating from the darkness of the windows. The chimney rests quietly along the right side of the structure empty, as no smoke billows from the top.

A shrill yip-of-a-bark has Willie turning his head toward the edge of the woods to the left of the cabin's structure near the outhouse. A small Pekingese scuttles across the grass toward him at top speed. Willie can't help but laugh as he stoops toward the oncoming dog. As it nears, the dog leaps into Willie's outstretched arms, alternating between nibbling at the bushiness of his beard and licking what little exposed skin it can find on his face.

"Hey there, Pearl," Willie coos, enveloping the shaking dog in his arms and patting the matted fur on her head. "You been ruttin' in the pig pen again?"

Pearl pants happily in reply and looks to her master with her bug-eyes wide with excitement.

Willie hugs her tighter. "I missed you, ole girl."

"Papa?"

Willie's head jerks toward the sound of the call. A skinny boy with a mop of black hair stares from the backside of a wooden fence where three small pigs rut around in a pale of slop. The boy holds a pail in both hands at his side, straining against the weight that is not much less than his own. He wears ragged dark pants with a cotton shirt covering his small torso. He is taller than Willie remembers, grown at least four inches since he'd last seen him, probably standing closer to his stomach than at his waist.

"Fletchie," Willie says under his breath. It's not a question; it's a statement, a chant of sorts. He lets Pearl jump from his arms and starts toward his son.

"Papa!" Fletchie exclaims, dropping the pail—splashing his pants leg with the goopy slop—and clumsily hops the fence to run to his father.

"Fletchie!" Willie chants it several times before letting it roar from his chest as the mistiness returns to his eyes. "Fletchie!"

Willie runs, Pearl yipping at his feet, and scoops the boy up in his arms. Tiny arms encircle Willie's thick neck as Fletchie buries his little head in his father's beard. Willie rocks from side to side, Fletchie's legs swinging like pendulums with each turn. The boy is crying, his back quaking under his father's hands. Willie feels the tears stream fresh down his own cheeks.

"Fletchie."

His son looks up at him as his father sets him down on the grass and kneels before him. "I missed ya, Papa." It comes out choked with happy tears that cascade down his smooth and dirty cheeks. The boy realizes he is crying and wipes at his eyes with a sleeve. Willie takes this opportunity to do the same; the smiles remain, though.

Willie sighs and looks toward the sky. He thinks about praying in thanks. It's the first time he's thought about God in a good way in a long while. He'd been angry. Angry for getting caught. Like so many other believers, instead of placing such blame where it belongs, he'd looked upward instead. As if in answer to his almost-uttered prayer, a cloud rolls along the sky to mask the sun's light from view, casting shadows in the clearing. The cabin looks darker now. Even darker than it did before with its shuttered windows and the absence of lamp or candle. The boy is at eye level with him as he kneels, certainly taller than he'd been before. Willie can't help but feel a bit frustrated and disheartened at the time that he had missed while being away.

Fletchie reaches out for his father's hand. "Ya back from jail now, Papa? Ya ain't gotta go back?"

Willie looks at his son surprised. Pearl walks to the boy and nuzzles against his pants leg. Willie shakes the thoughts from his head and rises. He looks down at his son. "Where's your Mama?"

Fletchie's finger stretches toward the dark cabin. "She's a-sleepin'. She's always sleepin' since she took sick."

Willie feels the weight of his heart plummet into the darkest pits of his stomach. He thinks he might vomit, but there'd be nothing to come up. He hadn't had much of anything in the means of food since boarding the train to head to Leslie. He turns toward the house, reaching out an over-large hand to mess Fletchie's hair. "Go on and finish your chores now."

The boy looks at his father longingly for a moment, hesitating, afraid that if Willie goes out of his sight, he will disappear once more. He yes-sirs, though, and starts back toward the pen at a run to finish as quickly as possible. "Come on, Pearl." The dog yips and takes off after him.

Willie's boots clump on the old boards of the porch. He reaches the door and closes his eyes, taking a few deep breaths to prepare himself for what he is to see inside. His hand takes hold of the handle, steadying his shaking, and pushes the door open. The interior is bathed in darkness interrupted by the letting in of outside light. All of the cotton curtains are drawn shut against the windows. Fine dust particles dance in the soft lighting streaming in and cover the wooden surfaces of floor and furniture alike. The main area of the two-room cabin looks more of a mess than Willie can recall it ever being. Even when they were putting the boards up on the foundation, wood shavings and leaves littering the freshly-laid floor, the cabin was in a better way than the sight before him. During the construction, Mabel made it her duty to keep his workstation clear and tidy, sweeping the roofless floorplan in an unending battle with progress.

Now Willie looks on pots scattered across the counters with flies buzzing around the caked-on remains of food neglected from brush and water. Cobwebs hang from the table and chairs and decorate the corners of each of the four walls at the top and bottom. Amid the chaos, the only ray of hope in sight is the small bed in the corner where Fletchie sleeps, the corners of the sheets tucked firmly and tightly to the straw mattress as his parents had taught him. Willie smiles despite the strangeness in the air at the sight of his son continuing to do as he is supposed to throughout the hard times that have clearly fallen on his family. Willie thinks of the resilience of such children before his eyes catch on the door to the bedroom across from him.

It is firmly shut off from the rest of the house, its wooden surface blockading what awaits inside with a foreboding feeling that only gets worse with the sound of the wracking cough echoing consumptiously from the other side. The noise breaks the silence that has moved into Willie's musty shell of a home. He freezes for a moment in sadness as the coughing continues for a long while. He wants nothing more than to burst through the door to the bedroom, take his wife in his arms and hold her through the pain, willing whatever ails her to pass into him and leave her be, but his legs refuse to stir from their place on the dusty wood floor. Only when the coughing subsides is he able to approach the thick door and push it open, letting it swing against the protesting hinges rusted from neglect and lack of use.

The sickening smell of heavy fever-sweat permeates his nostrils upon entering with a faint hint of what resembles rot. Two pots sit by the bed filled with shit and piss; the smell worse than anything Willie had experienced in the trenches across France. He puts his sleeve over his nose and mouth to blot out the horrid odor, so he won't throw up on the floor. He looks to the bed and falls to his knees with the weight of anguish washing over him. The sight of his wife, his sweet Mabel, being far worse than anything he could have imagined, sends a wracking sob through his body that vibrates him down to his toes. Her frail body heaves with shallow breaths that rattle in Willie's ears. Her once luminous brown hair now sits flat against her forehead, damp with sweat, flecking with gray from advanced aging or exhaustion, Willie cannot tell.

Why her? Why the angel that had saved him countless times from a self-destructive path that he would have surely headed down without her guiding him along the right one? It should be him. He should be the one rotting in a bed. After all he'd done, he deserves it. He wants nothing more than to take her place. He would gladly accept such a fate. She doesn't deserve this. Not this. Not like this, God.

He wipes furiously at the tears streaking his bearded cheeks and rises to his feet on unsteady legs. Quietly, he shuffles to his wife's side. Her mouth hangs open, panting from the heat of her slumber. Her neck and lower jaw run with jagged blue lines that seem to start mid-chest and move up toward her sunken cheeks. The areas that they spider across look inflamed despite the darkness of the room. Another tear falls unwillingly from his face as he imagines her angelic features on the day of their wedding: beautifully smooth and tanned from hours outdoors. She had one dimple on her right cheek when she smiled. Even at nineteen, her forehead showed the signs of laugh lines that she would fuss over with powder. But damn it, she was beautiful. The picture of perfection and love. He'd told her so on that day and countless others since. She had only smiled and told him that no one is perfect on this earth. That might have been the truth, but she was perfect for him. Still is.

He reaches down to her and rests his palm on her clammy forehead. She burns with a fever hotter than Willie has ever felt before. Her body shivers with the touch, and her striking, yet clouded eyes flitter open and look hazily up at him for the first time in so many months. She smiles up at him despite the obvious pain that she feels and closes her eyes for a moment.

"Willie," she croaks.

He kneels down beside her and kisses her slick cheek. "I'm here, Mabel." He chokes back more tears, trying to keep a strong disposition should she look at him again. "Oh, Mabel," he whispers, looking at her lying in bed and watching the quick rise and fall of her chest. "How could this have happened?"

Her smile returns with her eyes remaining shut. "It's so good to have you..." her voice trails off before she can finish as she falls back to sleep once more.

"Mabel?" Willie asks, concerned. He leans down to listen near her face, satisfied slightly at the rattling breath that he hears. She coughs again, specks of phlegm shooting out to hit his beard and cheek. He wipes it away and looks upon his ailing wife, distraught. He leans down and pecks her open mouth before rising and walking from the room. He leaves the door open to let in some fresh air and exits the house. He doesn't look at the mess surrounding him as his feet thump on the wooden planks of the porch. Instead he concentrates on the land surrounding him, a life of its own, perfect in its own way. It doesn't help much. He sits on the steps looking out at his property. He cannot think. He looks at nothing in particular. There is nothing to feel, nothing but a cold numbness.

Fletchie approaches his father from the side of the porch and climbs the steps to sit by him. The excitement for his father's return seems to have left the boy as, even at his young age, he seems to comprehend more of the situation than Willie would have thought.

He looks longingly toward his father who stares at his feet. "Papa?"

Willie closes his eyes and takes a deep breath to steady his voice. "Fletchie."

The boy looks to his dirty hands as if wondering where the dirt had come from before looking back. His face is screwed up in concentration, trying to find the right words to express what he is feeling. "Ya gonna fix it?"

"Fix what?"

"Mama."

Willie looks up from his shoes toward his son, defeat showing in his face. "How you 'spect me to do that?"

The boy thinks once more before smiling slightly. "Well, guess like ya used ta fix me."

Willie is becoming frustrated. "There ain't nothing that I know to do, boy. Why ya botherin' me with such questions?"

"Ya can to," the boy says back. "Just like ya used ta do with me. You'd rub some dirt on it and kiss the hurt and make the pain go 'way."

Willie's eyes mist again. He's cried a lot lately. His son looks at him expectantly. "I did used ta do that, didn't I?"

"Yessir." Fletchie says and looks to his feet, mimicking his father. "That how ya gonna fix Mama?"

CHAPTER IV

WILLIE DOESN'T SLEEP. He refuses to try. Instead he sits on the front porch steps and remains long after he has to carry Fletchie to his bed after falling asleep leaning against his shoulder, drool dripping on Willie's shirtsleeve. Pearl leaves his side after a time to take her usual place atop a rickety bench seat on the far side of the porch that Willie thinks is in desperate need of repairs at some point in the near future. His mental to-do list is already piling up before him, yet he doesn't mind so much. Tasks will help him keep his mind off certain things.

The crickets chirp a melancholy refrain as they hop about the grass already weighed down with the dew that will twinkle in the sunlight of the morning. A bullfrog croaks over toward the outhouse inconsistently until it too surrenders to the deepening silence of the night. The stars refuse to emerge from the dark expanse of cloud that had moved in on the drive over and seems to linger stubbornly as the night wears on. It seems the only constant in Willie's world at the moment. At least the clouds are consistent. The land is a mess.

He remembers little from his days working the farm with his father as a child in the terms of what to plant and how to plant the rocky patch where he sits. His mother's land is better for that. The soil is rich and has a good layer of topsoil before reaching the immoveable surface of bedrock that inhabits the ground of his home.

Mabel is far beyond anything he knows to do. Fletchie needs his Mama, that's for certain, not a man resembling the shell of a father forced to desperate actions resulting in consequential absence. And God. Where has his Father been throughout all of this? Does he not love the sinner as the saint? Have faith, he is told. Willie can't imagine a faith in someone so absent. The clouds, though. They are here now. They seem constant, something to put faith into.

Willie blames himself. He should have been here for his family. He shouldn't have been stupid. Being stupid means making mistakes. Mistakes mean getting caught. Caught means being taken away in that bus shackled to the floor and the seat in front of you with guards at both ends of the bus with shotguns in their laps. It means a farm where the fields grow with fertile soil to make a man envious for the irony of the situation to work and till and harvest the bounty of the state. It means the haunting hymnals of the man chained to your left and right, in front and behind, and the keeping of time with a pickaxe or a hammer. Moan, swing, sing, sweat, swing, swing, swing. It means a loneliness unmatched by his Daddy's passing and France together, worse than the town you know as home turning its back on the return of the prodigal son as if masked in the appearance of an unkempt carpetbagger.

He shakes his shoulders to clear the thoughts. He is home now. He looks to the cracked door of his cabin behind him with the glow of a single lamp burning on the kitchen table. He rises. Pearl lifts her head, wondering if she is to follow. Willie signals in her direction to stay where she is. Her head sinks back to her paws as he enters the cabin again. The mess is extensive, but he starts picking at what he can. He cleans pots and pans left atop the sink, taking them out to the well for washing so as not to disturb Fletchie's sleeping, him snoring softly in the corner. Pearl joins him for the scrubbing, licking at the flecks of tacked-on grease and chewing at some of the more solid pieces stuck to the dishes. He pats the dog's head as they finish the task at hand and move back to the house, Willie balancing the cleaned cookware in his arms.

He moves through the living room with broom and basket to pick up the remainder of the trash, knocking down thick cobwebs from their perches. When finished, he looks upon his work with a sense of accomplishment. It is small and menial, but it is something to help in the healing of his family, which makes him feel involved, slightly. Pearl sits proudly beside him, looking up to him with her tongue hanging from her mouth for a moment before moving to the other side of the cabin. She prances toward the bedroom door and stops; her head lifts as she sniffs the air for a bit. She whimpers and turns back to Willie.

"I know," he whispers to the dog.

Pearl stares up at him briefly before turning back to the door, letting out a small whine. Willie moves forward and opens it, careful of the creak this time. Pearl walks in ahead of him and makes for the bed where she hops up and curls beside Mabel's feet. Willie looks at his wife again, only the second time since being home. The bowls of sick near the side of the bed catch his eye and remind him of his mission once more. He scans the room and deposits the refuse into the basket he carries. He picks up clothes and brings them to the main room to be taken for wash. The pots he removes from the house and dumps into the pig pen at the back of the house. The hogs eye the sludge warily for a moment, sniffing the splattered contents before diving in, rolling happily in the new addition to their home. Willie leaves the pots on the porch before going back in.

Once everything is complete, he moves to Fletchie's bedside and looks down at his son. He watches the steady, healthy rise and fall of the boy's chest under the thick quilt tucked around him. He sleeps like his mother, Willie thinks. The way his mouth rests open in the center and closed in the corners. He'd mentioned her sleeping smile to her on one morning after their first several nights lying together. She'd jokingly told him that she was only awaiting his lips in the morning, first thing. He'd kissed her awake every morning after that. He leans down to his son, raking back the bangs of the boy's hair, kissing his forehead. The house is quiet. Pearl stays behind in the bedroom to keep a watch on Mabel, sleeping fitfully throughout his foray to clean up the house a bit. The idea of the dog staying with her makes Willie happy, makes him feel a bit more at ease. Pearl can watch over Mabel while she rests.

The dining room table is taller than he remembers as he sits and takes out the plug of chewing tobacco from his overall pocket. It had gone unnoticed since his homecoming. He rips a chunk and chomps down. Thoughts drift to the Sheriff. He will be trouble. No matter whether Willie means to make trouble or not, the Sheriff will certainly be happy to provide it. There is no trouble to be had, not as far as Willie is concerned, but if there is a possibility of the slightest chance, Baker will be on top of it. If someone in town so much as mentions prohibition, Willie thinks that Baker will come busting down his doors to happily haul him back before a judge and see him thrown to the farm for the rest of his days. Nothing would make Sheriff Baker happier. Not much to do other than keep his head down and accept it.

He'd been lucky the first time. Having sold to the Stone County Judge hadn't hurt his case any. He'd probably have gotten off with nothing more than a week or so in county if it hadn't been for that city prosecutor coming in and preaching sobriety and the right of the law. He figured that every citizen should go straight if he had, born-again Christian as he was. Having not found the still had helped, too. If they'd found where he'd stashed the manufacturing portion of his operation, there would have been no choice but to send him away for the long haul. Catching him with four jugs, however, why that could have been his own private stock he was transporting. Sheriff Dibbs sure blew the bust out of proportion from what he'd heard said in the papers, but that was to be expected after the trial verdict. Dibbs wasn't a bad man, Willie'd take him over Baker any day of the week—he just enjoyed the attention, is all. Besides, if the law arrested every person caught with illegal liquor, it wouldn't have been long before Mountain View's population shrank to the point of fading from existence. A lot of things had saved him, that's for sure. A lot had damned him as well. None of this would be possible now. Gone are the days of quick escapes and an early release. Baker would see to that. Baker was a completely different animal. Just do him good to go straight and stay that way. And that's exactly what he intends.

Willie pulls the basket filled with trash close to his feet and spits atop the contents. The chair creaks a bit and wobbles on its back legs as he sits back against the rough wood of the backrest. Willie spits again and rises from the chair, getting down on all fours to check the damage of the chair leg. It looks fine. A board of flooring sticks up from the rest a bit, though. Willie pushes down on it and the board springs a little, creaking. He smiles. It can't still be there. They wouldn't have missed it. He quietly pushes the chair out of the way and pries the board from its setting. It comes up easily to reveal the small cubby that he had built along the foundations of the cabin when he'd begun running liquor. A single jug lies on its side with dust caking its surface and the cork intact. A quilted bundle sits close by. Willie hauls them both out one at a time, setting the jug on the table beside the bundle and retaking his seat.

Wrapped tightly, as he had left them, Willie pulls an old Colt revolver from its resting place. He picks at some fuzz caught in the hammer and opens the chamber. Five bullets rest snugly in their places. He spins the receiver and slams the action back home, thrusting the pistol forward with both hands toward the door in firing position. The barrel points into the night for a moment before he relaxes his grip and sets the gun on the table next to the jug. A fiddle and bow wrapped additionally in an old shirt remain on the table inside the quilt. Willie checks the hairs along the bow, nodding his head. He plucks a string on the fiddle, which thumps through the quiet a bit out of tune. He rises from his seat, grabbing the jug in one hand and the instrument in the other and makes for the darkness of the night.

The fresh air feels good as he takes his spot on the porch steps. He looks to both the fiddle and the jug on either side of him. His eyes linger on the jug. He reaches for it, bringing it to his lap, uncorking the top and taking a whiff of his whiskey. The strong scent of alcohol sends a shiver through his spine. He circles his middle finger around the small finger-hold on the neck, rests the base of the jug on his forearm, and tilts it to his mouth and up. The liquor makes a *glug glug glug* as he drinks deeply for a few seconds. When he brings the jug back down, his face puckers with the strength and the burn deep in his chest. He tilts it back up for another drink and a *glug glug glug glug*, the liquor draining down his throat and clearing his sinuses and his mind in a few quick seconds. A fuzziness overtakes his body starting in his ears and hands, moving throughout his body with a warm, slow creep that has him sweating despite the chill of the night air.

He smacks his lips and thumps the jug back to the wood of the porch. His eyes move to the fiddle resting on the steps next to him. He takes it gingerly in his hands and plucks at the strings, turning the tuning keys as he goes until the hollow *thunking* resonates pleasantly in his ears. When he finishes, he takes the bow and brings the fiddle up to his chin. The first sawing motion sends more chills through him, similar to that of the liquor, yet purer. It's a haunting feeling. He looks out across his land in the dark of night. It seems to have softened a bit, the clouds moving quickly and breaking with the breeze. He thinks for a minute and begins playing softly—an old Irish tune that he had heard his Daddy sing when he was a boy. A ballad of a woman and her murder at the hands of the man who loved her. As the first verse comes along, he opens his mouth to let his deep baritone fill the night air.

Down in the willow garden
My true love and I did meet.
It was there we sat discoursing
My true love dropped off to sleep.

As he sings, the wind picks up and whistles through the thick branches of the pine trees, making for an eerie sound—a choir to match the sadness filling his voice and the world around him. The clouds disburse as if to listen, bathing the earth in the soft yellow light of a harvest moon. The tree limbs wave in time with the rise and fall of his bow. Falling stars blink in the night, the sky weeping in answer to Willie's song.

A SMALL HAND PRESSING AGAINST HIS SHOULDER has Willie slowly opening his eyes to the early morning glow of the sun rising, yet still hidden behind the tops of the pines. He blinks his eyes a few times to adjust and straightens, stretching a sore back and neck from falling asleep against a hardwood post. The jug of whiskey sits next to his foot with the fiddle and bow resting in his lap. A cold dew had developed through the night, making Willie's clothes slick and damp and heavy with the weight of it. He shivers and looks to Fletchie's hand resting on his shoulder.

"Mornin', Papa," Fletchie says, smiling down at him. He reaches out with his other hand and passes Willie a cup of steaming coffee.

Willie blows on the cup and takes a sip. It burns his tongue and there are grounds throughout the liquid making more of a sludge than an actual cup of coffee. It's hot, though, and helps to soothe the beginnings of a sore throat from staying out all night in the damp. He runs a finger along his tongue to scrape off some of the grounds. He spits. "Thank ya, son."

Fletchie's smile widens and he steps off the porch and begins walking toward the drive.

"Where ya goin'?" Willie asks as the boy starts off toward the road.

"School," the boy says without turning around. He totes a bundle of books tied together with a belt slung over his shoulder.

Willie rises stiffly from his seat. "Ya want me to take ya?"

"Truck ain't workin'," the boy calls back, still walking toward the road. "I'll see ya later, Papa."

OLD FIELD PINES

Willie looks toward the woods where a tarp halfway covers a rusted-up truck with a wooden bed. The exposed motor drips with the morning dew. He'll have to get it fixed. Probably a quick solution. He'd done some of his own modifications to the vehicle when he'd been running with it. Made it hard to operate and to start sometimes. He'll take a look at it later. He stretches once more and looks off down the way; Fletchie has already gone out of sight on toward the small schoolhouse a few miles down the road to the main part of town.

Willie's tool shed, attached to the house near the pig pen, is just as he left it. The doorjamb that he put on during the tornado season a few years back kept the door firmly shut during his absence. Cobwebs coat most of the surfaces along with a fine layer of dust. The sunlight streaming in shows a cloud of particles stirred up by the disturbance of the door after so long. Willie sneezes, and sneezes again, before moving farther in the small space with a sleeve over his face to block out the allergens. He grabs a few wrenches and a hammer from the top of a rough-hewn bench in the corner of the shed. A glint of metal catches in the corner of his eye, and he turns to a pile next to the bench where some copper wiring sticks out from underneath a dusty tarp.

Willie leans down and pulls at the moth-eaten material, revealing some of the tools of his past trade below. A large section of rolled-up copper wire sits underneath with a hand-carved thump pole. He bends to extract the thump pole from its resting place and runs his hand along the smooth grain of the wood. It feels familiar and there are sweat stains from where he'd had his hands countless times while working. His gaze runs along the handle length to find his initials he'd carved at the base with the word "THUMPER" etched in the middle. A good, handy tool needed a name. While he was no Shakespeare about such matters, the name given seemed to suit the piece just fine. He smiles. It was the only piece of his equipment that he'd instructed to be kept around after the arrest, along with the wire that could be sold back to Lackey's Store or another shiner, perhaps for a higher profit. The pole was just too sentimental to have buried in the dirt. Leeroy Iber, a fellow shiner and sort of mentor to Willie when he'd first been starting off, had carved it for him after telling him he was ready to start running on his own.

"Don't ya go stealin' my cus'omers, now boy," Leeroy'd said with a grin as he handed the pole over to Willie. He was a grizzled man, sporting a long gray beard that hung nearly to his waist. Looking at him, one'd never think much of him, but Willie'd seen him throw men twice his size and half his age off their porches and give them the whipping of a lifetime for shorting him on payment.

The memories of Leeroy make Willie smile again. He didn't hear anything of the man on the farm and figures he might still be out and about, selling his shine on the sly under Baker's nose. He thinks that he will look him up soon, check in to see how the old codger is faring. He fingers the pole absentmindedly for a few more moments. It didn't deserve to rot in a hole with the worms and the dirt. He'd intended on hanging it in his house somewhere, a commemoration of his past and a testament to his future endeavors. That is out of the question now. If he does, someone 'round town will hear about it and sooner or later Sheriff Baker will come knocking with guns and chains and a choice. Dead or jail.

Willie'd take dead. He's had enough of the farm. At least in Glory he won't have to work the land like a slave, or he'd be made to in Hell. Not really much of a choice. He throws the pole back down by the wiring. The tarp is set carefully over the items, and he gathers his necessary tools for fixing the truck and makes to exit the shed. Memories ain't worth dying over.

The morning passes quickly into the afternoon leaning over the engine of the GMC. Willie tinkers with the nuts and bolts of the engine, covering himself in grease and sweat despite the coolness in the air. Colorful leaves fall around him as he works. After a couple hours tinkering, he hops in the cab and makes to see how his handiwork has paid off. The engine rumbles and rolls over and over without catching. He gets out and leans back over the engine, thinking it might be the starter or the timing belt. As he busies himself with his work, a horse and buggy pull up the gravel road to his property. A man in a nice suit shirt, pants, and suspenders drives the ancient-looking mare and pulls to a stop in front of Willie's cabin. Willie comes off the engine and wipes his blackened hands on the legs of his overalls. The man steps off the cart and waves toward him, walking quickly in his direction.

"Howdy, Willie," the man says as he approaches. He doffs the wide-brimmed hat from his head.

OLD FIELD PINES

Willie lets himself relax, recognizing Dr. Ulysses Monroe. He sticks out his hand for the Doc to shake. "Dr. Monroe."

They shake hands and let them fall back to their sides. Silence reigns for a moment as both men busy themselves with looking at the stitches of their boots. Willie eyes the Doc's suspenders with the shiny buckles at his waist. They have his initials engraved on each of them in a brilliantly-scrawled script.

Dr. Monroe awkwardly clears his throat and takes out a pipe and a pouch of tobacco from his pocket. He fills up the pipe without looking up at Willie. "So, when ya get back home?" He lights up and furiously puffs ever-growing clouds of smoke from his mouth and nostrils.

"Yesterday."

The old man inhales deeply on his pipe, having gotten it to the desired temperature. "Good ta have ya home, son," he says, spilling smoke with every word. The silence returns for a moment. The doctor sticks his pipe in his teeth and puts his hands on his hips, surveying the rocky land around them and stretching his back. "How's your boy doin'?"

"Good. Off at school. Yers?"

The Doc nods. "Howard's good. Growin' like a weed." He chuckles and looks to Willie, his smile fading into a look filled with more concern than anything else. "How are ya really, son?"

Willie spits into the dirt again. "I'm all right, I s'pose. Glad ta be home."

Doc nods. "I bet. Pretty rough down there?"

"Ain't got a clue, Doc."

They stand in silence for a moment longer with Dr. Monroe nodding his head continually, a nervous tick that he does often during conversations that last more than two minutes. Willie wonders if there's something wrong with his neck, the way it continually bobs back and forth. He ain't careful, damn thing'll pop right off and roll back to town, nodding all the way.

Doc Monroe smiles again, "Well, ya look healthy. Ain't much I can see 'cept yer a bit hairy. Only thing I got for that's a trip to Ed Johnson's shop for a shave." He laughs at his own joke.

Willie runs his greasy hand through the thick mane of hair growing from his cheeks. "I don't know, Doc. Thinkin' I might keep it for a bit. Suits me."

The Doc's smile twitches a bit. "So it does." He slaps his hands to his thighs. "Welp, how's Mabel been doin'? Get to talk much when ya got back?"

"Not much. She was pretty well conked out. Checked on 'er this morning and she was still sleeping. Hadn't stirred today."

"Probably the meds I gave 'er. She ain't been feeling too good: fever, sore throat, lots of pain the past couple weeks. So, I gave 'er some opioids fer the pain and some heroin to bring down the fever. That's probably what's got 'er down. She needed rest. Gave 'er enough to keep a mule outta commission fer a week. The rest probably done 'er some good, though."

Willie nods his head. "Thanks, Doc."

"Don't mention it. Welp, I'm gonna go on in and check on our patient. I'll come back'n talk with ya here in a bit."

Willie says nothing as Doc Monroe turns and slowly makes his way to his cart, grabbing his medical bag from the seat and disappearing inside the cabin. Willie doesn't follow. Instead he turns back to the motor and continues his work. He would be useless inside anyway. Let the Doc do his job and Willie will do his.

For a time, absorbed in his work, Willie forgets the presence of Doc Monroe in his home. He tries the truck again and it continues the strange problem of turning over without firing. He dives into the problem with full force: taking off parts, inspecting them, cleaning them, putting the motor back together. He does not hear Doc Monroe emerging from the cabin, wiping sweat from his brow with a handkerchief. He does not hear the sigh the doctor makes as he watches Willie working on the truck. He does not notice him approach wearily up to where he is leaning into the hood of the truck.

"Willie."

Monroe's voice makes Willie jump, banging his head against the raised metal hood of the vehicle. He rubs at his injured scalp and hops down, a bump already forming. "Damn it, Doc. 'Bout had me ready to jump you." He smiles at the doctor, who isn't looking at him, but at his shoes once more. "How she doin'?" Willie's smile fades as the Doc looks up into his eyes, the old man's own vision blurred from mistiness. His face is clouded with worry and clearly exhausted. "Doc?"

OLD FIELD PINES

Doc Monroe looks Willie in the eyes sorrowfully, quickly averting his gaze at the concerned look stretching across Willie's features. "I'm sorry, son."

Willie steps toward him. "What ya mean, Doc?"

The doctor doesn't answer. He scratches uncomfortably at the back of his neck.

"Doc?" Monroe doesn't respond. Willie reaches out and gently shakes the older man's shoulder. "Ulysses. Look at me." The doctor's eyes slowly move up to meet his own. They are different. They were always cheery eyes to look at with half a smile present in the corners. The smile is gone from them. "What's wrong with Mabel?"

Monroe sighs. "From what I can tell..." he trails off for a moment, clearing his throat. "The symptoms seem to point t'wards Diphtheria." He shakes his head in shame and looks back to his feet. "I shoulda caught it sooner, Willie. She just started displayin' symptoms. I'm so sorry."

Willie's hand drops from Monroe's shoulder. His head sinks. He can feel the pain welling inside him for a minute. And then he remembers. He remembers the Deputies' story, having picked up the Doc after first coming to see Mabel. Willie thinks about their initial meeting, how awkward the man was. Like he didn't really want to meet Willie's eyes or see him, for that matter, after what he'd done. He remembers the last words that Baker said to him before slamming his office door shut, the look of triumph in the Sheriff's eyes, knowing that he'd gotten in the final blow during their meeting.

Willie's hands clench to fists and he grinds the chew in his mouth until his teeth break through the wad and gnash together. He spits. "That what you told the Sheriff?"

Monroe's head shoots up from where it had rested on his chest. "Beg your pardon?"

Willie looks at the man in disgust, wondering at the depth that the people of this town would sink to spite one of their own. "That what you told Sheriff Baker when he had you brought to his office?"

Monroe is shaking his head even before Willie can finish. "I didn't go to the Sheriff with anythin', Willie. I jus' diagnosed 'er this very day."

Willie snarls like a feral animal, the rumbling coming from deep in his chest. "Liar!" he shouts, lunging at the doctor. The elderly man deftly side-steps him. This surprises Willie, but only for a moment before he turns and goes back in again. This time, Doc Monroe swings his medical bag at him as he passes, knocking Willie into the dirt. He lies there for a second, gathering his senses. He looks around and sees the hammer he'd brought out lying a foot or so away. He grabs for it, but Doc Monroe's boot smashes down on his hand and remains there. Willie's yelp of pain turns back into the harsh rumbling as he thrashes about, trying to get at the doctor.

Monroe calmly squats before Willie, keeping his foot firmly planted on Willie's hand that grasps the hammer's handle. "Look at me, son."

Willie continues his thrashing until Monroe rears back and slaps his face. The blow stuns him. There was power in it, a hard throw, making stars dance along Willie's vision. He tries blinking them away.

"Now look at me, boy." Willie obeys the command this time. Monroe is shaking his head. He spits into the dirt away from Willie. "Didn't your Pappy ever tell ya never to tangle with an old man? We ain't gonna fight fair. 'Sides, I pulled ya from your Mama kicking and screaming. I'll be damned if you gonna whip up on me or insult my practice."

Willie's emotions get the better of him, and he only feels anger looking up at the man, knowing deep down that he's trying to be sensible. Anger and sadness. Then he thinks of Mabel. There is only Mabel.

Doc Monroe shoves his crooked finger into Willie's face. "Now, you look at me, son. I've known you all your life. Considered your Daddy a friend, as I do you. Ain't no betrayin' trust with me, son. I was called before the Sheriff after visiting Mabel the first time, that I'll say for sure. I told him the truth: I didn't know what was wrong with her, and if I did, I sure as shit wouldn't be talkin' to him 'bout it. Ain't his business. This thing's 'tween your family and I, just as any case of mine here in Stone County is with any of the patients I see."

Willie's anger calms some. He knows the Doc is speaking true with him. He takes a deep breath, smiling at the thought of the Doc telling Baker off in such a manner. "Bet he didn't care for that."

"Nope. He didn't."

"Probably don't wanna go pissin' off the law, Doc."

OLD FIELD PINES

Monroe's smile returns and he looks down at Willie lying on the grass. "Think I can handle myself, don't you?" He rises, removing his foot from Willie's hand and extends his own to haul Willie back to his feet. He reaches over and checks Willie's wrist that he'd been putting his weight on and nods, satisfied that there was no damage done.

Willie rubs a hand through his bristling hair. He looks back to Monroe, a bit embarrassed for his actions. He sighs. "What's there to do?"

"I can give her antibiotics, but I'll have to get them from the house. I won't be able to be back for a few days. She'll need to remain in bed."

Willie nods.

"It ain't gonna be cheap, Willie."

"I'll manage."

Monroe sighs again, "Ain't all, son. Her neck's developing swellin' pretty bad. I don't know how long the infection's been workin' in 'er. The antibiotics might not do the trick. Might have to hospitalize her." He looks to see that Willie is processing all of this information. "If that's the case, gonna be even more expensive. Real expensive. Closest treatment facility I know of's gonna be cross the state line in Missouri. Healin' folks ain't cheap. Not with something this serious. Few years 'go this woulda been a death sentence." He looks away from Willie. "Could still be."

Willie shakes his head. "Ain't gonna happen, Doc. Not my Mabel."

Doc Monroe smiles half-heartedly and pats Willie on the shoulder. He walks the short distance to his buggy and climbs up. He brings the horse around and has him trot up beside Willie, turning toward the road to the highway and back to town. "You keep on fightin'. See Mabel does, too. We're gonna get through this one way or 'nother."

Willie looks up at Monroe in his buggy. "Thanks, Doc."

Monroe nods his head in reply, donning his wide-brimmed hat. "Oh, and just so ya know. Not everyone 'round here agrees with Sheriff Baker. Damn shame what happened to ya. Your shine was the best in four counties. I should know. I travel a good ways for my work."

He smiles and whips the horse into motion, the buggy rocking along the rough dirt road until it disappears into the trees. Willie looks after it for a long while, not doing anything. Pearl joins him where he stands and rubs against his leg in support. He ignores the dog and slinks back to the truck where he slides into the bench seat of the cab. For a few minutes, he rests his head on his hands that are draped wearily over the steering wheel.

He then rises up and slams his palms against the wheel. Once, twice, three times, until he feels a blood vessel rupture on his palm. He yells hoarsely and hits the wheel once more before settling back and closing his eyes. His bills are piling up, his debts deeper than he cares to think. He owes the state, conveniently charging him for his incarceration and his crimes. He owes the doctor; he owes the store where Mabel'd been charging groceries and other such supplies to a tab until Willie made it home.

He looks about the rocky soil and woods that make up his so-called-farm. Planting crops ain't gonna cut it. Not in the area he is. Can't farm land that doesn't want to be farmed in the first place. Good Lord made soil and he made stone. The Bible says to build your house upon the stone, and that's exactly what Willie had done. Bible didn't say nothing 'bout farming in stone. Sheriff on his tail and Mabel's sickness in front. He's running out of options and places to turn.

He reaches down and, on a whim, turns the key in the ignition. The truck sputters to life, the idling of the modified engine shaking the truck's cab. Willie looks around the small farm once more, the cabin on the little hill where he knows his wife rests inside with a disease he can't cure on land he can't farm in a world that seems to not want him to win. He throws the truck in first. Pearl looks up to the cab of the truck longingly and lets out a small whine. Willie shakes his head and bends to pat her head.

"Not this time, girl." She whines once more but drops her paws back to the dirt and trots back to the porch to watch. Rocks and dirt rain from the churning of the back tires before they catch and barrel forward down the road and off the property.

CHAPTER V

THE LANDSCAPE OUTSIDE OF MOUNTAIN VIEW, going down Highway 65 toward Batesville, is flat and relatively free of the thick overgrowth in comparison to the dense slopes that incorporate Willie's property. He finds that he is envious, cruising through the golden fields of hay and corn with small plots of vegetables near quant farmhouses with fires burning in their stoves and soft smoke billowing from the chimneys. Peacefulness. Prosperity. They are one in the same. States of being that Willie is relatively unfamiliar with. He imagines fathers and sons bailing hay and ripping ears of corn from their stalks. These figures laugh and smile to each other, knowing full-well that while the work is hard, they have something to be thankful for; they are called home from their fields and labor to laundry on the line with the mother, a healthy woman, forking food onto plates from the stove and placing it on the worn wooden table before the tired and sweaty men. They talk and laugh and smile and enjoy their lives, thanking God for their blessings and prosperity.

The familiar turn flashes in front of him and Willie slams the brakes and cuts the wheel, grinding the gears downward, narrowly missing a tree as he turns up the drive to the moderately-sized white house. His father had added onto the place around the time Willie turned fourteen. It used to be a one-room shack where his mother and father shared a large bed in the corner, forcing him to make his bed on top of or underneath the kitchen table. The top was uncomfortable, but the floor had been nearly as unbearable with the dogs rolling around in his blankets. When his legs began to hang from the end of the table with his head dangling from the opposite end, his father took pity on him. Their harvest had been good that season—their harvest was good most seasons that Willie could remember—and his Daddy set down at the breakfast table one morning, moving the blankets and pillows from its top to the floor.

"Damn house's too small, Mama," his father had remarked.

"Well," his mother had said from the stove, stirring a large pot of oats, "why don't ya build it up bigger, then?"

His dad had skipped breakfast that morning, rising from the table and going to work immediately on the lumber needed for the project.

Willie slips out of the truck's cab to gaze upon the now-large house where he'd spent his childhood. A wrap-around porch had been added at the request of Willie's Mama with a swing swaying in the breeze close to the front door with a matching one on the far side by the back door. The swing is empty at the moment, but Willie can make out a figure moving in the window of the kitchen along with the sound of the rattling of pots and pans.

So I'll cherish the old rugged cross
Till my trophies at last I lay down...

Her singing voice echoes to the front door, a beautiful twang of the Ozarkian dialect mixed with the lilt of the Irish in between and on the ends of the words, bringing the ending sounds up cheerfully as she sings. Willie walks through the house until he leans against the doorframe of the entrance to the kitchen, watching the frail form of his mother bustling back and forth from counter to cupboard, kneading dough and flouring her hands.

I will cling to the old rugged cross,

"And exchange it someday for a crown," Willie joins in on the final line of the chorus.

His mother turns with a smile, her head of short gray hair bobbing with a slight curl around the edges. She opens her thin arms covered in flour to her elbows. "William."

"Hello, Mama." He walks toward her and they embrace, her head resting against his sternum. He towers over her now; he lays his head down on top of hers and breathes in the scent of her washed hair and sniffs the familiar perfume that she'd worn for as long as he could remember. Her hair tickles the edges of his beard.

"My own baby." Willie shakes in his mother's arms, feeling the pain of the past and present coming to the surface, grateful to have her still, grateful for the familiar embrace. She pats his broad back soothingly. "Now, now. Ain't gonna have that." She gently pushes him out to arm's length and looks him up and down with a smile. "You could use a shave."

Willie grunts in reply, wiping at his nose with the back of his hand.

"Well," she turns back to the counter, "I'm making a pie. Make yourself useful then and cut up them peaches for me."

Willie rolls up his shirtsleeves and starts toward the counter where four ripe peaches sit waiting next to a knife as if she had expected his arrival.

"Eh," his Mama hisses, pointing a flour-coated finger toward the door. "Wash up."

"Yes'm."

Upon his return, they work in silence for a time except for the knife sliding through the peaches and knocking on the wooden counter surface mixed with the soothing hum of his mother's soft voice switching from hymnals to old Irish tunes in no particular order. They put the pie in the woodstove to bake. Willie seats himself at the kitchen table that he'd made his bed on for the majority of his childhood as his Mama puts a pot of water on the stovetop to boil for coffee.

When the pie is complete and the water boiling, his Mama silently cuts a large slice for her son and places it on a plate before him with a fork resting on the side. She cuts one for herself, setting across the wooden table from him, gathers two mugs from one of the open-faced cabinets. She sets the small table, bringing the pot of bubbling water and placing coffee grounds inside. She drops bits of eggshell into the pot to settle the grounds toward the bottom, pouring Willie a cup before pouring some in her own. During this process, Willie stares hungrily at the steaming slice of pie in front of him. It takes all he has not to dive into the gooey treat before his Mama is finished, but she'd trained him good and he waits patiently for her to finish. When everything is set and ready, she sits silently looking at Willie and smiles. She glances down at the pie in front of him in a go-ahead manner. He takes a bite; it is deliciously warm and oozing with the sugary syrup of cooked fruit. He washes the warm pastry down with some hot coffee. It is only after he smiles at her that she takes up her own fork and begins eating.

"Good pie, Mama."

She smiles again, blowing on the rim of her mug and taking a sip of the coffee. She places her fork gingerly on the edge of her plate and dabs at her upper lips with a cloth in her lap. "What're ya doing, baby?" She looks at him sweetly with her dark eyes behind the mounds of wrinkles in her skin. She looks much older than when he'd left, more fragile. He knows better, though. Even with the stooping back and the age spots going up her arms and neck, Willie knows there to be power left in her bony frame, a strength that had scared him a bit as a boy. He thinks it might have scared his Daddy a bit, too.

He sips his coffee. Grounds grit in between his teeth. He has an urge to spit them on the floor but knows better, so he swallows them down with another mouthful of pie. "Came to see ya."

"I can see that. I mean, why're ya here, son? Shouldn't you be at home with Mabel?"

"She's sick, Mama."

"I know."

Willie sighs. Of course, she knows. His Mama knows everything, always has. "Doc says it's the Diphtheria."

She picks up her fork and takes another bite of pie, acting like what he'd said made no difference to the matter at hand. A sting of caramelized peach hangs from her lip. She wipes it away with her kerchief. "And why aren't ya taking care of her?"

"I don't know what to do, Mama." He looks across the table to where she sits, pleading with her for any kind of advice or help that she can give. "She's gonna need treatment."

"So, get her treatment."

"It's gonna be a lotta money."

"So, get the money."

"How the hell you 'spect me to do that?" Willie asks, his voice rising in frustration.

The old woman thrusts her fork in his direction, a gooey piece of pie balanced on its surface. "Don't ya go raisin' yer voice with me, son. I know you's a grown man, but ya ain't too old for me to make ya go cut me a switch."

Willie's head sinks. Frustration and sorrow mix with an overwhelming feeling of helplessness. "Sorry, Mama." He picks up his mug and leans with his elbows on the table. "I just don't know what to do. Land ain't hardly any good up there. 'Sides, it'd take too long to be getting crops in and make a profit. Season's over. Startin' to get cold already."

"Start shinin' 'gain," she replies happily, spooning up the last bit of pie on her plate and bringing it to her lips.

Willie's eyes darken, "No."

"Why not?"

"I got caught."

"Yep," she slaps her bony hand against the tabletop, making the mugs rattle. "You did 'cause ya gone and got stupid." Willie sits silently, taking the rebuke. "Ya didn't listen. Ya got cocky 'cause ya thought having that little town in yer pocket and buying yer likker made ya some kind of invincible. What did I tell ya? I told ya something bad was bound to happen. Just 'cause yer from somewheres don't mean they won't throw ya to the wolves the second the damn road gets rocky."

Willie is silent for a moment, staring at the remnants of his pie. "I know."

She smiles, the look of anger in her eyes fading a bit. "And it only took ya being locked up to figure it out."

"That ain't fair, Mama."

The look in her eyes flashes back into existence. It terrifies Willie just as it had when he was a child. "Life ain't fair, Willie." She smiles, her eyes relaxing again as she brings her mug to her lips. She picks up the pot to refill her mug and then holds it out to Willie. "More coffee?"

Willie offers his mug. "It ain't gonna work anyway."

"And why would ya think that?"

"New Sheriff ain't gonna give me any leeway."

His Mama laughs. "Ah, this Sheriff Baker from Searcy County giving ya a fright. What's so special 'bout some hack Sheriff from Marshall anyhow?" She leans over the table toward him like she's about to let him in on a secret. "Some folks say he didn't even serve. What kinda lawman ain't gonna go when 'is country comes a'callin'?"

Willie remembers back to his conversation with the Sheriff, his coolness in ignoring Willie's comment about the war. "That don't matter none. He's good, Mama."

"Yeah, he is." She takes a drink of her coffee. "Got John Henry while you's was away." Her head sinks as her mouth opens to continue, but she hesitates.

This is news to Willie, but he'd expect nothing less. John Henry was careless with his shining, and it was only a matter of time after the crack down that he'd have been caught. This isn't what bothers him, though. It's her hesitation—her unwillingness to continue—that makes him nervous. "What is it, Mama?"

She shakes her head. "I'm sorry, honey."

"What is it?"

She sighs, looking up at her son. "Baker gone and kilt poor Leeroy Iber."

Willie feels his heart plummet toward his stomach. He grabs at a pain that flares up in his chest as his chin sinks. "What?"

She nods. "Awful. Shot him dead. On his own land. Damn shameful."

Willie looks up at her from across the table. He rubs at his temples where a headache begins to form. "How long?"

"'Bout three weeks or so. He's buried out by the Methodist Church."

Willie nods. There is nothing to be done about it now. He'll still go visit his friend, no matter the change in circumstances. "Baker ain't gonna allow for shinin' to get stirred up 'gain in his county."

His Mama smiles morosely across the table and reaches her hand to place it over Willie's. She grips his fingers with that strength he knows she has. Damn near hurts the way she holds him. "Ain't his county, Willie. This here's our county. Folks just don't remember it right now, and he just don't know it."

Willie sighs. He is thinking about it. What other way is there to make a living out here? Farming ain't working anymore. He couldn't get a crop going and harvested fast enough to make the money he's going to need, not before the frost hits. Not if the good Lord himself came to help him till the rocky land his house sat on.

"What're ya thinkin', honey?"

His Mama has been looking at him, studying his face, the way his eyebrows raise up when he's concentrating real hard. "We can't do it on my land. Sheriff'll be spectin' that. Plus, if he's as good as I think he is, probably already got Jack or Tommy to squeal 'bout the ole still site."

"So ya do it here."

"Where? Ain't no water. You knows we gotta have cool water close by."

"Roastnier Creek borders my land."

It's Willie's turn to laugh. "Yeah, down a fifty-foot drop off the cliff. Won't work."

"Lester mighta found a way."

He laughs a second time. "Lester Thompson? That poor boy is part drunk and part whipped hound. And a fool to boot."

Her wrinkled face slips into a frown, and she squeezes his hand harder. "Lester's kin. Don't go talkin' 'bout yer kin like they's heathens. 'Sides, he might be a drunk, but the boy's got some workin's 'tween them ears of his."

"I don't even know where to start lookin' fer 'im."

His Mama smiles as she takes a sip from her coffee mug and points out the kitchen window. "Might try startin' out by yer Daddy's ole smoke shack."

"He's here?"

His Mama nods over her mug. "Been workin' on our water problem for a few weeks now."

"You been out there?"

She shrugs, rising from the table. "Once or twice." She begins collecting the plates and mugs.

Willie smirks. "Prolly out there passed out drunk in a—"

"That's enough." She doesn't raise her voice. Willie doesn't know if she can. His Mama'd always been a soft-spoken woman. It was when her voice dropped and got real quiet that he knew he'd messed up. It had terrified him, like her eyes when they went to darkening when he was a boy. Still scares the hell out of him. "You listen. You gotta sick wife and a baby at home that needs you to take care of 'em. Grants for shit land that ain't worth plowing aren't gonna do it. Ya got a talent. Ya make the best shine Stone County's seen, and we ain't gonna let no damn law, or some swanky lawman, or yer doubt in Lester get in the way of us makin' our livin'."

His head sinks. "I just got out, Mama." He rubs a hand over his buzzed hair and scratches at a spot on his chin under the bushy beard. His eyes are drawn as he looks up at her. "I don't wanna go back there. It's worse than any foxhole I's holed up in over…"

"Shhh," she soothes, plopping her load down and wrapping her arms around his head. "You're a good boy. You got yer Mama again." She pats his head, bringing a hand under his chin and lifting his face to look at her. She is smiling at him sweetly. "Your Mama ain't gonna let nothing happen like that again."

She picks up the remnants of their food, leaving him sitting at the table as she busies herself in the sink. She doesn't turn around as she continues. "Now, you go on back home and tend to yer wife. Ain't gonna be able to start all this today anyway."

Willie rises, the conversation over, and makes for the door. He turns back to her and smiles again. "Thank you, Mama."

"You run along, now." She waves from her spot next to the stove with the half-eaten pie and the pot of coffee.

Outside, Willie doesn't make for his truck immediately. He looks off toward the thicker woods where he knows his Daddy's smoke shack sits within the trees next to the cliffside. It always had a pretty view of the sunset from what he can remember. You could see for miles from there, looking on at the hills and valleys below, watching as the last rays of the evening sun shone on the tops of the trees, reflecting the color of the leaves back toward the sky and giving everything a golden hue. He would sit there for hours as a child, just looking. The leaves would be that perfect mixture of reds and yellows, the colors in the mid-afternoon sun glinting off them like so many luminescent diamonds. He starts in that direction, thinking about the dangers, the rewards—he thinks about Mabel and Fletchie. The trees grow thicker around him as he continues his walk, lost in the thoughts of what he could do, or not.

A grunting sound faintly floats to his ears, the sound of earth being dug into, removed, and shoveled away. The shack comes into view first. A small structure, it sits in the middle of the grove of pines and oak trees with a partly-shaded view of the valley below. It's an older structure than Willie remembers, its rough-hewn planks looking dingy and rotted from lack of use for the past several years since the passing of his father. A stale smell of smoked pork fat has soaked into the planks, and the coldish breeze wafts the faint scent toward him as he walks. He closes his eyes and can see the smokestack billowing with the gray smoke from the pigs; the smell grows stronger for a minute and he smiles.

On the backside of the smoke shack, hidden by a clump of brush with a pipe leading to the shack, Willie finds the source of the grunting noise. A slender, wiry young man with a bare-shaven upper lip and a patchy beard works a small trench with a spade leading to a strange barrel contraption that Willie cannot make out.

"Lester!" he shouts, sweating over his task.

Lester Thompson jumps at the sudden disturbance of the quiet, jittering about to try and find the source of the call. His twitching eyes settle upon Willie and he smiles—missing a front tooth, wiping at his sweaty face with a dirty shirtsleeve. "Willie Henderson," he drops the small shovel and hops out of the trench, walking Willie's way, dusting his hands on his filthy jeans. "How the hell are ya, cousin?" he sticks out his hand. Willie shakes it absent-mindedly, staring at the contraption and the trench.

Willie points to the barrel-like thing next to the small shack. "So, this it? Gonna solve our water problem?"

Lester nods his head up and down violently with a wild grin on his face. "Yeppers."

Willie looks it up and down. "What is it?"

Lester is still nodding his head. "Pump. Uses tight places and pressure ta suck up the water from Roastnier and bring 'er up to that there barrel. Should give ya plenny water fer yer still."

"It gonna work?"

Lester has not stopped nodding his head. He smiles his missing-tooth grin and says nothing in reply to Willie's question. "Gonna have some likker soon?"

Willie looks to his cousin. Is he even his cousin? Second maybe. He looks more a mangy dog waiting for scraps at a table than a man. Man, shit. Boy's no older than nineteen if he's a day. Drinking too much from a young age got him looking rough, though. Acting it, too. Willie hadn't cared for him much after he'd been unable to pay his staggering liquor debt that he'd accumulated when Willie was still shining. Selling to family has never been one of his favorite business policies. With a town like Mountain View, though, where everyone's somebody's something, he didn't have much a choice. Willie looks down to see the copper line leading to the smoke shack. "You thinkin' of running that line through the ole shack, then?"

Lester smiles. "Yessiree. Ain't nobody gonna see ya in there. Pertty good cover."

Willie chuckles softly, shaking his head. "Ya tryin' to blow me sky high?"

Lester's grin remains on his face and he nods his head again. It takes him a moment to register the actual question. The smile fades gradually and his head switches motions from up and down to side to side. "Whatcha mean?"

"Can't shine in confined spaces like that there shack. Fumes could leak and reach the flame. It reaches any flame source, BOOM. Gotta have some wind moving through." Willie turns and surveys the land around him. The shack just won't do. Any idiot knows that. 'Cept Lester, apparently. His gaze settles on a small notch in between two rises in the rough landscape. The remains of a small...it can't be still standing. Willie's memory whirs and he heads over the short distance to the spot, Lester trailing behind while scratching at his ass conspicuously. The rough structure against the small hill is a bit worse for the wear, yet Willie runs his hand along the low roof thatched with tree bark that still acts as a decent roof in some places. His Daddy had quickly made the little lean-to one day so Willie could have a place to play while he tended to the pig smoking: his father had told him it was to be his own smoke shack. It was nothing. A play area to keep him occupied and out of the way while the old man drank and worked. It was a bit dilapidated, in need of a hammer and a tender hand, but there was cover enough to be had, and the light breeze blowing against his whiskers told him of the good airflow through the space. Willie pats the old structure and looks back to the smoke shack. Those boards were good, at least some of them, as was the roofing material. It could be sturdy. It could work.

Willie turns to Lester who is clearly puzzled. "Can you pipe that contraption here?" he asks pointing to the lean-to.

Lester looks from the pump to where they stand, his gaze going along the ground and looking up to the sky, doing his mental calculations. "It'd be tough, but I might be able ta get 'er running thisaway."

Willie nods. "When can ya have it done?"

Lester pulls at his patchy whiskers, eyeing the distance once more. "Dunno, probably 'round two days, I reckon. Pump's damn near finished."

Willie smiles, patting Lester's bony shoulder and starting back the way he'd come toward his truck. "Get it going, then."

"Where ya headin'?"

"Got some thinkin' to do." It could work, though. He knows it. It'd be a risk, but not one that he'd be unfamiliar with. He goes back and forth on his walk to the truck, climbing into the cab and pointing it toward home.

HE IS PARKED OUT A FEW HUNDRED YARDS from the turn-in that he'd watched Willie go down quite some time ago. Half the job is waiting, but Sheriff Michael Baker doesn't mind waiting. He is a patient man. He can certainly sit around waiting for Willie to mess up. And he will mess up—they all do eventually. It's just a matter of being there waiting for them when they decide to get stupid. Michael Baker will be around and watching when such a moment comes. He sits and rolls cigarettes, smoking them as he works and putting the remainder into a silver holder that rests in his lap. He glances up every now and then to make sure Willie's truck hasn't reappeared. Smoke fills the cab of his pickup. Part of him wishes that the trees weren't so thick around the property, perhaps then he could see into what Willie might be doing. It can't be good, whatever it is, and Baker can't stand when people are up to no good. It's against the rules, and everyone must follow the rules.

Rules are important, after all. His father was a horrible teacher, yet he'd made that part of his early education clear with belt and fist and rake. Whatever was available to him to use in teaching discipline and the rules to his son. He was a horrible drinker. One that starts early and continues until he is either passed out or mean. Usually mean. It was when he was mean that his lessons on what the rules consisted of were dealt out in the swinging of objects and beatings. It had worked, though. In a way, at least. Michael Baker understood the value of the rules. He'd never cared about prohibition, did not hate the consumption of alcohol surprisingly enough. He'd never needed booze as a crutch. He could be mean enough without it. It was the breaking of the rules that ground his gears together in a grating manner the screech of a mad stray cat.

He smiles at the lessons that his father gave him as he smokes, grateful for the teachings and the day that those lessons stopped. The booze his father had liked to self-medicate with was highly flammable, after all. That afternoon he'd been too drunk to even wake up as Baker had doused his prone old man with the remainder of the liquor in the jars that had been in the barn. He didn't feel him reach for the book of matches in his pocket or hear the scraping of the match lighting along the rough surface of the package. He'd only woken when the flames licked his body, melting skin and clothing and sending flame up in a stinking smoke that filled the confined space. It had sobered the bastard up quickly, and he'd woken screaming.

IT TAKES A MOMENT FOR WILLIE TO REALIZE that he is being followed on his drive home. A truck that he doesn't recognize makes every switch-back curve behind him far enough where Willie can't make out a face, but close enough that it isn't losing sight of him. Willie takes another route home, an out of the way dirt road going around the turnoff to his property to circle back through Mountain View's township before doubling back on the road toward his property. Willie even stops off at the Lackey Store to look around the shelves for a minute before getting back in his truck and heading out of town. The truck pulls out directly behind him and follows him out of town.

At the turnoff to his house, Willie stops his truck in the middle of the road and gets out. The cowboy hat he sees through the glare of the windshield has him throwing his hands into the air. "Right here, Sheriff!" he shouts at the driver. "What ya got?"

The door of the strange truck opens in front of him, Sheriff Baker stepping out to lean against it with half his body hidden from view. "Howdy there, Mr. Henderson."

Willie stays silent for a moment, chewing the tobacco in his cheek and spitting on the dusty road. "You got somethin' to ask me, Sheriff?"

"Just out for a drive then, Mr. Henderson?" He looks up at the clear October sky. "Beautiful weather for it, ain't it?"

"Don't believe that'd be any 'a your business."

Baker's eyes grow dark at this. The cigarette in his teeth glows with his furious puffing as he steps clear of the truck door. His right hand hangs loose-ly by the pistol grip strapped to his belt. "Where ya been, Willie?"

Willie's eyes shoot instinctively to the cab of his truck—still running—where his own pistol rests on the seat. Too far to move toward. He looks back to the Sheriff and spits in the dirt at his feet again. The tobacco juice hitting the dirt reminds him of blood as it congeals with the dust. "Gonna shoot me, Sheriff? An unarmed man on the edge of his own land?"

Baker stays in the same ready position for a few more seconds, eyeing Willie, probably trying to think of the spot where he could bury the body without anyone in town finding out, wondering whether the sound of the shot would send anyone running out curious. He sucks on his cigarette hard, making the cherry burn red and dwindling the butt down to a nub, threatening to catch his voluptuous mustache aflame. He laughs, smoke billowing from his lungs and moves his hand from his side, resting his arm on the door of his truck casually. The butt of the cigarette falls from his lips to extinguish in the dirt at his feet. His laughing continues for some time before silencing completely with his eyes narrowing once more. "Ain't gonna ask ya again, son."

He'd do it, the crazy sumbitch. Hand's moving back down that way. "Went to see my Mama. Owed her a visit after my long absence."

"Nice long visit, then?"

"Yep."

They stare each other down for a few minutes. The silence makes Wil-lie realize the absence of the woodland noises, the barking of squirrels, the chirping of birds, and the sound of leaves falling that normally encompass the nice, quiet moments in the woods. They must be holding their breath, waiting to see how the current situation will play out, he thinks. He never breaks eye contact with the Sheriff.

The Sheriff laughs again, this time the fakeness of it coming out, keeping his eyes on Willie. "Well, sure does warm the heart to hear about a happy reunion." He slinks back into the cab of his truck, closing the door and letting the truck roll forward into Willie's drive. The gall of the bastard. He backs up and gets the truck turned back toward town. He is facing Willie again, his arm resting out the open window of the truck cab. "Well, I'll be seeing you,

Mr. Henderson. Give my best to the missus."

He pulls out and is gone before Willie can say anything. He watches the vehicle bump along the uneven track, hit a curve, and disappear from view. He spits and lets the wad of tobacco roll from his lips before walking back toward his truck and heading up the drive home.

The farm is as quiet as he had left it earlier that morning. There is a laziness about the air as Willie steps out of the cab to the silence that isn't silence as the noise of the surrounding woods has returned with the lack of tension that had been there a few moments before. The wind is still dead, though, as if the land knew of his encounter with the Sheriff. Willie shrugs this off and makes his way up the porch steps where Pearl waits, her body wagging with the rapid movement of her tail. He reaches down and pats her head with a "good girl" before opening the front door. He stops in shock in the doorway, seeing Mabel, gaunt from her condition but looking more like herself, sitting at the dining room table. A ghost of a smile passes over her lips with his entrance.

"Willie," she greets him, her voice croaking out his name around the small, but visible swelling of her throat.

It takes him a moment to find his own voice. Tears fill his eyes, forgetting her sickness for a moment, as elation fills him for her having this lucid moment. "My Mabel."

Her smile grows. She pats the chair next to her invitingly. "Are ya gonna sit?"

Willie moves to her side and sinks to his knees in front of her instead, burying his head in the skirt of her nightgown. "Mabel," he says again with a sob. He brings his face up, his hands clinging to the loose garment. His eyes are wet. "I'm so sorry."

The smile on her face fades a bit.

"I shoulda been here," Willie blubbers, his words spilling off his lips at a rapid rate. "I shoulda been here. I got stupid. It's my fault."

She reaches out, cradling his bearded face in her hand. It's a cold, bony hand. She lifts his chin to bring his eyes back up to hers. Her head shakes slightly, her own eyes brimming with tears, the same look he'd seen on the day that he was hauled out of the courtroom a guilty man. "No."

Willie opens his mouth to speak again but is silenced by a slender finger sliding in front of his lips.

"No." Her smile returns a bit through the tears, a crooked, familiar grin that had made Willie crazy from the first moment he'd seen her. She had smiled that way on their wedding day, looking at him with their hands intertwined in front of the preacher as he repeated the words of their vows after the minister. "This ain't your fault, Willie. Good Lord only knows such things." She rises from her chair; Willie can feel the shaking of her legs with the effort as she does. Her hands gently push his chin up and Willie rises with her, towering over her small form. They look into each other's eyes for a long moment. "None of this is your fault."

Willie's face sinks into her shoulder as their arms wrap around each other. He can feel the remaining heat of her fever radiating off her cheek through the fabric of her dress. Her legs wobble a bit and lose their small strength, no longer able to hold her. Willie keeps her upright with his grip around her waist.

"Mabel?"

Her eyes are swimming in her head and take a minute to find his. "Just a little dizzy."

Willie scoops her up in his arms and moves toward the bedroom, carrying her as a man carries his bride over the threshold of their home after nuptials are performed. He sets her on the mattress and pulls the blankets around her. She shivers and coughs. Willie brings one of the bowls on the floor up to her face and she spits, resting her head heavily back on the pillows with her eyes closed. Willie believes her to be asleep after a time. He moves to rise from the bed, but her hand reaches out and grabs his. Her eyes are open again, pleading.

"Don't you go leaving me again, William Henderson."

Willie's heart breaks anew. "I won't," he says, though knowing full well he may not be able to keep that promise. He leans down and listens to her uneven breathing. Her eyes are closed again. "I'm gonna fix it, Mabel. I'm gonna make all this go away. Just gotta trust me." She is asleep again, her breaths wheezing with the tightness of her throat. Willie kisses her hand and gently extracts his from her sleep-weakened one. Her hand opens and closes with the absence of his own for a moment before settling with her body and surrendering to the state of rest that either the sickness or the drugs seem to keep her in.

The sun is lower in the sky when he walks into its soft glow on the porch of the cabin. Fletchie sits on those steps, having returned from his studies for the day. Willie joins him and the boy reads from a book that Willie doesn't recognize. He never was one for reading and all that. The words would jumble, and he had hated reading aloud since he was his son's age. Mabel was always the reader, sitting with Fletchie and teaching him his letters at a young age. Willie likes that his son has picked up this habit from his Mama. Grateful that the few habits he sees of himself in his son aren't harmful in any way. The book is thick and weighty with a lack of pictures from the page that Willie can see. The text is tiny.

"Whatcha readin'?"

"Peter Pan and Wendy," he says, smiling up at his father. "It's a story 'bout a boy who never grows up and fights with pirates."

Willie smiles back, "Sounds pretty interestin'."

"Yessir. He lives in a magic place. He can fly, too."

"Sure sounds fun. Like it, then?"

The boy nods. "Yessir." He is silent for a minute, closing his book, careful to mark his page. "Papa?"

"Yes?"

"Did ya mean it?"

"Mean what, son?"

"You gonna fix it? You gonna fix Mama? And ya ain't gonna leave no more?"

Willie sighs, looking out over the land before answering. "I'm gonna do my best."

Fletchie continues to look at Willie sitting next to him, his small face gazing up with worry beyond his years. "You gonna get in trouble 'gain, Papa?"

Willie looks down at his son, shaking his head. "I hope not." It's the only way. He knows it. It's not about him; his family comes first. If that means going head to head with Baker, he'll do it. It's clear now. He rises from the porch steps and reaches down and ruffles Fletchie's black locks. "Go on in and do yer readin'. I got some work I gotta do."

His son stomps into the house as Willie makes his way to the shed. He opens the door and lets the fading light of the afternoon sun filter through the door. He doesn't need it, though. He knows where everything is. He rips the tarp from the bundle of copper wire and his thump pole. He picks them both up and sets them on the workbench that they were under and grabs at a shovel hanging on the wall. He knows where they would have buried it. Before heading out, he grabs a kerosene lamp hanging on a nail by the door and closes everything up. He whistles, making for the trees that lead uphill from his cabin, a walk he's more than familiar with. Pearl barks and runs after him, catching up as they submerge into the growing darkness of the trees.

Pearl yips beside him happy, jumping ahead several steps. She knows where they are going. She'd been there, with him, every trip he'd made into the woods to go to his still. Saved his life a time or two. Nothing ever got past her in the quiet, familiar darkness encompassing them as they worked by the light of the moon and a few lanterns on the darker nights. Your eyes adjust, eventually, to where the dark is welcome. It is too light at the moment. Everything looks strange to the point where he almost passes the spot. If it hadn't been for Pearl, Willie would have walked right on his way farther, continuing into the tranquility of the woods. Her knowing the area, whether night or day, she alerts him to their arrival by plopping onto a soft pile of leaves covering the rocky ground.

Willie brushes the ground with his booted foot to scatter the leaves around, studying the ground closely. A small rock buried enough to where it juts from the ground at a strange angle catches his eye. He starts digging. He works for a while, shoveling dirt over his shoulder as the sun sinks and the night looms in the air. The ground is soft from having been worked around not too long ago, short enough to where roots haven't made their way back into the soil, and the digging by lamplight soothes Willie for a while, and he forgets his troubles and worries: there is no sickness, no Sheriff, no money problems. There is only piercing the ground, grabbing some dirt, throwing it over his shoulder where Pearl darts back and forth among the flying earth to sniff and roll around in the dust and muck. Dig, throw, dig, throw, dig, *thump*.

The metallic clink muffled by a thin layer of dirt has Willie stopping to wipe at the sweat dripping from his brow and hair. He bends down and takes handfuls of dirt, scooping them away until he can see the dull, metallic glow of copper in the flickering light of the lamp.

CHAPTER VI

EXHUMING THE BULBOUS EQUIPMENT FROM THE EARTH had been difficult, Willie having dug well past midnight until he could drag the metallic corpse from the mass grave. He'd stopped a few times in thought, remembering back to the many graves he'd dug of far greater size in France. For a moment during his work, he'd mistaken a gnarled root for the bones of a hand clutching the dirt. He'd sliced down hard on the root with a quick *thwack* of the shovel, severing it of its hold and tossing it over his shoulder to join the growing pile of dirt behind him.

While the digging was tough work, the transporting of the mud-encrusted still to the backside of his home was far worse. He'd tied a rope around the circular cape of the main vat, attaching several of the smaller pieces—cap, piping, and the like—and dragging it through the rough terrain like a mule drags a plow. He'd been caught in several places, heaving and cursing until the still would break free and continue its slow drag onward. His breath clouds before his face as he stares at the mucky remains of his past moonshining operation caked with mud and leaves to the point of being unrecognizable. Pearl, panting, walks around the mass of dirty metal and piping, sniffing happily before licking at a particular patch of dirt, cleaning a spot on the cape of the still and trotting back to sit at Willie's feet.

Willie leans, sweaty and dirty, against the equipment and sinks to his bottom in the dirt. He is exhausted far beyond anything that he'd felt on the farm. He wants to sleep and his eyes sag as his screaming limbs get the break they have been aching for most of the night. He shakes himself a few times to keep awake. He can't fall asleep here. He has too much to do. Too much to think about before he gets to rest.

Transportation is going to be an issue. With Sheriff Baker surely having eyes on him when he is off his land, hauling the large pieces of the still—let alone a run of shine—to his Mama's land himself was out of the question.

They'd have him pulled over and shackled, Baker smiling behind the cigarette in his teeth, quicker than a blink. That won't work at all. Willie won't
allow that smug smile to be directed at him. Not this quickly; not like that. An
idea comes to him, kickin'm like that mule when he was a boy. If it were to
work, he could be running shine all the way through Stone County, possibly
reaching into Cleburne, Izzard, Independence. Hell, folks might be guzzlin'
his liquor in the backwoods and streets of Searcy County before it's all said
and done. That'd get the Sheriff right and riled and no mistake. Piss 'em right
the hell off to see his own sipping from Willie's jugs. Willie chuckles at the
thought of this. Wouldn't that be a hell of a sight?

He creeps into the house in the silence of the pre-dawn hours, trying his
best not to wake Fletchie in his small bed in the corner as he rummages in
the hole in the floorboard. He grabs the jug that sloshes with the remnants of
his last moonshine run. He'd put a heavy dent in it on his first night home,
but there might just be enough for two good glasses yet. He leaves the fiddle
to lie in its blanket where it sits underneath the floor. He kisses Fletchie's
forehead and goes in the bedroom to check on Mabel, sleeping in that fitful
manner with sweat caking her forehead as the sickness runs rabidly through
her body. He realizes as he leaves the cabin that he has not yet lain in his own
bed. After months of being away, not being able to feel Mabel's arms as they
sleep, he'd yet to go to her at night and lie with her as he had every night of
their marriage before being hauled away. He starts the truck and pulls onto
the highway with these thoughts rattling in his head, giving him a bit of a
headache that his hard work and lack of sleep had helped to build into a dull
throbbing in his skull.

The sun shines through the windshield of the old truck as he rumbles
along the rough roads, passing the wooden sign indicating his entrance into
Searcy County. He'd passed through Stone County without seeing hide nor
hair of the Sheriff, or anyone for that matter, following him on the road. He
enjoys the drive. It's a beautiful stretch of road, really, with heavy vegetation
and tree limbs hanging heavy and low along the switch-backs. The leaves
drip and drop, splattering his truck like a soft rain with the dew of the early
morning. It might as well be frost, Willie thinks to himself as he blows on his
hands to warm them in the chill of the cold air blasting through the open cab

of the pickup. It had been a chilly night of working. He plops the last chunk of tobacco from the pouch into his mouth and spits out of the truck, finding the turnoff a few miles from Leslie almost too late. He pumps the brakes and whips into the narrow driveway, passing the fence with the curious cow chewing cud and staring at the strange vehicle bumping along its drive and disturbing its peaceful breakfast.

He pulls in and slides to a stop next to the GMC mail truck parked in front of the white house with its muscadine vines crawling to the sky from every wooden surface it can latch onto. He hops out of the truck. The screen door creaks open slightly and is closed softly as if a hand is guiding it back into place so as not to alert Willie of the exiting of someone from the house. He is expecting the click of the rifle action before he hears it. He casually strolls out from behind his truck to greet Ms. Davis with her wobbling barrel swaying jaggedly to follow Willie as he approaches.

"You can just stop right there," Ms. Davis greets him, spitting a stream of tobacco juice from the side of wrinkled lips.

"Mornin', Ms. Davis," Willie says, smiling and stopping at the foot of the porch steps. The rifle barrel sways in circles a few inches from his face. If she fired from this range, he'd surely be no more. Willie stares into it, though, keeping the smile on his face.

"Knew you's from the guvment." She looks behind him, her eye scanning back and forth between the thick line of trees that surround the property. Her hair is still done up in the curlers from the night before. "Where'n the rest of 'em hidin'?"

"Who's out there, Mama?" Clyde's voice asks from inside the house. His voice is groggy as if he'd only just woken from his sleep.

She spits again. "That guvment fella you gave a ride to 'way's back. I told ya ain't gonna be nothin' but trouble."

The clomping of feet approaching comes from farther inside. Clyde emerges smiling and fastening suspenders over a dirty shirt.

"Mornin', Clyde."

Clyde points to Willie's vehicle, holding his friendly smile. "Seems ya ain't here for a ride. How ya doin', Willie?" He looks to his mother still pointing the tottering rifle at Willie's head. "Put the rifle down, Ma. He ain't from the guvment." He smiles at Willie apologetically.

The old woman begrudgingly lowers the rifle and rests the hammer home, muttering about her son's ignorance.

Clyde chuckles and sticks out his hand. "Ignore her. She ain't all there no more. Can't even comprehend that I technically work for the guvment myself." They shake. "What can we do ya for, Willie?"

"Got a minute?" Willie holds up the jug. "Got some business to discuss."

Clyde eyes the jug hungrily. "Come on in. Mama, get some glasses, will ya?"

The house is surprisingly tidier than Willie imagined it would be, sparsely furnished with a table and chairs in the center of what is mostly a kitchen with a woodstove sitting along one end of the wall. A few chairs sit in a makeshift living space on one side with a curtained area able to hide a claw-foot tub from prying eyes and for privacy of bathing. Bottles line the floor next to the tub in a neat row with a cloudy liquid filling the tub almost to overflowing. Ms. Davis walks over to it with a wooden spoon and stirs the liquid, shooting suspicious glances back over her shoulder toward Willie.

Clyde takes a seat at the rounded table in the middle of the room. "So. Wha'cha got?"

Willie plops the jug on the table and pushes it in front of Clyde. Clyde removes the cork and sticks his nose to the lip of the jug to get a whiff of the contents. He breathes in deeply and sighs, a visible shudder running through his body. Ms. Davis brings over two glasses and sets it on the table, moving back to stand behind her son protectively, keeping a clear view of Willie in case he is to try something guvment-like. Clyde pours a glass and slides it across the table toward Willie, pouring himself some in the other. The liquor comes out clear as spring water and Clyde lifts it up in the light from the open windows to admire the clarity. He takes another sniff and then raises the glass toward Willie.

"Cheers." They both clink glasses and bring them to their lips. Willie takes a small sip and sets his back down to watch Clyde. The other man's drink becomes a gulp, and then another, until he tilts the glass up and taps the bottom to free the last remaining drops to drop onto his tongue. He jumps from the table and does a quick jig. "Woooiee!" he exclaims. "Holy hell fire, that's some good likker. Way better than anything I've had since they out-lawed the stuff."

His mother looks at him with furrowed eyes. "Lemme see that." Willie holds out his glass to her, but she ignores it. She grabs the jug in her bony hands and tilts it back on her elbow, taking a loud pull so that the liquid audibly rushes down her throat. Her eyes open wide in surprise as she slams the jug back on the table, dry as a bone. She squeals in delight and smiles for the first time since his arrival. "I'll be damned."

"Smooth, ain't it? Way better'n anything we got, Mama."

She ignores the comment, looking back at Willie with suspicion. "Where'n ya get it?"

"Made it."

Clyde laughs and slaps the table, rattling the empty glass next to him. "Ya got talent, Willie. Got anymore?"

Willie slides his glass across the table. Clyde greedily takes it and tilts it back.

Ms. Davis pops her son in the back of the head. "Give it here." He obeys, and she finishes the glass off in a few seconds, smacking her lips when finished.

Clyde looks over at Willie in admiration, a question in his eyes. "So, ya just come by here to share a drink?"

Willie shakes his head, preparing himself to make the pitch he'd rehearsed on the drive up. "Gotta proposition for ya."

Clyde smiles. "Well, I'm in a good mood now. Whaddya got for me?"

"You 'member what you told me on the ride toward Mountain View? After we passed the Sheriff car?"

Clyde scratches his chin, looking to the ceiling in thought. He's slept since that ride.

"'Bout no one wantin' to piss off the postman?"

Clyde laughs. "Ah, yeah. I ain't been stopped on delivery ever."

"Well, I need a favor."

Clyde nods for Willie to continue.

"I'm gettin' started back up. Movin' sites and everything. But I gots a problem. New Sheriff is givin' me some guff and I don't think I can get my still to the new site without him swoopin' in and taking my happy ass back to the farm. Plus, there's no way I could be the one to deliver the product when it's all said and done."

"And ya think I might be able to do it, then?"

Willie nods.

Clyde sits back in his chair in thought. He scratches at the stubble on his cheeks. "I don't know, Willie. That's a lot of risk fer some likker. What's in it fer me?"

"Cut of the profits. Little extra money on the side."

Clyde leans his seat back on its hind legs, the chair creaking. He looks at Willie for a moment. "I don't know, Willie."

"There'd be free likker in it for ya, too."

This has Clyde smiling. "Now, that's a pretty good offer. No more of that bathtub swill." His Mama's hand connecting to the back of his head makes a yelp escape his lips. "Damn, Mama. I don't mean nothin' by it." He turns in his chair to look up at her. "You've had it. Way better than anything we've made."

She looks drawn at her bathtub of insipid booze, contemplating whether her son deserves another smack. She glares at Willie instead. "How much we talkin'?"

"Money or whiskey?"

"Both."

Willie smiles. "I plan on takin' this beyond Stone County. With Clyde's help, we could deliver here in Searcy and on to Cleburne, Izzard, Independence, you name a county and I want to see my likker in it. I think we can have people drinkin' this all over. And everyone's in need. With prohibition and everyone else either locked up or too scared to challenge Michael Baker, we'd have run of the market."

"Baker's a dangerous fella," Clyde muscles in. "Never liked the look of that man when he was Sheriff over these parts. Glad to be rid of him, honestly."

Ms. Davis takes a plug of chewing tobacco, ignoring her son, and rips a chunk with her stained teeth. She spits on the floorboards. "What's that mean, anyhow?"

"I'm talkin' good money. Plus, I'll give ya enough booze to fill that tub up right," he says pointing toward the bath. The room is silent for a moment, Willie looking back and forth between the faces across the table, trying to gauge what they might be thinking. "Whatcha think?"

Clyde sits looking at him sternly for a moment. "Well," he looks up to his Mama. She nods her head. He smiles at Willie. "When can we start?"

THE MAIL TRUCK PULLS THROUGH THE TOWN of Mountain View around three in the afternoon. No one notices its presence except to stay clear from the path of the typically-riotous driver. Sheriff Baker sees this as he walks about town and pays it no mind, finishing his rounds and making back for the quiet sanctity of his office. There is nothing out of the ordinary as Clyde screeches to a halt in front of the Lackey Store and unloads bundle upon bundle of brown-sacked mail into the building, the only peculiarity being the truck making toward the unpaved road leading away from the direction it would take back to Leslie, though most do not notice. The driver is a bit on the awkward side if his hectic driving has anything to say about him, and for the majority of the town it does indeed, so if he decides to make a wrong turn and go in the opposite direction from what is normal, there is no concern shown.

SHERIFF MICHAEL BAKER SEES THE FAMILIAR TRUCK parked outside of the County Jailhouse long before he makes to investigate it. Instead he sits and watches as Willie exits the vehicle and casually leans against the hood, producing a pouch of chewing tobacco from his pocket and gnawing down on a good-sized chunk. Baker smiles. This is all a game to Mr. Henderson. If he wants so bad to size up his opponent, Baker will be more than happy to oblige him. He leaves his office, shutting the door firmly behind him, and exits the building into the brilliant sunshine of the day. The temperature has risen to around the mid-sixties with the heat of the sun, and a slight breeze blows through the town, making standing outside to stare at one's adversary a pleasurable-enough experience.

Baker makes sure he is not the first to speak, yet Willie refuses conversation from his end as well. He leans and stares, and spits and stares, meeting

Sheriff Baker's eyes with an ease and sharp smile behind his unshaven face. Baker doesn't like that smile; healthy teeth stained with the tobacco juice working through his jaws, a delicate string of spittle clutching to one of the long hairs on his hidden chin. Willie makes no move to wipe the spit away from his hair. Sheriff Baker has never cared for beards. A finely-trimmed mustache is statesmanlike, shows just the right mixture of grooming and manliness. A beard, though. Those are unclean, unkempt, lazy.

Michael Baker lights a cigarette he produces from the silver case in his pocket. He stands smoking and staring while Willie leans spitting and staring. Something about Mr. Henderson deciding to pay him a visit doesn't sit right with Baker. Something is happening, for sure. He can feel it in his bones without a doubt, yet Willie's presence presents a challenge to him, and Michael Baker is not about to let Willie best him in any sort of challenge. The idea of such makes him sick to think about. After a time, Willie removes himself from the hood of his truck, gives a peaceful wave toward Baker, and gets in his truck. Baker's eyes remain on the vehicle as it backs away and drives off toward Willie's home. Baker watches until Willie Henderson is out of sight. He thinks about getting in his own vehicle and following him. Is it part of the challenge that Willie had laid before him? It very well could be.

After a few moments' indecision, Michael Baker makes for his truck waiting nearby. Before he can start the vehicle, Jack and Tommy run up to him, bent over in front of his vehicle out of breath. Baker gives them a moment to gather themselves. Jack, finally, is able to gasp out about the brush fire having caught near the schoolhouse. His mind leaves Willie as he whips on his cowboy hat and springs into action. The cigarette butt drops from his lips into the dirt to smolder and die.

WILLIE LAUGHS AS HE TAKES THE CURVES IN THE ROAD toward his home. He laughs at the Sheriff, he laughs at the situation, the beauty of the land around him as the sun seems to shine a bit brighter now and the clouds part farther in a blue sky brings him joy. The fire will keep Sheriff Baker and his boys busy for some time. Plenty of time for Willie and Clyde to do what needs to be done. He pulls onto the narrow track of his property. The mail truck is parked behind the house waiting on him, Clyde finishing tying down a tarp to cover the equipment from any curious eyes as they transport it to his mother's farm.

Willie laughs again, thinking of Lester Thompson. Lester might be a no-good drunkard. He might be a bit of a fool, and he might not be able to solve Willie's water problem with the crazy pump-contraption that he'd dreamed up, but Lester was a drunken fool who knew how to set something ablaze and keep it burning for a good, long while. Willie breathes in, and in his joy, he can almost smell the sweet smell of burning field and shrubbery. He knows this to be ridiculous, a trick of his mind, but damn it, it smells good.

As Clyde finishes up, Willie makes for the house to go in and check on Mabel. Thankfully, she is sleeping in bed. She'd not heard Clyde approaching or loading the equipment into the truck. Willie hadn't expected her to, but anything was possible. For once, he is grateful for her deep sleeping. He doesn't want her finding out this way. He will tell her in his own time. Before he'd left Mountain View, he'd gone by and left a note for Dr. Monroe at the Lackey Store as he bought another pouch of tobacco.

Whatever she needs, see she gets it.
-W. Henderson

Willie looks in on her sleeping in the dark of the bedroom, as she so often does now. Her neck is swelling more, and she thrashes uncomfortably in her sleep from bad dreams or fever or a combination of the two. Willie can't decide which.

"You're gonna make it, Mabel," he whispers into the darkness before gently closing the door and walking out to finish the work at hand. He means it, too. More than anything else, this is a promise that Willie Henderson tends to see through. No matter the consequences, no matter what comes, he will see his beautiful wife restored to health. Her labored breathing had continued as he closed the door. Her eyes had remained closed. He'd wished for a moment that she would open them. Just once. Though they did not.

Once the truck pulls onto the gravel road of his mother's property, Willie sits back up on the bench seat of the mail truck. He breathes a sigh of relief from both trouble and pain. He'd taken a jolting, possibly dislocating his left shoulder on one of the wild turns that Clyde had taken. Willie checks himself for other kinks and stretches his back. His shoulder is sore, but it will manage. Clyde smiles over at him with the same crazy look in his eyes that Willie had seen the first time he'd ridden with him.

"Yeeehaaaw! Helluva ride there, ain't it?"

Willie grunts and points to a spot near the front porch of the house where his mother is emerging, bending her back and using the cane that Willie knows she doesn't actually require. It's all for show. "Park there. Ya gotta meet 'er."

Clyde brings the truck to a sliding stop, surely rutting up the grass in the yard. Willie winces at this and looks to his mother for some sort of disapproving glare. "All righty. Let's go meet yer Mama." He makes to jump out of the cab, but Willie's hand catching his shoulder stops him.

"Let me do the talkin'. She ain't real keen on bringing nobody but blood in on family matters."

"Hell, Willie. I live with—"

"Just keep yer mouth closed, will ya? Ms. Davis may be a mean old cuss, but she ain't got nothing on her," he stabs his finger toward his Mama, hunched over and waving jollily to the unknown inhabitants of the vehicle.

Clyde only nods in reply.

Willie steps out of the truck first, waving shyly like a small child might toward his mother who seems to straighten a bit at the sight of him.

"Willie," she says sweetly, leaning back heavier on her cane as Clyde emerges from the mail truck. "You've brought a guest. How lovely." She turns back toward the house, shuffling in a manner expected of someone her age. "I'll just go in and put some coffee—"

"Cut it, Mama. We're here to work."

"I beg yer pardon, son. I don't know what ya insinuatin', but ya better watch that language 'round—"

"Clyde, meet Ms. Betty Henderson," Willie interrupts her. "Mama, this here's Clyde Davis. Runs the postal route from Leslie up through Timbo and Onia and down through Mountain View."

Clyde walks up and sticks out his hand. "Mighty nice ta meet ya, ma'am."

Willie's mother delicately accepts his hand. "Well, it's nice to meet ya, too. But—"

"He's gonna be our distribution. Hauled the still from my house to here."

Betty Henderson drops Clyde's hand and straightens to her full height quickly enough to make Clyde jump. Clyde stares as she moves toward Willie, brandishing the cane she'd been leaning on like a weapon now, making him wonder if she'd been bent over at all in the first place.

"You damned fool. You thinkin' you're just smart, ain't ya?"

"Yep," says Willie.

She brandishes the cane and pokes him in the chest, shoving him back a step. "Excuse me?"

"Yes'm."

"You hauled that damn still out here's? In the light 'a day? You plum lost yer damn mind, boy. Even covered up with them damn sacks, ya coulda been—"

"Sheriff ain't followin' us," Willie interrupts again.

"How ya s'posed to know that?"

"I got it burnin'!" Lester's voice shouts from behind them. They turn to see the wiry form of Lester Thompson high-stepping across the fields toward them. He totes a bag across his back that bangs against him with each step. He reaches them after a moment, smiling despite his heavy breathing. "I… I got it… burnin'," he spits out between gasps. "Damn near set…set the schoolhouse ablaze." His smile widens as Willie pats his back a few times.

"What the hell you on about?" Betty asks, annoyance breaking through.

"Lester kept the Sheriff busy while we made our way out here."

"How?"

"Set fire in the field 'cross the schoolhouse."

Lester grins stupidly. "Had it burnin' good 'fore I left. Sheriff Baker and Tommy and Jack had themselves a good ole time gatherin' up 'nough people ta get 'er under control 'fore it reached the school." His smile fades a bit. "Shoulda just set the damn buildin' on fire. Woulda like to see the sparks fly off them schoolbooks."

"And what of the children?" Betty shrieks, rounding on Willie and whacking him with her cane. "My own grandbaby. Stupid. Stupid. Stupid." She punctuates each stupid with a *thwack* of the cane. She rears back for a good swing, and Willie puts up his hands to fend it off.

"They weren't there."

She stops mid-swing.

"They were on some kinda walkabout today. Fletchie'd been all excited 'bout it earlier." Willie takes a deep breath, rubbing at the sore places that she had already beaten on. "We got it here's, all that matters. Kids are safe."

Willie grabs his mother's shoulder and moves her a few feet away from Lester and Clyde who introduce themselves and blabber on about their new ventures and their love of moonshine. He tells her of his plan that he's cooked up for distribution of the product. He details how they will move the shine throughout the counties through Clyde's postal route and how he'd witnessed the man's dangerous driving while not being stopped by police who would have taken anyone else straight to jail for such reckless behavior. When he finishes, he looks his mother in the eyes, waiting. They shine back at him with a mixture of understanding and doubt.

"Whaddya think?"

She looks at him and then doubtfully lets her eyes cross over to Clyde next to Lester. Her look is a bit sour. It is clear that she doesn't trust him, or the plan fully, for that matter. "So, he runs it in that there mail truck and plays it off as his regularly scheduled deliveries? What if he mixes them up?"

He'd anticipated the question. "Goes right in the back of the truck inside some of the mail sacks with a small black dot to mark them from the rest. He won't get 'em confused."

"What if he does?"

"He ain't going to, Mama. He knows the risk he's puttin' in."

She points her bony finger at her son and then at her own chest. "We're. Risk we're putting in. Who you think they'll come after if'n he screws the pooch? Sheriff's already got yer scent."

"He ain't gonna get caught," Willie says, pulling his arms up to his chest and crossing them. "Plan'll work. 'Sides, I ran this business pretty well 'fore everything went wrong."

"No," she barks sternly, making Lester and Clyde glance awkwardly in their direction. "Things didn't go wrong, ya got stupid. Plain stupid, and you didn't listen to me. That's it. Sooner ya get that through yer thick skull and learn from it, sooner we can move on with this business in a profitable manner."

Willie doesn't say anything for a moment. Her preaching makes his fists clench. Never liked being preached at. The anger fades to shame. It's her stare. She got a way of just looking at him that makes him feel lower than horseshit. Her anger was one thing. He can handle the anger and the whoopings as a child. Her disapproval, that's something entirely different, something he can't take. Couldn't take it even as a boy. "I'm sorry, Mama." He knows her to be right, because she's always been right.

She knows his mind. She lets him wallow for a minute with her silence, looking at him with her pursed lips as she did when he was small, her eyes narrowed. Best he knows his place as far as she's concerned. She stands in stern silence. "All right," she finally replies. "I don't like it one bit, but I'll give it a chance."

Willie smiles a smile of triumph, a smile of forgiveness, and makes to walk away to get to work. Her bony hand reaches out and grabs his with a strength she shouldn't possess. Willie turns back to her and she pulls him in close. "I don't like folks that ain't our kin in our business." She's whispering, barely audible, but her quietness demands his attention. "I hope ya know what yer doin', boy."

Willie nods. "It's the best shot we got."

She shakes her head resignedly, rustling the short, gray curls on her head. She leans in good and close so only he can hear her. "If he gets outta line, you're the one gonna have to put him down." She smiles her usual smile and her face is back to normal. Any sinister thoughts seem to have vanished from her with that smile. She pats his scruffy cheek lovingly and turns to Lester and Clyde waiting awkwardly by the trucks. "I'll get you boys some drinks out there promptly." She turns back to the house without another word or glance toward her son.

Willie almost thinks for a minute that his mother might be just the slightest bit crazy. Maybe she's always been like that. Was he so blinded by his love and devotion for her that he hadn't noticed it as a boy? Had his father seen that side of her? These thoughts are fleeting, however, and soon out of his mind. She is his Mama. She'd done more for him than he could count, and he couldn't let her down again like he did before. 'Sides, he had Mabel and Fletchie to think of. If his Mama was going to give him the means to provide for them both, he'd take it for the gift that it is. No matter her flaws, Mama knows best.

He turns to his rag-tag gang waiting by the mail truck with their hands in their pockets and looking to him for instructions. "All right, boys. Let's go and make some money."

CHAPTER VII

A DIFFERENT FEELING SEEMS TO FILL THE AIR as Willie works setting the brass-colored cap onto the cape of the still, slipping the collar on over the main body and bolting it into place. Peace. That's what he's feeling. The troubles and worries of his life melt with the precision and concentration and the menial labor of lifting and hauling heavy pieces of metal and piping that the performance of his trade requires. That's what it is, he supposes: his trade. He chuckles to himself at the thought of this. Was it respectable? Maybe not. Not so much like that of a shopkeeper, a postal worker, or a Deputy Sheriff, for that matter. It was honest, though, despite any law that might say otherwise. He was providing a product that people he knew—good-natured folk—wanted and would pay good money for. He remembers back to his Bible studies on Sundays as a child, particularly thinking of a passage about judgment: "For with the judgment ye judge, it shall be dealt to you twice over." Or something relatively along these lines. He is rusty with his Bible study, but it is the general gist, none the same. It was in Mark-something, maybe Matthew. He can't remember, but it says it. He's never judged nobody for their lot in life. Why should he be judged for his? He likes his trade, this making and selling of liquor for folk's enjoyment and pleasure. This is biblical to him. Maybe not the product, but the action. 'Sides, Jesus drank. Made wine for that wedding. If Willie'd been around back then, Jesus woulda liked his shine just as good. He's sure of it.

He'd sent Clyde home after the unloading of the still equipment with instructions to return in a week to check on the processing and to allow for his longer periods of presence in the area to become routine. Willie figures he'll have the still going by nightfall if his Mama still keeps all the necessities in her cellar as he figures she does, but it'd be a long road from any kind of product. He's particular, and these things take time. Like any good artist waiting on inspiration to strike, you gotta let the masterpiece inform you when it's ready, not you inform it. It don't work that way. The mash has to cook for a certain amount of time before he's ready to let the beer settle, then the settling process takes several more days before he's ready to even think about the cooking time, for which he plans a nice, slow cook. Most of the shiners he's heard of get impatient. They want that liquor as soon as they can get their hands on it, but the secret is to let the damn thing set for a good while before even beginning the second run, so the beer gets a good fermentation going. Without it, Willie thinks, he might as well be selling piss water directly from the shithouse. Folks 'round Mountain View love his brew because it's the best. He give'um anything less than his normal high-quality product, and he's sure they'd rat him down the line and he'd be kissing shackles before he could blink. Folks are finicky like that when it comes to their liquor. Clyde had left a bit disappointed. It's understandable, thought he'd be trying some shine before the sun went down, Willie thinks, but there's a process to this. An artistry. Sorry, Clyde. You wanna have quick liquor, you can go drink the stuff floating around in your Mama's bathtub. If you want the art to turn out right, just go on and leave the artist to his work.

Lester'd stayed behind. He stands awkwardly with his hands in his pocket as Willie connects the cap-arm into place. He'd offered his help, several times in fact, but Willie'd refused him. He'd just get in the way with his questions and ideas and his foolishness. He's a good enough kid, for sure, but Willie doesn't have time to be holding the boy's hand through the process, only to have Lester drooling over his shoulder and waiting on the first taste. Willie doesn't need that at the moment. He needs silence and to be left alone to practice his craft. Funny thing is, Willie needs him here. Once he gets everything set up, it'll be useless if Lester's contraption fails to pump water up to the still. Part of Willie thinks it to be a futile plan in the first place. Lester had been a real smart kid. Willie remembers him back before the booze got ahold of him before Willie'd gone off to France. Lester had been bright, probably the only one of the family that was worth anything at the book-learning stuff—everyone except Fletchie; Willie knew that he got that from his Mama, though—and was on a clear track to going off and getting him some kind of fancy education out of the hills and country he'd known. Maybe that's what had sparked the drinking, his discovery for his love of booze. Maybe if Lester hadn't been afraid of leaving home, he wouldn't be the twitchy, half-crazed bastard standing awkwardly a few feet from him.

Maybe it had been the lack of a father figure in Lester's life. No one even knew who his father was. Lester's Mama, his mother's cousin or something, had been pretty open with her legs from what Willie could remember. A drinker herself, she probably couldn't remember which man had ended up fathering Lester. Sure enough, though, out popped Lester near twenty years back. A kid without a man to help lead him right, without a Mama to really care for him and teach what it meant to behave and how to act. If there'd been someone there to take care of him, maybe he would have turned out different. Maybes and ifs and buts. No use thinking of all that. The case is, Willie needs him. Without his crazy scheme, all this work would be for nothing.

Lester continues to watch uncomfortably a few feet away. At one point, he makes to help Willie lift a particular piece into place on the still and Willie waves him away with the crescent wrench in his hand, struggling with the load in his arms and resting it on his knee.

"Ya just stay over there an' outta my way," Willie says maybe a bit too affecting. He'd meant to keep him away, not terrify the poor boy. Willie's a big man. Him standing up from his work and brandishing an oversized wrench is surely a menacing sight. Lester'd squeaked a bit and stayed frozen where he was. Willie doesn't need his help with this. Kid'd just screw it up anyhow. He'll get too excited, thinking of the liquor that'll be flowing before too long and will right mess something up. This is a process—and Willie doesn't trust anyone interfering with his process.

Willie looks over at Lester now, standing as he'd been instructed to stand, awkwardly staring at his feet and kicking up some twigs littering the ground at his feet. Willie sighs. He'd been too harsh. "Lester, why don't ya go get that hose pumping some water to your fancy machine over there? Gonna be 'bout ready to start once we get everything set up. Need to see that thing workin' before I go get the supplies."

Lester jumps into action with a smile. "All right, Willie," he chirps excitedly. "All right, all right." He moves to the machine which he'd moved as Willie had asked, extending over the edge of the cliff, apparently reaching down the seventy-five to one hundred feet to the bubbling waters of Roastnier

Creek below. Willie still has his doubts. There is no motor so it uses knobs and suction in the place of electrical power. If it works, Willie will bend over and kiss Lester's ass. Hell, he'll put his head between his legs and kiss his own if that contraption gives them the water they need for the still's operation. Willie's mind doesn't work that way. He prefers the simplicity of a creek nearby, like the one that ran through the mountains on his own property near his old still site. Water running naturally: clear and cold and simple. That is out of the question, though. That'll be the first place Baker'll check when the shine starts running through the county once more.

Willie pushes the Sheriff out of his thoughts; instead he watches Lester almost comically bounce around the heavy box-contraption: attaching a copper wire to a spout hole on one side and running the pipe to the flake stand that Willie had just finished setting up. Once he's finished, he bounces on the balls of his feet nervously, looking to Willie in anticipation.

"A-All right," Lester stutters out, "it's ready."

Willie nods, still not believing the stupid machine will do much more than fail. "Fire 'er up, then."

SHERIFF MICHAEL BAKER SURVEYS the scorched ground before him that continues to smoke with the remnants of the blaze that had jumped around nearly three acres of land. The tall grass that once swayed in the cool autumn breeze was now no more than a blackish-gray dust that swirls to be breathed in and coughed out in wracking fits. He rolls a cigarette and places it between his lips, tickling the ends of his long mustache curled up on the ends ever so slightly with a bit of beeswax. He lights the cigarette with his lighter: a brass device that clicks downward against a flint that fires the wick soaked in oil. The lighter was not a family heirloom, something his father had given him as a man, passing it down to future generations. His father hadn't given him more than bumps and bruises throughout his childhood. No, Michael Baker had taken this particular lighter off the man from his first arrest in Searcy County as a Deputy. The man, a moonshiner from up in the hills of the Missouri area up around Branson, had been delivering illegal liquor into the county for some time. Long before prohibition had even been thought of, this man made and sold his liquor. It wasn't the selling of liquor back then that had been the issue with the man's enterprise, it was the toting of large amounts over state lines to be sold without the payment of tariffs and taxes or anything of the like. Everyone around the area had liked what he was producing, and there really wasn't any movement in catching him. The case had been given to him by the Sheriff at the time, supposedly just to keep him busy and out of his hair. No one thought he'd come close to stopping the infamous shiner. Shit, was the Sheriff surprised when he walked the man in, cuffed and struggling like a boar. Michael Baker smiles at the memory of the look of surprise on the fat Sheriff's face. The shiner was trouble. Baker'd taken him down. Sadly, he'd never made it to trial. He'd died the first night in his small jail cell. The cause was still, as far as anyone was concerned, a mystery.

Baker takes a long, hard drag off his cigarette. The familiar smell of tobacco smoke replaces the stale fire smoke in his nostrils and purges his lungs. It's cleansing, in a way. Tommy and Jack continue pouring bucket after bucket of water on the smoldering remains of the fire, dousing the areas around where they'd stopped the blaze to prevent any more spread from a spark catching on the wind and sailing farther into the dry grass. Incompetent idiots, the both of them. They'd splashed around with the buckets when they first arrived on scene, soaking each other instead of the spreading flames. Michael Baker had about lost it and shot them both just to be rid of them. He could've used their bodies as breakers to keep the raging grass fire at bay, maybe. He'd taken to yelling instead. After a good lickin' from him, they'd gotten in line and got everything under control. Just in time, too. They were only around twenty yards from the schoolhouse when they'd gotten the fire under control. If it had reached the dried wooden structure, there would have been no stopping it from burning the old wooden building to the ground. They'd have just had to let it burn out. Luckily, though, he'd been there to get his two idiot Deputies working, along with the five or six volunteers who had shown up, and gotten the job done. The children would still get their education, all thanks to the tireless efforts of Sheriff Baker.

"Really get those edges around the scorching good, boys," Baker points to the area for his two Deputies with a smile. He smiles more now. He's always liked the thrill of games that take a bit of skill to come out on top. It's like chess—while the white pieces get to go first, the black is the one that gets to come in and clean things up. His opponent had made the first move, allowing Baker to measure the playing field and plot quietly across from him with a smirk. This was Willie's work, Baker's sure of it. It was awful clever. He'd not even put it together until they got out to the burn site and had begun working. Baker had stood watching the flames for a moment, watching the scrambling of his Deputies and the men from town. He laughed. He couldn't help it. It was so well-played that he couldn't help but laugh at his own simple mistake, his misstep. That's why you came to see me; right, Mr. Henderson? That's why you stood there just staring at me with a smile. His Deputies and men from the town had looked to him as if he'd lost his mind. Perhaps he had. Willie had played him. He was up to something, had been up to something, while they were screwing around with a fire. This was a mechanism for time, Baker thinks. Time for what, Mr. Henderson? He isn't sure, but it had been a carefully-constructed buy for time.

I'll give you this one, Mr. Henderson, Baker thinks to himself. Well played. But you made a critical error, that's for certain. In chess, knowing your opponent, learning his moves and the way he thinks, why that's half the battle. Once you know how your opponent moves—once you know the way he thinks—you can predict his moves before he makes them. I know you now, Mr. Henderson.

"My move."

"What's that, Sheriff?"

Michael Baker realizes that he had spoken aloud. He looks to Tommy's simpleminded face, a face that shows concern, that contemplates—if it really can contemplate past the baser instincts—whether or not his boss has lost his mind for real. Baker sucks on his cigarette. "You play chess, Deputy?"

Tommy scratches at his head for a moment, considering the abrupt question.

"Chess? The game you play with those little pieces?"

Tommy's eyes light up with recognition. "The ones with the little castles and horses?"

"Yes."

"No, Sheriff. Can't say I do."

Sheriff Baker nods knowingly at his Deputy's response. It was a long shot, after all. "It's about strategy, boys. We have to be ready for our move now. Mr. Henderson's played his hand."

Jack steps up with a smile and a small laugh, sloshing a bucket of water as he steps beside Tommy. "Ya think Willie had something ta do with this?"

Sheriff Baker takes another puff from his cigarette, blowing smoke out of his nostrils. "I know he did, son."

"But I seen 'im leavin' t'wards Onia early this mornin'," Tommy replies a bit defensively. "He couldn't a' been anywhere near the schoolhouse. I been watchin' 'im just like ya's told me to."

"Of course, *he* didn't do it, you idiot."

Tommy and Jack look to each other, clearly confused. Jack scratches his head, "But I thought you said this was him?"

"Just 'cause he's behind it, don't mean he did it."

The two men continue looking confused.

"He had someone else do it," Baker says, exasperated. This has the boys nodding. Idiots. "I know it was him behind it all. He came to see me right before the fire got started. Just stood out by his truck and stared at me outside the jailhouse." Baker looks off to the blackened field before him, remembering the earlier part of the day. "He just stared with a smile. I know it. He wanted to let me know he'd made the first move. Not a very stealthy opponent, but maybe that's just his game. No…maybe it was a message."

Jack and Tommy stare at the Sheriff. A look passes between them. It's official. Baker must have lost his mind. Maybe it was the smoke. Excessive smoke inhalation can make people act a little crazy, can't it?

"You all right, Sheriff?"

Baker ignores the comment and continues his mumbling. I'm coming, Mr. Henderson. You just know that. The soft sound of children's voices coming from behind him breaks him from his revelry. He was imagining Willie Henderson raging behind a thick set of iron bars. He turns toward the sound and smiles a little at the looks of awe and excitement on the small faces that peer at the scene before them, the teacher trying to gather them all back into the schoolhouse to complete their final lessons of the day before releasing them for home. Their smiles and pointing makes Michael Baker smile in return. He's never had any children of his own. He's married to his job, married to the law. The law is his lover, his mistress, his true love. He enjoys the thought of children, though. They are the future. They can be shaped and molded to allow for the best future of this world. A world that, if Michael Baker has anything to say about it, will be without crime and the infectious nature of people like Willie Henderson, at least in his county. Children hold an innocence that goes missing with age. It happened quickly for Michael Baker, and he decided long ago to make it his mission for children to get to keep that innocence. It is what God intended.

A small black-headed boy catches the Sheriff's eyes. The boy darts in and out of the line of children, pulling girls' hair playfully and pushing his friends back and forth with a laugh. This boy, Baker recognizes. He looks just like him. Except for a few features, surely coming from his Mama before she took sick, and the disguise and innocence of youth that shields all children from the horrors of sin and the crimes of their fathers. It's him, no doubt. Baker had seen him before, kept an eye on him.

He points to the boy. "Deputies, that boy there. That Willie's boy?"

Tommy looks over toward the line of gawking children. "Fletcher Henderson. Yeah, that's him. Seems like a good boy, don't he?"

Sheriff Baker isn't listening. He starts toward the group of children. Mrs. Halliman sees him and waves politely.

Baker waves back and puts on a smile. "Howdy, ma'am."

"Sheriff Baker," she smiles at him shyly, her eyes sinking to the hem of the dress she wears. She fusses with a non-existent stain. "Say hello to the Sheriff, children."

A chorus of hellos and small waves greets him. He smiles down at them in turn. "Hello, kiddos."

"Thank you for getting that fire under control here, Sheriff," Mrs. Halliman says, turning back and forth to count the busy children around her.

"Oh, it was no problem, ma'am. Can't have these young'ins going without a school now, can we?" I'm sure some of them wouldn't have found that such a tragedy, Baker thinks to himself. "Listen, ma'am. I think my Deputies still have a bit of work to do to make sure this here fire don't start back up. Would you allow me to escort you and these little rascals downtown to have us some Coca-Colas? My treat for disrupting your school day." Michael Baker's eyes fall on Fletchie. "Would you like that, kids?" They erupt with enthusiasm. Fletchie smiles, but he continues to meet the Sheriff's eyes curiously. He's got a bit of his father's darkness in there, Baker thinks. Poor, wretched innocent. I'll save you from the devil. Never fear, little one.

Mrs. Halliman smiles politely. "Well, that would be lovely, Sheriff. I believe that they would just go a bit crazy after our walk about town if they had to go back in and sit at their desks today. Thank you."

Michael Baker's eyes are still on Fletchie. "Oh, it's not a problem, ma'am. Shall we go?" They begin walking in the direction of Mountain View's town square. Mrs. Halliman talks to him excitedly about their walk around town and the discussion of such and such about the town history while herding the children together into a mixed bunch in front of her. She holds a long string in her left hand that the children all take ahold of for the walk. Sheriff Baker politely nods and smiles at the comments without really hearing any of the conversation. He looks at the black hair in front of him. It is so deliciously simple that he can't believe that he hadn't thought of it earlier. The best way to get to his target was to find a way into his inner circle. The pieces on the board are set. Michael Baker surveys the imaginary setup with rapt interest. In chess, it's not about going after the king from the start. A good player slowly weakens his opponent by taking out as many of the opposing pieces as he can. If the pawns fall, the more important pieces will follow. Besides, an angry player—someone flustered by the moves of their opponent—he is easy to beat. He will make mistakes before it's all said and done. Sheriff Baker smiles again at the thought and absently rolls a cigarette as they walk. It's my move, Mr. Henderson. Are you ready for me?

LESTER TURNS THE FIRST VALVE on the machine connecting the pipe to the river. Willie watches, seeing no water. He chuckles a bit: at Lester's ineptitude, at his own belief that it might work. "Told you this wouldn't..." A sound somewhere between a high-pitched hum and a sucking noise starts to come from the pipe. Willie steps closer to watch while Lester remains next to the last valve with his eyes closed, listening intently to the noise. Willie listens with him. He hears...no, it can't be. Sure sounds like...

Lester's eyes pop open with a smile and he cranks the last valve. A gurgling bubble starts from the spigot of the pump. There is a brief moment of silence followed by the sound of running water through a copper pipe, ending with the spilling of clear, cold water onto the dirt in front of Willie's feet. He stares in amazement as the flow splashes his boots and seeps into the drying leaves, making them move with the snaking of the spreading puddle. He sticks his hands underneath the spigot, running them through the flowing water. It's cold and fresh just like the creek it comes from. Cupping his hands, he brings the trickling water to his lips and takes a sip. It tastes perfect, just as if he'd grabbed a pail full from the very banks where it flows. His eyes move to Lester standing there waiting impatiently for Willie to respond, his fingers interlocked near his chest with his thumbs fiddling around each other in circles.

Willie dips his hand back down to the cool water, cupping more of it, some spilling through his fingers, and throws a splash Lester's way. The boy seems a bit taken aback with the assaulting splash, thinking that Willie might be displeased, that something might have gone wrong—was the water too warm?—before Willie envelops him in his large arms. Lester gasps in shock and pain from the crushing of his spine. He relaxes after a moment. He'd been victorious. For once in his life, just maybe he'd done something right. Something that really makes someone happy in his work. He closes his eyes to take in the moment. He feels useful. Willie sets him down and smiles at him, turning back to the flowing water and slapping his cousin on the back.

"Well," Willie begins, coughing in his hand, embarrassed at his sudden burst of happiness and affection. He smiles again. "What are we standin' 'round waiting on? Let's get to makin' us some likker!"

Lester only nods, the smile stretching his bearded, hollowed face. Willie's arm remains across Lester's shoulders as they walk toward the house. Lester remembers the water and escapes Willie's arm to run over and turn the valve to close off the flow. Willie waits on him. He returns to Willie's side and the bear-of-a-hand slaps his back once more as they walk through the pines and the shrub on the narrow track back toward the house.

THE CHILDREN'S HAPPY LAUGHTER brings a smile to Sheriff Baker's face as they sip from their big glasses of Coca-Cola with ice cubes. He'd even sprung for a few of them to get a scoop of ice cream on top if they'd wanted it. He feels good. Normally, Baker hates events like this, mainly because he is usually in the wake of a group of constituents when these kinds of things happen. They would gab to him about things he never cared to talk about in the first place, make him discuss policy that didn't really matter. He does the job. He does the job right. Why isn't that enough for them to hear? The children, however, care nothing for his politics or his run as their town's Sheriff. They don't want to shake his hand or discuss the rising percentage of speeding through the sleepy little town, or, Lord forbid, the weather. They are perfectly content to sip their sodas and laugh at their own jokes, leaving him and Mrs. Halliman to sit happily watching.

Mrs. Halliman is still talking. Damn, that woman can talk. Baker reckons that she hasn't shut up once since the offer to take them for drinks in the first place. He isn't really bothered by it. He just doesn't listen. He smiles and nods politely every few minutes, looks her in the eye with an affirming expression on his weathered face, acting as if he cares deeply for what she is saying, but it doesn't matter. None of it matters. The only thing that truly piques Michael Baker's interest is getting to speak to little Fletchie Henderson: sitting among his friends at the moment and laughing along with them, sipping from his soda and stealing a spoonful of ice cream from his fellows' glasses when they look away. Baker's eyes darken a bit at this. Innocent or not, kid has a little too much of his father in him. Perhaps Baker can set him straight when this is all said and done. Take him under his wing, maybe. The boy deserves someone to look after him and teach him right. His father is certainly not going to oblige in that manner. He could be promising. Just need to get learnt a few lessons is all.

Baker looks at the pocket watch he keeps in his shirt pocket, another present that he'd claimed off of some unfortunate troublemaker fate had allowed to cross his path. It is gold with silver trim around the edges and a silver engraving with the name, Alfred, on the front.

"Was that your father's?"

Baker shakes his head and looks up confused at Mrs. Halliman. "Pardon?"

She smiles. "The watch," she points to the finely-crafted time piece in his hand. "Was it your father's, Sheriff Baker?"

"No, my father's name was Josiah."

She looks at him confusedly. "But the watch says Alfred on it."

"My Grandpappy, ma'am," the lie coming smoothly to him. No one needs know the truth about his trophies. Some might find it a bit grotesque, yet they are precious to him. More precious than anything his grandfather had ever given him. His grandfather was a drunk. "He gave it to me when I went off to college. Sadly, he passed shortly after that."

"I'm sorry to hear that," she looks down shyly for a moment before looking at him excitedly. "So you went to college, Sheriff?"

"Yes, ma'am. Up in Missouri."

"An educated man. That's so refreshing around here. Did you go before or after the war?"

Michael Baker's eyes narrow for a moment. She looks away from those eyes, alarmed by their darkening glare. Baker catches himself and smoothly wipes the look from his face, burying the look and feelings deep. He takes out his cigarette case. "Did you go to school, ma'am?" He puts a cigarette between his lips and lights it.

She looks to him again, his change of mood quickly forgotten. "No. I finished the secondary school 'fore helping my father 'round the farm. A few years later, the schoolteacher in town retired and I was able to take her place. I done a good bit of reading…"

Michael Baker stops listening. He lights and puffs at his cigarette, letting his eyes roam nonchalantly around the room before they settle back on the messy head of black hair a ways away among the laughing group of children. They seem to be slowly finishing up with their treats. Baker clicks open the watch and looks at the time.

"Well, I hate to cut this off," he says, interrupting Mrs. Halliman, "but I believe it's about time for me to get back to work. 'Bout time for you to let these young'ins run off, too." He shows her the watch face reading 3:30 in the afternoon.

"Oh, Lordy," she says, rising from the chair. "It sure is. Shoulda had them on their way half an hour ago." She turns to the group of children and asks for their attention, snapping her fingers in a rhythmic manner a few times. The children echo back with their own chorus of snaps, turning to face her. "It's about time for us to head home for the day, but first let's all thank Sheriff Baker for his kindness."

A chorus of thanks greets the Sheriff as he makes for the door, dawning his cowboy hat, giving the kids a big wave. He'll drive around and wait toward the edge of town for his moment to arrive. "It's no problem, kiddos. Y'all stay out of trouble. Don't want me to be comin' after ya." The children and Mrs. Halliman laugh at his joke. He exits the shop and jumps in his truck, pulling down the road a spell before whipping it around and heading out toward the edge of town on the road leading to the Henderson house. He'll pass this way, for sure. Friendly Sheriff Baker will be waiting to offer him—no, insist—on giving him a ride home. That'll work. That'll work just nicely. Then they'll be able to have their chat. Talk about his Daddy's line of work, maybe. No. Best not bring his father into this just yet. Just get to know each other a bit better. No need to spook the boy. Make friends. Friends aren't afraid to talk to friends. Friends tell each other everything.

He thinks of Willie Henderson and smiles at such a thought, pulling off the side of the road on a narrow dirt track to wait for Fletchie to pass him by. Baker rolls a cigarette and smokes it with the windows down, enjoying the cool fall breeze and admiring the colors of the changing leaves. Many of them have fallen already, and more will follow if the wind continues building as it has over the past few days. Baker likes wind. It reminds him of change, of the coming of something better, something new. He has dreams sometimes where he is the wind. A powerful, righteous wind that catches Willie Henderson on the edge of a high cliff one day and blows him off the face of the earth. The dream always has him waking up smiling.

He doesn't have to wait long. Fletchie's approaching footsteps reach his ears before he sees him. The boy walks along the dirt track whistling a lively tune and beating the bushes and overhanging limbs on the side of the road with a stick that he twirls in his left hand, his schoolbooks slung over his shoulder tied together with a belt. Baker sits up and throws the nub of his cigarette out the window. He doesn't immediately follow after him. He lets him pass by, not noticing the truck parked, and continue down the road a little ways before he starts the truck and pulls out after him.

Fletchie doesn't turn around as the truck slowly approaches, only thinking it someone passing him on the road. Baker pulls up beside him and rolls down the passenger window of his truck. "Young Mr. Henderson."

The boy looks at him a bit startled at first, perhaps deciding whether or not he should run into the woods to his right, before recognizing the Sheriff in his shiny truck. Papa'd told him not to talk to strangers. He obeyed Papa on this normally. But this was the man who bought him the soda with the scoop of vanilla ice cream. He had talked to Mrs. Halliman while they'd enjoyed their treats. He wasn't a stranger. He was nice. "Howdy, Sheriff."

Baker smiles down at him from the truck. He leans over and opens the passenger door. "How 'bout a ride, son? Good, long walk from here."

"My Mama says I'm not s'posed to get in nobody's truck 'cept Papa's."

"Your Mama's a smart lady. But I'm sure she won't mind. I'll let you turn the siren on. How 'bout that?"

"Neato!" Fletchie exclaims, jumping into the cab of the truck without a second thought and slamming the door shut behind him.

Baker pulls out back into the middle of the gravel-dirt road and points to a switch on the dash. "Just that one right there."

Fletchie eagerly reaches toward the switch.

"Oh wait, wait, wait," Sheriff Baker stops him. The boy looks up at him confused. Baker stares ahead, pursing his lips and shaking his head softly. "I'm sorry, young man, but I just remembered; only sworn Deputies and I can use the sirens."

Fletchie's face sinks to mirror the look on Baker's face, his chin drooping to touch his chest. "Oh."

Baker smiles a little. It is so easy to get children to want something. It was just too easy. "You know what?"

Fletchie's eyes tilt toward the Sheriff. He looks as if he might cry.

"It could probably happen. I'd just have to…no, that wouldn't work."

The boy's head shoots up off his chest and he stares at the Sheriff excitedly. "What?" What won't work?"

Baker looks down at him with an eyebrow raised before sighing and looking back toward the road. "Nah. You wouldn't like it all that much. 'Lotta responsibility."

"I'd like it. Promise, sir. I'm good with 'sponsibility."

"Well," Sheriff Baker begins, drawing out the word for added suspense.

It works. The boy nearly sits on the edge of the bucket seat waiting for Baker's suggestion to drip from his lips. "I s'pose I could just deputize ya. Make ya a real Sheriff's Deputy. But that's a lotta work for a kid like yourself."

"I can do it. I swear. Honest, sir. I'll be a good Deputy. 'Sides, I'm grown. Nearly seven years old."

"You really think ya can handle it, son?"

The boy nods in earnest in the seat beside him.

"All right, then." Baker pulls the truck to the side of the dirt road under the shade of a hanging pine limb. A few needles fall down on the windshield of the vehicle almost immediately after the automobile comes to a halt. He turns to face the boy with a serious look on his face. It's not an act, either. Baker takes what he is about to do incredibly serious. He grabs the worn Bible he keeps on the dash of the truck and places it solemnly before Fletchie. "Put your left hand on the Bible and raise your right hand." Baker raises his own right hand to mirror the small one shooting up into position, the small left hand slapping on the face of the Bible, nearly knocking it from Baker's clutch. "Repeat after me. I... I'm sorry, son, your friends call ya Fletchie. Your real name Fletcher?"

The boy nods again.

"All right. I, Fletcher Henderson."

"I, Fletcher Henderson."

"Swear to uphold."

"Swears ta uphold."

"The laws of God and men."

"The laws of God and men."

Baker smiles down at the boy. He smiles for himself some, having made up the oath on the spot, thinking it was pretty damn good for a spur-of-the-moment swearing in. Yet he is proud. The boy has taken a large step in the right direction. He might not know what exactly this oath is intended, but he seems to take it seriously none the same. This is good. There is hope for him. He knows he has the boy, too. Fletchie will do just about anything he says now. Best not to push it so quick, though. "I now deputize you as an official Junior Deputy of Stone County." He puts the Bible back on his dash with reverence and reaches out his hand for the boy to shake. "Congratulations,

Junior Deputy Henderson."

The boy beams up at him with pride. "Thanks, Sheriff. This is really neat. Can I play with the siren now?"

Yep. He has him, for sure. He pulls back onto the road heading toward the Henderson homestead. He points to the siren once more. "Be my guest, Deputy."

The siren blares through the quiet of the wooded area outside of Mountain View all the way to the narrow drive leading to the quiet farm where Willie Henderson is concocting his evil schemes away from the Sheriff's eye. Michael Baker puts down the accelerator a little farther than he normally would, mainly for the boy's amusement. He looks over several times throughout the ride to see Fletchie grinning wildly, ear to ear, and whooping along with the sirens as they go. He shuts it off as they round the last curve to the mountainous farm home and pulls the truck to a stop.

"All right, Deputy. This is where I guess we part ways for now."

"Ahh, do I have ta?"

In his pocket, for sure. "'Fraid so, Deputy. But I'll be checking in on you real soon. Gotta be available for you to report back to me, don't I?"

The boy nods eagerly again from the passenger seat. Sheriff Baker reaches over and ruffles his black head of hair. "Now, off with you."

Fletchie gets out of the truck, turns about, and gives Baker a stiffened salute.

"Listen, Deputy," Baker says, leaning out his window. "I think we should probably keep your swearin' in a secret for now, even from your friends and your folks. Wouldn't want nobody gettin' jealous now, would we?"

The boy nods stiffly, still keeping his rigid salute.

Baker salutes him back from his seat in the cab. "Dismissed, Deputy."

The boy breaks and runs up the dirt path toward his house. He stops at the crest of the drive and waves exhaustively toward Baker. The Sheriff returns the wave and pulls out back onto the road toward town. It has been a productive day, he thinks to himself while rolling a cigarette, steering the vehicle with his knees. He lights up and hums through the smoke as the cool wind of the moving vehicle sends the pine needles on the hood flying away.

OLD FIELD PINES

Willie ARRIVES BACK HOME as the sun sinks below the treeline. The exhaustion he feels is deep, yet it doesn't seem to show on his face, smiling at the orange-purple tincture of the skyline through the canopy of limbs on the wooded road. He feels good. It was an honest day's work. He could always tell an honest day's work when he got home tired, sweaty, fulfilled. Lawyers and the like of those professions surely don't have such ends to their workday. They don't sweat; they don't feel the product forming from the calluses of their hands. They swindle. Yet this is legal. Legal to take honest folk for their money with only paper to show for it in return. This is legal, yet working all day on a product to sell isn't. Willie doesn't understand this. His mind won't wrap around that philosophical stuff.

It doesn't matter, though. The day is nice and cool with just the right tinge of warmth that doesn't have you running for the woodstove to thaw your aching hands like it will when December rolls around. No. This has been damn near the perfect day. The sight of his son sitting on the porch reading a book as the truck rolls to a stop puts another smile on Willie's face. Fletchie's a smart boy. Gonna be something to reckon with when he gets him an education. And he'll take to it. It'll stick with him. His brain's made for stuff like that. Willie thinks to himself that perhaps his son might pursue a dishonest career, like law. It's not the position, he supposes, it's the man. Fletchie will be a good man 'cause he's got the right raisin'. Be the only damn lawyer that Willie'd ever trust if he so chooses to go such a route.

Fletchie looks to his father as he gets out of his truck and smooshes down the top edge of the page he'd been reading from. He sets the book on the porch carefully, with reverence, as if it's something holy, before running over to hug his father. Willie lets him grab onto the leg of his pants and pats his back for a moment before ruffling his black head of hair. The hair was just about the only feature that he'd inherited from his father. The rest—the smile, lips, eyes, nose—that came from his Mama. Willie sees so much of Mabel in their son.

"Hey, boy. How was school?"

Fletchie nods, his smile spreading. "Good."

"Good trip 'round town, then?"

"Yessir."

Willie looks to the grinning face, near to burstin' looks like. The boy wants to tell him something. Good news, from what it looks like. Willie wants to tell him some good news as well. Tell him they ain't gotta worry no more. That money will be coming before too long. They'll get the medicine for his Mama real quick and she'll start doing better. The smile fades from Willie's lips. He can't tell his son that. Too young for all that mess. He'd probably have to lie to the boy. This thought makes his frown crease farther into his face, making him look older than his thirty-five years. The thought of lyin' to his own son, the thought of lyin' at all, that don't sit right with him. He tries to push the smile back on his face.

"Your Mama asleep?"

Fletchie shakes his head. "Nosir. Been hackin' up somethin' awful. I went in ta see how she's doin' earlier, and she just told me she was fine." His eyes sink to his shoes, losing the spark that was in them only moments ago. "She don't sound fine ta me."

Willie pats his son's head. He's just like his Mama. Takes the weight of the whole world on his shoulders like it's his responsibility. His ability to feel, to feel for someone absolutely, that's Mabel in him. No doubt about that. Willie's always been able to look at the world a bit more calculating, face value for what it is. Not Mabel. She feels for everything, questions the wrongs and shows compassion for everyone. Fletchie gets that from her. The way he stands now, taking his mother's sickness on his mind, compassionate, trying to figure out a solution, it makes him look like her even more than he already does. He even tends to wrinkle the space between his eyebrows like she does when thinking of the injustice of it all.

"She's gonna get better. Imma goin' to see to that, boy." He points back to the front steps where his books sit. "Go on and finish your readin' and do your chores. I'm gonna go check on your Mama." The boy stands in the same spot, his eyes continuing to look down at his feet as they kick at a dandelion poking out from a patch of weeds. "Here in a bit I'll come back out and ya can tell me 'bout your day."

Fletchie's eyes light up at this. "All right." He takes off at a run, yelling back over his shoulder. "I'll go get the hogs slopped and be done 'fore ya know it."

OLD FIELD PINES

Willie smiles at his boy's small frame as it disappears around the corner of the house toward the attached pen where they keep the hogs. Might be time to butcher one for some meat. They could have a big feed once Mabel is doing a bit better and enjoy the last of the good weather to boot. They could always salt and store the rest for the colder winter months. He walks up the steps. Pearl stands at the door waiting on him, wagging the puff of her tail in the air.

"Hey, girl." He bends down and gives the dog a nice pat. She rolls over for him to rub the soft fur of her underside. "You ready to go back to work, girl?" He obliges her the tummy rub, watching as her eyes perk up at the mention of work. She knows what he means. She'll be ready to go whenever he is. She'll come with him, for sure, when he goes back over there. Gotta have his alarm system near at hand. She looks up at him with the loyalty of any good animal. "Gonna go in and check on Mabel."

The dog rolls over, circles the porch, and lies down near the steps, looking out over the hilly fields toward the treeline.

He can hear her coughing before he even steps into the house. He stands for a moment with the door cracked, looking back at the woods and rolling hills with a grimace. This breaks his heart. Despite everything. Despite all of the devastation and death, his time locked up and kept far away from his family, the sound of Mabel suffering almost sends him to the edge. If he could do anything—take her place, anything at all to possibly take away this sickness that plagues her, he'd do it. No doubt about it.

He is doing that, though. He's doing everything he can. Of course, there will be risk. God knows that with Sheriff Baker on him like he has been, the chances of success are slim, even with the different delivery system and the moving of the still site, there would still be risk. But he'd walk through Hell and back again, walk right up to that ole devil and spit right in his eye if that's what it would take. He doesn't realize that he is at the door to their room until his hand reaches for the knob and pushes it open. Mabel sits hunched over, her body wracking with the horrible cough, her neck swelling even farther than it had been that morning. She sees him and wipes the spittle away from her mouth. She tries to hide it, but Willie sees the coagulated blood on the edge of her hand before she can cover it with the handkerchief.

She leans back into the fluff of her pillows, exhausted. "Willie."

"Hey there, honey." He stands there awkwardly in the door for a moment. Perhaps the treatment will be coming too late. No. He can't think like that. She'll get her medicine despite the risk and get well before he knows it. He believes this. He has to.

She clearly senses his discomfort. Her neck puffs with purplish veins running along the puffiness of her throat. She pats the bed beside her. "Come on and sit with me a moment," she croaks, going into another fit of coughing.

Willie comes and sits down beside her while she finishes. When she is finally able to take a breath, it rattles in her throat, and spittle mixed with blood dots her lips and chin. She makes to wipe it away and avoids eye contact with him. He says nothing, catching her hand before she can wipe it away. He takes the handkerchief delicately clutched in her bony fingers and dabs at her chin and lips gently. She smiles at this and he smiles back at her. Her smile is filled with the physical agony that he can only imagine she feels and tries not to reflect it back at her, knowing he is failing miserably. The look on his face makes her chuckle: a lilting, beautiful sound that has Willie laughing in turn. They sit a moment in the bliss of shared humor, letting their laughter fill the room as it once had. Before her sickness. Before he'd been taken away from her. Another coughing fit comes with the laughing, and the smiles die quickly from their faces.

Willie waits patiently until she finishes, sitting and twiddling his thumbs, unsure of what to do or how he might help her. He doesn't notice she has stopped until she reaches out with her sweaty, fevered palm and takes his hand in hers. Willie doesn't mind the sweat or the heat. He's just glad to have her awake for a moment. He'll take it. He'll take as much of her as he can get.

"I'm gonna fix it, Mabel."

She smiles up at him, drawn, moving her head until she is able to catch his fleeting eyes. "What do ya mean?"

He gestures with his hands at her and the bed. "This. I'm gonna fix it. Just wait."

Her smile grows even more drawn than before. She is doing that compassion thing, that thing that she'd passed on to Fletchie. Even in this, bedridden and sickly, she isn't thinking of herself, but the sadness that Willie is feeling for her. "I don't know if there *is* a fixin' it, Willie."

Willie shakes his head, refusing to believe such a thing. "There is. I talked to Doc. He's gonna be gettin' you some treatment real soon. I told him to do it, anything he has to." The smile he gives her is one of hope. "I've got a plan, Mabel. It's all gonna work out."

She studies his face for a moment, turning this way and that—her swollen neck making movement difficult. "Oh, no. No, Willie..." her eyes begin to water, and her words dissolve into tears.

Her crying surprises him. He'd expected happiness, hope in return, not tears. He reaches out his hand to touch her arm, but she shakes it away a bit harshly. "Mabel?"

"No," she sobs. Even her crying sounds different with everything happening to her throat. It still fills Willie with pain hearing it. "You can't, Willie."

He is almost in hysterics with her. He doesn't know what he did or how to make her stop. He just wants her to smile. Just once more up at him, tell him that she believes that everything will be all right. "What's wrong?"

"No. Please say you're...please tell me you're not...please." It's uncontrollable now. She lets out a pained wail that has Willie burying his own face into his hands, laying his head down onto her shaking arms, reaching for her. He does all he can to comfort her and make whatever is hurting her go away.

Willie is not only hurt but frustrated. He is terribly pained along with her, but he doesn't understand. "Can't. Can't what, Mabel? Can't what?" He spits the last question out a bit more harshly than he intended to, but she won't answer him. She won't stop crying. She won't tell him what is wrong. She only cries in her hands for a few minutes, refusing his comforting touch as if it is something poisonous. This hurts him worse than when he was watching her in her fits of coughing. "What do you mean?"

Her breathing comes in gasps now, but she is able to take her hands away from her tear-stained face. Her eyes meet him, pleading with him. "Please tell me I'm wrong."

"Wrong? Wrong about what, Mabel?"

She sniffles, looking in his face, scanning for truth. "Tell me you ain't running shine again."

The question catches him off guard for a minute before he answers. "No, Mabel. Of course not." It surprises him how easily the lie, to Mabel nonetheless, comes to him. It isn't really a lie, though. He isn't running moonshine at the moment. They'd only just got the first bit of mash ready and set that day before he'd come home. There wouldn't be any running for some time. And he wouldn't be doing the running anyway. That would be up to Clyde. He was only doing the production side of everything. He was just the master chef of the operation while Clyde was the delivery system. It was a lie nonetheless, though. He knows that. Deep down, he knows that he is lying to her, to the one he loves more than anything on this earth. But isn't a lie easier, more soothing at this point in time? It's safer this way. The less she knows, the better. Just in case—well, just in case the worst happens.

Her tears slow for a moment. She goes into another coughing fit and then sighs when it is over. She looks tired, old even. Far older than she actually is. He can't tell if she can see through his falsities. He wouldn't be surprised if she could. "Promise me."

He looks at her and wipes away the tears running from her cheeks. He cups her chin with his large hand and smiles at her while the bile rises from his stomach and into his throat, threatening to send him running for a bucket to be sick in with what he is about to say. "Promise."

He can't tell if she believes that either. Hell, he wouldn't believe him if she was in her shoes. But he's doing what he has to. It's all for her and Fletchie. Maybe one day, a day a long time from now, she will understand if she learns the truth. That is, if she doesn't see beyond his lies in the moment, if he doesn't slip up or let the guilt crushing him overcome him and spill his guts to her. He can't tell, as he looks in her eyes, what she believes.

She sighs, though, and leans back into her pillows. "How ya gettin' the money, then?"

This also takes him aback. He hadn't thought much about that. "What you mean?"

"How ya gonna fix it, Willie? How you gonna pay Dr. Monroe for any treatment?"

Willie thinks quickly. "I'm working with the postal service delivering some packages, and I'll be helping Mama out on the farm."

She looks at him quizzically, her eyebrow raised in her unbelieving fashion. With that look, she almost looks to be well again. Willie can't help but smile at her. "The postal service and your Mama's farm?"

"Yep. Met a man who gave me a ride from Leslie that works for 'em. Said they were looking for some folks to help with the delivery process. I went and saw him the other day and told him I'd take the job. Plus, Mama's got me workin' her fields for her and selling some of her crops for my own profit. She can't do it by herself, and we sure as shit can't grow nothing worth anything out here. I'll harvest and take her stuff into town for her. I've already talked with John Lackey about him selling her produce and gettin' some folks in town that would be willing to buy her hay 'stead of grow their own." He pauses to see if she is believing any of it. He still can't tell. "I'd have told you about the postal thing sooner, but you've been pretty well out of it. Plus, it just kind of happened. Didn't think it would pan out to much of anything."

She continues her quizzical staring, trying to decide whether or not she believes his story. Another coughing fit brings her low once more, and she loses the look and the thoughts of disbelief with the pain that clearly shows on her face. She closes her eyes and lays her head back on the pillows.

"All right, Willie. I'm glad you're finding work so quickly. Thank you."

"Trust me, honey. I'm gonna make this all better. No more leavin' ya and Fletchie behind. I promise." He leans in and kisses her, rising from the bed afterward. "I'll go start on some supper here in a minute. Would ya like something?"

"No," she says, her voice sounding more and more groggy. She is drifting toward sleep again. "No. Think I'll just sleep a while."

"You really need to eat."

"Just bring me some of whatever when it gets done. I'll eat."

"Thank you," he says, standing and watching her for a moment, his shadow casting toward the bed from the soft light emitted from the other room of the cabin. He believes her to be asleep after a time. Her breathing has softened more, and her breath loses some of the rattling that accustoms it when she talks too much these days. "I love you, Mabel." And he means it. Despite his lying to her. Despite having to deceive the one person in his world that loves him fully and truly in return. It is for the best. It is because he loves her. He makes to close the door behind him.

"I love you, Willie."

Any good feeling, any at all that he might have possessed, fades with that. The guilt is almost overwhelming as he closes the door and stands in the soft light of the main room. He moves to the stove, trying to confirm in himself that what he is doing is best. A lie meant in good purpose is not such a bad thing, is it? No. It can't be. He can't worry about such things anymore. He's already too far gone down the path he chose to walk, and there is no turning back at this point. Too many people are involved, too many cogs are turning. I do this for you, Mabel, he thinks to himself while looking back at the closed bedroom door. It's all for you.

Willie puts another log into the slot in the stove. A low, comfortable heat comes from the shimmering coals inside. He takes a cap off of one of the iron burners. He finds some potatoes in the pantry. Many of them have sprouted the strange tannish arms of new growth, but they smell fine—earthy even—to Willie. He chops them and places them in a pot that is already filled with water. He doesn't know if the water in it is clean or not, but it doesn't matter. The heat will boil anything malicious out. He is no chef. By any means. If it hadn't been for Mabel taking the brunt of the cooking work all these years, they probably would have all starved a long time ago. When the going gets tough, though, the tough need to get their asses in the kitchen and make some supper for their child and sick wife. He sets the potatoes on the stove to boil and walks back outside on the porch where Pearl sits next to Fletchie—having completed his chores—reading his book as he had found him when he came home.

Willie takes a seat beside his son, Pearl circling next to him for a moment before curling up against his right leg. "So," Willie starts. Fletchie puts aside his book, careful to mark the page that he is on. "What y'all go see and talk about today?"

"It was so fun. We went 'round town and to the courthouse and talked about how long it'd been there and went inside for a minute. Then there was a fire."

"At the courthouse?" Willie asks in mock surprise.

"No. At the schoolyard."

"A fire, you say?"

"Yeah. Almost sent the school up in flames. The Sheriff and his Deputies caught it before it reached the building."

Willie tries to hide his smile. "That musta been something."

"Yeppers. I'd have been real sad about that. School's where I get all my books. They coulda burned up."

"I'm sure that nobody'd allow for all them books to catch fire now. Good thing they caught it when they did."

"Yessir."

Willie takes out a fresh plug of chewing tobacco from the pocket of his overalls. He undoes the wrapper while Fletchie watches for a moment, trying not to let his dad see his eyes wander over the plug. Willie bites off a chunk and chews for a moment thoughtfully. He spits in the dirt and looks at his son staring at the tobacco pouch in his hand. Willie breaks off a small piece and offers it to his son with a grin.

"Really?"

Willie nods and offers the chew again.

Fletchie reverently takes it and pops it in his mouth, chewing furiously. He can't help the sour look washing over his face. Willie laughs at this, a hearty, full laugh.

"Don't swallow none. You don't want it, just spit it out there on the ground."

Fletchie tries to settle his face back to normal and continues to chew. He leans forward and spits. It's stringy and dangles from his lips. He spits and spits, trying to get it to fall from his lips. He ends up accidentally spitting the small wad out of his mouth, leaving some of the brownish spittle on his chin. Willie wipes it off, laughing again.

"Then the Sheriff took us all out for sodas."

Willie's laugh dies at this. "Did he?"

"Yeppers. Bought everybody in the class a soda. Even let us have a scoop a' ice cream in it if we wanted one."

Willie is getting angry. He can feel it building in his stomach like a cancer. He spits. "Idn't that nice of him."

"Seems real nice."

"He say anything to ya?"

Fletchie hesitates for a moment. He can tell his father, can't he? But the Sheriff told him not to. He's not s'posed to tell about the ride home or about him becoming a Deputy or nothing. He can't tell him. He made an oath. "Not really." It surprises him how easily he is able to lie to his father. It would surprise the boy to know that his father has felt similar feelings about the ease with which lies cover the truth recently. He feels low, though. Lower than dirt. And after his Papa let him have some of his chewing tobacco. None of the guys at school were going to believe that. It's quite the privilege to get to chew like a grown up, and here he is turning around and lying to show his gratitude.

Willie notices the boy's hesitation, though. He knows something is wrong. He can't help but feel a little angry at his son. Why would he want to talk to someone like Baker anyway? 'Cause he's a kid, you idiot, he thinks. He's a kid and someone was nice to him. How the hell he s'posed to know any better?

"You sure he didn't say nothin' to ya? Nothin' at all?"

"I mean, he said hey to us. He said it to everybody. Asked us if we wanted ice cream in our Cokes. Seemed like a real nice man. He did ask 'bout you, Papa. Said to tell you hi."

Willie sighs. He sighs to try to keep the anger out of his voice. That son of a bitch. The gall of that bastard. He can do whatever he wants to Willie himself, but he sure as shit better leave his family out of the mix. They have nothing to do with this. This ain't their fight. This thing's between them. Fletchie's so much like his mother, so trusting. So kind. He'd talk to anyone who seemed like they wanted to. Just like his mom. And, damn, he's smart, too. Probably can't get enough conversation on his level with kids his age. An adult wanting to pay him attention would be almost too much for the boy to pass up. Of all the things Fletchie could have taken after Mabel for, Willie hates his friendliness the most right now. It could get him hurt. Get all of them hurt.

"Listen, son." He looks down at Fletchie who refuses to meet his eyes. He acts ashamed. "I don't want ya talkin' to the Sheriff none. He ain't a good man."

"Why ya say that?"

"'Cause he don't like your Papa none. I just don't want him tellin' you things 'bout me that ain't true. Bad things."

Fletchie leans his head against his father's arm. Willie looks down at the scraggly head of black hair, hair like his own, against him. "Ya ain't bad, Papa. I know that."

Willie's mind goes through his life. The war. What he'd done over in Europe to survive. He remembers the bullets. He remembers the screams of the dead and dying. The stink: piss, shit, blood, death. He'd caused some. He'd caused a lot of death. He remembers some young boy dying in the mud at his feet, screaming—for his Mama, more than likely—in a foreign language that Willie couldn't understand. He remembers bringing the butt of his rifle onto the boy's forehead to end his life. He'd told himself that it was for mercy. The kid was only suffering. Really, it had been to stop the crying. It drove him mad, homesick and starving and hurt as he was. The shinin', too. Runnin' from the law and polite society alike to make a little money. He spits in the dirt. It's hard to imagine himself as a good man.

"Papa?"

Fletchie is looking at him. Willie didn't realize that he was crying until the small hand comes up to his cheeks and swipes at his tears.

"Why ya cryin', Papa?"

Willie grumbles as he wipes at his eyes with his shirtsleeve. "Just got somethin' on my mind is all. Think I'm tired."

They sit in silence for a few minutes, the only break in the quiet being the small snores of Pearl next to Willie and the occasional spit of tobacco juice.

"Papa?"

"Yeah?"

"You mad at me, Papa?"

"No, son."

Fletchie looks at his feet. "I didn't know about the Sheriff. I'm sorry."

Willie puts a muscled arm around his son's tiny shoulder. "Just want you to be careful 'round people. I'll take care of everything else. You just be careful. Got it?"

Fletchie nods.

Willie pats his shoulders and rises from his seat on the porch. "You go on in and get ya some supper. Take some into your Mama, too." He walks out into the yard. Pearl awakens with the movement and trots after him.

"Where ya goin', Papa?"

"Just gotta run an errand right quick. Go on and get ya some taters in the house."

Fletchie goes inside without another word. Willie walks to the truck and hops in the open cab. Pearl sticks her front paws on the edge of the truck and begins scratching for him to pick her up and take her.

"Not this time, girl. Ya go on back to the house."

She whimpers in reply.

"Go on." Willie reaches across the bench seat and finds his pistol strapped there. He takes it out and flips the chamber open and checks the bullets inside before slamming it home and starting the truck up. He pulls out of the house with a rising of dust in his wake.

Fletchie watches from the window of the kitchen as the truck disappears into the fading dusk. He feels bad for lying. He had to. The Sheriff had told him he had to. He's a Deputy of the law. The thought of this excites him and he soon forgets having to lie to his father. He spoons some potatoes onto his plate and goes in to take one to his Mama.

SHERIFF MICHAEL BAKER SITS BEHIND HIS DESK in his office at the jailhouse. Everyone else had long since gone home. He'd elected to stay behind, feigning responsibilities involving certain documents that needed his immediate attention. There is a window in his office that looks out onto Mountain View's downtown square with the towering courthouse of brick and stone taking center stage to the menagerie of shops and stores bordering the giant building. He likes the view. He can see everyone coming and going, all the business of his town right under his nose, just a quick glance out his window. It is a fake view, though. He knows this. It is like an act of a play, everyone milling about on their way and trying to pretend that deep down they aren't wretched. Baker knows this. Baker can see right through the act, a trait that he is rather proud of and feels should be an ability of all those who choose to go into law enforcement. Everyone puts on their masks, though.

OLD FIELD PINES

Even him. It is part of the job.

The view is empty now, all of the lights in the downtown area having been extinguished an hour or so ago with the passing of the last of the roamers through town square. All the lights in the shops have gone out and the square is peacefully quiet, a time of day that Sheriff Baker enjoys. It is the purest time of day when no one is around to pollute the silence with noise and refuse and lies. There is only silent darkness broken by the sound of squirrels running about to collect what someone might have dropped. A raccoon digs through a trash bin somewhere unseen, yet Baker can hear its paws ripping through the cans, and an owl hoots somewhere in a tree near the courthouse, safe from the prying eyes of humans and predators alike, waiting for a nice meal to scurry out into the open so that it might snatch it mid-flight.

A bottle of liquor sits on the desk in front of him. It is unopened, glinting in the light from his desk lamp. Another souvenir. He'd been saving it for a special occasion. It feels like tonight will be the night. He waits as the truck pulls around the corner of Main Street and disappears from the sight of the window. Baker pulls two glasses from a drawer to his right and sets one before himself and the other on the opposite side of the desk where a chair sits empty. The main door opens quietly. He'd left it unlocked, knowing that he would have company. He doesn't know how. It had just been one of his feelings. The door of his office stands open.

"Mr. Henderson." Sheriff Baker does not rise from his chair as Willie's shadow blocks out the soft light of a few lamps from the main room of the jailhouse. He'd left these burning as well so Willie wouldn't stumble on his way inside. It was charitable of him. "Come on in and take a seat." He reaches for the bottle in front of him and pops the top. He smells it, taking in a good whiff and shuddering at the harshness of the alcohol. He pours into the glass on the opposite side of the desk. Willie remains standing where he is, peering in through the darkness, shrouded in shadow. The revolver hangs limply at his side. He is surprised to see Baker so welcoming.

"Now, don't be shy. Come on in and take a seat. Have a drink." Baker points to the revolver in Willie's hand. "You won't be needing that, Mr. Henderson. Just go ahead and put your gun away for now."

Willie doesn't move. He had been angry on the ride over. Angry knowing just how cunning Baker is. Angry enough to drive off his farm in the growing evening, drive around to try and cool down, and ultimately decide to come to the jailhouse with the intent of murder. The welcoming attitude that greets him has him trying to find that anger once more. He masks its absence with a show of it, nonetheless. "You son of a bitch."

Baker laughs. "Now, Mr. Henderson. No need for such vulgarity. We are gentlemen, aren't we? Please, take a seat and have a drink. Let's discuss our business as gentlemen are ought to do, shall we?" He offers the glass once more in Willie's direction.

It's a trick. It's got to be. No way this man would be sitting here smiling if he didn't plan something. Perhaps the drink is poisoned or some kind of thing like that. Maybe Baker has a gun underneath the desk pointed at Willie, and the finger is just itching for him to take a seat so it can throw the hammer back and let loose.

As if reading his thoughts, the Sheriff smiles. He takes a tentative sip from the glass he offers to Willie. His mustache curls up with his lips as his face screws together. "Ugh. Never really liked the taste of it myself. Potent stuff, though." The Sheriff reaches for his side where the pistol sways on his hip. He takes it in his hand. Willie points his gun toward the Sheriff. Baker holds up his left hand in a stopping motion, taking the pistol from its holster held between his thumb and forefinger and sets it in a drawer of his desk. He slams it shut with a *bang*. "There," he says, closing the matter. "Now we can talk without any bad thoughts."

Willie begrudgingly takes the available seat in front of him. Baker tips the bottle to Willie's glass, replenishing the slug he had taken. They sit for a moment in silence, Willie and Baker staring at each other from across the desk. After a moment, Willie picks up the glass in front of him and takes a whiff of the clear liquid. Its smell is strong with just a hint of copper tang mixing subtly beneath the surface. It smells familiar. He takes a careful sip, his eyes never leaving the smiling image of Baker across the way. It's not bad, not as good as his own brew, but it is relatively pleasant and most certainly familiar. He leans forward and examines the bottle more closely, Baker's smile widening a bit at the corners. Willie feels the heat in his eyes, remembering back to his long summer nights of tutelage under his friend making moonshine. He tries to force the hot tears back, keep them from falling. The liquor was of someone who knew their way around a still, a professional in all aspects.

"Leeroy," Willie says to no one in particular.

Baker laughs, picking up his own glass and taking his first sip. "But of course, Mr. Henderson. I'm rather fond of this particular vintage as the architect of its design has sadly passed on." He rises from his seat, leaving Willie to stare at the bottle. Baker goes to a shelf littered with various books and mementos from his career. He picks up a beautifully-crafted wooden box and returns to his seat, opening it for Willie to see. Willie swallows what sadness has flooded him, keeping his composure, and looks at the robust cigars sitting on a bed of black velvet. He nods, impressed.

"I'm honestly glad that you recognize this particular make, but I was almost certain that you would, Mr. Henderson," Baker says, selecting a cigar from the box and sliding it Willie's way for him to pick one for himself.

Willie reaches in and grabs a cigar, not particularly sure if one is better than the other. The hospitality is surprisingly fetching for such an encounter, in the sickest way possible. It makes the hairs on his neck stand on end, testing the air for the inevitable moment of chaos that will surely ensue. "How could I not? Only two or three folks 'round here make liquor that well, and it ain't none of mine."

Baker laughs again, clipping the end of his cigar and offering the cutter to Willie. "No. Not nearly the quality of what yours was from what I've heard. They will be an interesting comparison." He smiles. "See if the student surpasses the teacher." He lights his cigar, puffing the end into a glowing cherry, smoke billowing to form an eerie halo over his combed hair in the soft lighting. Baker clicks his lighter to life and holds it out across the table for Willie to lean in and light his own smoke. "It's really a good batch for such a small-time operation. Poor bastard, had to shoot him for resisting."

Willie leans away from the lighter's flame and reclines in his chair, puffing away at the long cigar in his teeth to hide the anger that he truly feels. His teeth are barred like fangs against the nib, smoke billowing furiously from his mouth and nostrils. His eyes blaze through the smoke.

"What was that poor bastard's name? Aber? Kiber?"

"Iber."

The Sheriff snaps his fingers. "That's it. Iber. Leeroy Iber." His smile widens at the glowering look in Willie's eyes. "Friend of yours, right?"

Willie blows smoke and reaches for his glass on the table. "Good man."

"Dead man."

Willie quaffs back the drink and slams the glass down on the desk. Baker refills him. He holds his own glass up to Willie in a form of toast. "To good, dead men." He slams back his own drink and pours himself another one. A giggle issues from his lips—sounding far more childlike than the elderly gray figure from which it originates should—when he looks over to Willie who hasn't bothered to raise his own glass at the toast. "Come now, Mr. Henderson. It's all part of the trade. He knew the risks—just as you do yourself—of becoming a part of such an industry. Only he'd underestimated his opponent. He made mistakes and when he was caught, he decided that fighting was a better option than spending his time on the farm. It was quick, Mr. Henderson, I promise ya that. BANG!" He slams his fist on the table, rattling their glasses. Instead of making Willie jump, it only makes him clench his teeth. "And that was all she wrote for Mr. Iber."

Willie grinds his teeth against the stub of the cigar. He wonders at the possibility of reaching for his gun, cocking the hammer, and putting a bullet between the Sheriff's thick eyebrows—or perhaps in the middle of the bushy mustache, just for the sport of it—before Baker could reach his own pistol to stop him. The odds are against him. He continues smoking, watching the Sheriff's grinning face, the yellowing of his rather straight teeth beneath the manicured hairs covering his upper lip.

"This why you waited for me, Sheriff? Talk about some of my friends you killed? Talk about good men put in the ground before their time? Good men just trying to make a livin' for their families when most the land out here ain't worth the pieces of paper the deeds are printed on? That your plan, Sheriff? Anger me into actin'?"

"I don't believe I had to anger ya too much, Mr. Henderson. I never called you to my office. You showed up on your own, and I just happened to be waitin' 'round. Whatcha plan on doin' with that cannon anyway?"

"Meant to come kill ya."

Sheriff Baker leans over the worn desktop on his elbows. "Ya still wanna, Willie?"

Willie picks up his glass and brings it to his lips. "'Course I do."

Baker grins behind the smoky haze from his cigar. "What's stoppin' ya, then? Skin it and let's see what ya got, war hero. I wanna see what it is ya think you're made of." He breathes in deeply, sniffing the air in a strange, maniacal action as if tasting something. Tasting the tension. "I would relish the opportunity."

Willie grins back. "You'll get it. I promise ya that, Sheriff. You'll get it. Wanna know what my life—the war, prison, everything—has taught me?"

"What's that, Mr. Henderson?"

"I'm pretty damn good at waitin'."

Baker nods, the smile covering his face seeming to fade just a bit. A lessening of the curvature of his lips. "As am I, Mr. Henderson. I'm rather good at waiting around for something to happen. For something I want."

"That what you did when the war came a'callin', Sheriff? You just sit 'round waitin' for it to pass?"

This wipes the smile completely from Baker's face. He glares at Willie sitting smugly across from him, inhaling a large cloud of smoke from his cigar. "Watch yourself, Willie. My patience and hospitality only extend so far." He takes another puff from the cigar and reclines back in his seat, keeping his eyes locked on Willie's bearded face. "I have been a life-long servant of my country and state, Mr. Henderson."

"Yet you didn't go to Europe?"

"I went, you bastard!" Baker yells, slamming his fist firmly onto the top of his desk. His eyes seethe. The suddenness of it startles Willie a bit. These sudden outbursts of anger are surely the real Michael Baker bubbling to the surface. It happens around Willie, he thinks to himself, quite often. Baker takes a calming breath and blows out more smoke from his lungs, the cigar having burned down quite a bit from when their conversation began. Willie glances at the clock on the wall to realize they'd been sitting together for longer than it had seemed, the night speeding by around them.

"I was there, Mr. Henderson. I was there for quite some time. Nothing really too dangerous, no more than a correspondent, really: delivering orders and letters, back and forth correspondence, things of that nature. Saw some action, too." His stare is no longer on Willie anymore. Willie recognizes what he is looking at. He is looking back. Willie recognizes it as he has stared like that himself a time or two since coming home from France. Baker looks off toward the wall of his office and beyond, back to the war. Willie knows the awful nature of having to relive everything for no particular reason at all. Relive the horrors of those days in the shit and the mud and the blood.

Baker shakes himself awake from his stare. "I don't talk about it. There were…" he clears his throat, "complications. I was sent home. End of story."

Willie says nothing for some time; he forgets why he had come in the first place for a few short moments. What is it that he feels? It feels almost… no, it can't be. But, yes…that's it. Sympathy. Sympathy for the one man who if he caught him for real, caught him doing what he knows he has to do, would haul him smiling to the courthouse and even to Hell if the devil'd give him the chance. Willie can't help it, though. He knows all too well the horrible feelings that come with the memories from his own time at war.

"Don't s'pose this changes much?" Willie asks. He doesn't have to ask. He knows the answer.

"Nope. Don't guess it does."

Willie looks down at his glass. "Pretty hypocritical of ya to be drinkin', Sheriff," Willie comes back, changing the subject with a bit of humor returning to his voice. "Evil likker might be sneakin' into yer heart."

"Evil is relative, Mr. Henderson. I'll answer for my crimes." His voice and eyes are harsh now. "I'm gonna make sure you answer for yours, too."

Willie grins again. "I'll drink to that."

It is silent for a moment before Baker replies. "Got yourself a good boy, ya know it?"

Willie nearly chokes on the liquor in his throat. The anger comes back in a wave. He looks to his gun on the table and has to take a few moments to calm himself before he does something he knows that will lead to trouble. This is why he came anyway. Baker back to trying to provoke him into acting, making a mistake. Willie isn't going to give him the satisfaction. He slowly rises from his chair, putting his cigar stub on the table and draining his glass of liquor. He collects his belongings and stares at Baker, his eyes confidently smiling.

"I'll give you this one time, Sheriff. Just this one warnin'. This here situation is between you and me. Ya come near my family again, I'll burn you alive for the whole town to watch."

"Threatenin' an officer of the law is a crime, Mr. Henderson."

"Ain't no threat, Sheriff. That's a damned guarantee." Willie heads for the door. "Ya can take that straight to the bank."

THE GRAVEYARD IS QUIET THIS TIME OF NIGHT. Even the small woodland creatures seem to have called it in and are sleeping soundly out of sight of Willie's wandering. He'd not known he was going to come until his truck had stopped in front of the wrought-iron gate out behind the Methodist church. His legs move of their own accord, following the family names that he knew so well until he reaches a row that he is more familiar with. Many of the stones are old, some he's sure he couldn't even read the inscriptions in the light of day, having faded with the wind and rain and weather. It's peaceful here, though. And his legs are thankful for the exertion as he continues down the long row.

He stops at a newer stone. He's unfamiliar with this one, but the light from the large moon is bright enough for him to read the inscription carved into it. He pats the stone lightly and with care.

"Hey there, Leeroy." He sinks to his knees in front of the stone. His forehead finds the cool, rough surface. No tears come, surprisingly. He was sure that there would be once he realized what he was looking for. He only sits, his forehead resting on the gravestone in silence, searching for a comfort he knows no longer to be a part of this world.

PART TWO

PART TWO

𝕿𝖍𝖊 𝕾𝖙𝖔𝖓𝖊 𝕮𝖔𝖚𝖓𝖙𝖞 𝕯𝖊𝖒𝖔𝖈𝖗𝖆𝖙

20 November 1925

Moonshine Epidemic Sweeps Stone County

The people of Stone County have seen a rise in distribution of illegal moonshine liquor. Authorities claim to be taking action to uncover the perpetrator and the source of the problem. Despite the prohibition on alcoholic substances, it is clear that the production—and consumption—of moonshine is rising in the area.

The effects of the rise in volume of the bootlegged liquor have been seen throughout the county as arrests for illegal intoxication have risen by thirty percent over the last three months. Sheriff Michael Baker discussed the issue with us.

"We are working hard here to determine the source of the illegal production and are tirelessly searching for evidence to be able to put a stop to those who would disturb the peace of the good citizens of Stone County."

The Sheriff continued, "I know in my heart that the citizens of this county are being taken advantage of by this evil substance. The recent arrests have been good people, many of whom have only fallen trap to the devilish temptation that we see every day. As their Sheriff, I pray for these folks, good folks all, and will fight for them during this time of tribulation."

No arrests have been made at this time in the search for the culprit, but the Sheriff assures us that he and his Deputies will continue their...

The Stone County Democrat

30 November 1925

Search for Bootleggers Continues

Despite efforts of the Stone County Sheriff's Department, moonshining operations have flourished. Arrests for illegal consumption and possession have risen further. Last week, six arrests were reported from local townsfolk of the county seat alone. The perpetrators had the liquor on their person at time of arrest.

Mixed feelings on moonshining arise in citizens of Stone County. Some residents feel the ban on alcohol has done nothing but good things for the well-being of our citizens and applaud the federal and local governments for their passing and enforcing of the prohibition.

Southern Baptist minister, James Earle, and Methodist, Donald Waldrup, spoke out about their opinions on the ban and the continuation of moonshining in the county.

"Times are hard," Father Waldrup said. "Devil's trying to make his way into Mountain View through the hearts of our congregations. We encourage our fellow Christians to stay far away from that liquor. Keep the faith and know that the Good Lord is watching you."

Other community members feel the ban to be an infringement on basic human rights and applaud the efforts of the illegal distributors. One citizen, having asked to remain anonymous, commented on the current situation. "Well, I figure it's about every man's God-given right to make a living on this earth. Can't say I fault whoever's doing it. They are just trying to make a living."

Another citizen, also anonymous, said that they are happy with the actions of the bootleggers. "Government ruling on what we can and can't do just seems plain wrong. We should be free to do as we please. I say, keep it flowing and raise a glass to the fellow taking the time to provide a service."

Sheriff Michael Baker commented on the situation this past Thursday. "We are working every lead we can to find the perpetrators and rid our county of this disease. We are working tirelessly in this endeavor and hope to come back with some good news soon."

There were no further comments on the current leads and actions being taken. With the continuation of such actions, we can only hope...

The Stone County Democrat

4 December 1925

Local Bootlegger Brought to Justice

John Travett of Stone County was arrested on his land last week at the site of an illegal moonshine still. Travett was taken to trial. Circuit Court Judge Derre H. Coleman ruled a guilty verdict this Tuesday. Travett was charged with production of bootlegged liquor with intent to distribute.

Travett was sentenced to 15 years at a state penitentiary. The sentence will be carried out without the opportunity of parole as he serves his time for his crimes against the state.

The courtroom was crowded for the sentencing: some folks believed the spectacle to be justice, while others thought the punishment harsh, given Travett's role in the community as Baptist Church Deacon and his exemplary record thus far.

John Travett spoke out at his sentencing. "I refuse to apologize for my actions. We had fallen on hard times, and I did what any man would do to provide for the family whom he loves. Any man in here who would say different is a liar and a coward."

Travett was escorted out of the courtroom in chains after sentencing in a fit of rage.

Sheriff Michael Baker spoke after the trial was over. "This is a true victory for the good people of Stone County. This is not just a win for my department and office, but a win for all law-abiding citizens of this county. I am looking forward to seeing the effects of such an arrest in the community. Arrests for illegal drunkenness will drop, the absence of illegal substances will bring out the best in our citizens, and I'm sure that further arrests will follow in the war against moonshiners."

Sheriff Baker was confident that the moonshining activity will quiet with the recent conviction. "Many of the recent arrests for possession have contained certain jars of the substance. The liquor found within these jars has been of superb quality and make. Many of the jars found on Travett's property matched the jars previously obtained from other arrests, and his liquor seems to be of similar quality. It seems that we might have rid the county of one of its more notorious shiners."

The Stone County Democrat

11 December 1925

Moonshine Presence Strong as Ever

Illegal substance abuse continues in the Stone County area. John Travett's operation seems to have not been the big player that the Sheriff's Department had previously thought. In past weeks, distribution of moonshine has seemed stronger than ever, and arrests pertaining to the consumption of the substance continue to rise.

The peculiarities pertaining to recent findings—particularly with the jars recovered and quality of the liquor—seem to be relatively the same despite predictions of Stone County Sheriff Michael Baker. We can only speculate whether the arrest that was made involving Travett was the arrest that the citizens of Stone County were particularly hoping for.

Sheriff Baker refused to comment on the subject when asked. However, he wants to assure the citizens of Stone County that his department is tirelessly making efforts to overcome recent hurdles and bring justice to those subjected to this horrible substance.

If any citizens have information regarding the illegal liquor, you are encouraged to contact...

CHAPTER VIII

WILLIE NAILS THE LATEST NEWSPAPER CLIPPING to the wooden frame of his still shed. Previous clippings detailing the Sheriff's consternation at coming up with nothing in the hunt to catch him in the act flutter in the cold breeze. His breath comes out in puffs and frost crunches under the sole of his boots as Lester helps Clyde load the last of the next run into the mail sacks and into the bed of the mail truck. Pearl lies curled up on a ratty blanket that Willie'd brought along for her. She sleeps soundly in the warmth radiating from the stone and mud structure of the furnace. Willie looks up to the gray sky with the heavy clouds moving in. There will be snow soon. More than likely be a white Christmas this year, or at least an icy one. A rarity for this section of Arkansas where snow only comes in slushy small batches that do more damage than make the landscape picturesque. Ice has always been the real issue in the area. He whispers a small prayer for the weather to hold off long enough for them to finish up and get back to their respective houses before any kind of bad weather hits.

It surprises him how much better he has been since the night of his conversation with the Sheriff. He finds that he thinks of that night often. What it was that made him feel better, he has no idea. Whether it was the actual confrontation, the thrill of needing to kill and denying it, or his ability to say farewell to an old friend after so long, it isn't clear, but he is happy for once. He looks around at the steaming contraptions and workings of the still, Pearl snoozing comfortably with the furnace's heat despite the chill in the afternoon air, and at Clyde and Lester finishing up their work and talking lightly over the latest run or some small-town gossip that they'd heard at whichever place from so and so, and he is grateful.

"What 'bout these three jugs, Willie?"

Willie turns to where Lester points at the three jugs of freshly-made moonshine standing near the shed and shakes his head. "Leave 'em. Them are goin' with me."

Clyde stuffs some newspapers into the sack in between the jugs and jars of shine to keep them from rattling and busting on him on the highway and loads it into the bed of the pickup. "All right," he says, looking around, his breathing heavy and coming in thick clouds. Despite the cold, sheens of sweat drip from his thinning hair. "Think that's the last of it." He wipes at his brow and goes to the cab of the mail truck with the county symbol painted on the side. Opening the door, he produces a thick package and walks to where Willie stands gazing contentedly at a squirrel with fat cheeks bringing what might be the last of his winter stash into a small nook in the trunk of a large oak.

Clyde extends the package to Willie, who continues to stare up at the tree, ignoring him for a few moments. "Willie?"

Willie shakes his head, making his beard wag from side to side, coming out of his dazed state. He spies the package in Clyde's hand. "Oh." He takes it, pulling out his pocketknife and slicing it open.

"Pretty good haul this last run. Made drop offs all over Stone County, over toward Searcy County, and even as far down as Cleburne." He laughs. "People really like yer stuff, Willie."

Willie ignores the praise and pulls out the bundles of cash from the package. He walks to the cover of the still's shed to stay clear of the wind and enjoy the heat from the furnace and begins counting in silence, leaning on his haunches and working carefully. The warmth from the still is nice on his sweat-slicked skin with the furnace smoldering from the run he had just finished. Lester joins Clyde as they watch Willie count the money and divide their percentages into separate piles. Willie's and his Mama's piles are by far the largest with Clyde's coming in a close second and Lester's being a bit smaller than the others. This was all agreed upon previously, but even Lester's meager pile adds up to a nice sum of money. Willie double checks his math, ticking off the numbers in his head and on his fingers when they get a bit confusing, and gathers up the piles and rejoins the two men waiting in the cold.

Willie hands Clyde his bundle, careful not to let any of the bills slip from his hand in the icy wind. "Here ya go, Clyde. Pretty hefty sum for the effort."

"The rewards are greater with the risk."

Willie hands Lester two piles: his smaller share and the larger bundle for Willie's Mama. "Here. You got yers, and make sure ya give Mama hers. Don't go squelchin' any neither. You know that woman won't put up with nobody swindling from her share, and it's yer ass if ya do."

Lester fidgets uncomfortably. Willie can't decide if it's from his nerves or the cold or the slight rebuke. "I-I-I'll g-get it to h-her, Willie. D-don't worry none."

"Be sure ya do."

"Ya sure ya don't wanna g-give it to h-her yerself? She k-keeps sayin' how she don't ever get to see ya m-m-much, and ya being over on the p-property and all."

Willie turns back to the shed and produces another couple of large jars from the base of the furnace. "Nah. Gotta run back to the house here in a bit. Doc Monroe should be out before too long to give Mabel her next round of medication."

Clyde rubs at the back of his neck. An uncomfortable gesture, but Willie never sees it. He don't like the mentioning of sick folk. Makes him nervous. "How's she doin', Willie?"

"Better. Had the first round of antibiotics come in 'round mid-November. Last Doc saw of her, said she was respondin' well to the treatment. Swellin's down in her neck a bit, but can't really tell much difference other than that. Still coughin' and hackin' bit much for my likin'. Doc's been givin' her stuff to sleep a lot, too. Says the rest will help her to gettin' better quicker."

"That's right good news, Willie. She's gettin' better."

Willie smiles. The first smile that either Clyde or Lester had seen all morning. She might just be out of the woods. He hands the jars to the men waiting. "Here. Saved these from the last bit. Should be 'nough in those to last y'all two a while." Willie hands over Clyde's jar. Lester reaches for his and gets his hand on it. Willie's grip remains strong on the jar, and his eyes meet Lester's. "Don't go gettin' caught with this neither. If ya do, I sure as hell can't come bailin' ya out of trouble." His brows lower as Lester's eyes sink uncomfortably to the pine needles at his feet. "Ya get caught, yer on yer own."

OLD FIELD PINES

Lester's eyes dance over the jar as he nods his head. Willie releases it and wraps his arms across his chest, blowing out a long cloud of warm air from his lungs. He worries for Lester. The boy has come a long way since they started working together a few months back. Maybe it's his eyes caressing the bottle of liquor as if it is something truly precious. Perhaps it was just the boy's sketchy path through life so far. Willie'd gone back and forth over giving it to him but had decided it might be better coming from him rather than Lester going off to find some on his own. At least this way he will be able to keep an eye on him.

"Welp," Willie says with another sigh, looking up at the dark expanse of sky with the thick, puffy clouds threatening some nasty weather. "I reckon that's it then, boys."

Clyde puts his money and jar in the cab of his truck and starts it up. He pulls on a pair of gloves that had been sitting on the dash. "When ya wantin' me back for the next haul?"

Willie pulls out a plug of chewing tobacco and rips off a chunk with his teeth. He thinks and chews for a moment before spitting in the dirt. The cold makes his spit glob together, and a string of the stuff hangs from his lips into his beard. He wipes it away with the sleeve of his coat. "What day is it?"

Clyde thinks for a minute, ticking off the calendar in his head. "It's Saturday, so the 19th. December 19th."

Willie looks to the still and then to the barren trees once more. He searches for a moment, but he can't seem to pinpoint the squirrel's location. "Well," he spits again and wipes his wind-chapped lips. "Don't reckon I can get another load done 'fore Christmas anyway. I can have two done, I think, by the 1st of the year maybe. Be nice to have a double load. See if we can't get some more folks to buy up a bit of stock. Think ya can carry double?"

Clyde thinks for a moment, looking back at the bed of the mail truck brimming with overloaded bags of moonshine and letters. "I'd have to get more mail sacks, but I don't see why I couldn't carry more. Might take a bit longer gettin' rid of it, though. Be a good bit of cash when it's all said and done."

"Think that'll be a good plan, then. If Lester helps," Lester looks up from the jar in his hand when Willie mentions him, "then we'll be able to get it done. Be a busy next couple weeks, though."

Lester's head twitches into a nod that continues as he speaks. "I'll help ya, Willie. No problem t'all."

Willie nods. "It's good, then. Clyde, I'd say ya just plan on being back here early January, the 2nd maybe, for the big load. We'll stick 'round here and get everything started for it. If Mabel's up to it, we'll probably come out here on Christmas Day. Lester and I can even sneak away then to get a run of beer cookin'."

"Sounds good to me." Clyde sticks out his hand to Lester who takes it and gives it a good shake, more like a tremor, as his other hand feverishly grips the jar of liquor so as not to drop it. Clyde moves to Willie and offers his hand, which Willie accepts with a smile. "Ya know, I think I could get used ta this making money thing. Really not too bad of a gig."

Willie disagrees but doesn't say anything. He's got plans that don't involve a risk of him ending up in jail. He continues smiling, though, and nods his head in affirmation. "Just make sure everything stays safe and ya don't mess up yer mail-carryin' job. Without that mail truck, this whole plan goes to shit."

They let go of each other's hands, and Clyde waves as he walks back to the cab of his truck. He turns back as he is halfway in, smiling at Lester and Willie. "Merry Christmas, boys." With that, he closes the door and slams the truck into gear.

Willie waves as the truck jumps forward—tires spitting dirt and leaves, almost spilling one of the bags of product onto the earth. It stays in place, though, and Willie watches—not the slightest bit worried—as the truck bumps away, going a bit too fast for the heavily-wooded area, dodging trees and stumps alike as it barrels out of sight. Willie isn't worried, though. Why would he be? Everything is going as planned and he has two good men to help him. He can't allow himself to be cynical. He won't do it anymore. That is a dark path that he's gone down far too often in the past. He refuses to again. Everything is gonna be all right. He has no complaints. The delivery system is working to near perfection, his Mama isn't botherin' him all the time as long as she gets her share of the profits, and Mabel is gettin' better. That's the best thing. Even though she isn't quite good yet, the slightest bit of improvement is a damn sight better than where she had been.

Lester stands awkwardly next to Willie. His eyes have hardly left the jar in his hands. Willie might be a bit hard on him, but he can't help but worry for the boy. Likes his liquor a bit too much to make him completely trustworthy. If he were to mess up, get drunk, and find himself wandering into Sheriff Baker's sight, Willie don't know whether or not his resolve would hold. God knows what Baker would do to get answers out of him. That's why he told him to help with the next few batches. Best to keep him close, 'specially if he's gonna be imbibing in the product. Despite the harshness of his actions, though, Willie has grown quite fond of Lester. The young man might be half-damn-crazy, but he is loyal to Willie to a fault. Probably jump in front of a bullet for him if it came down to it. He reminds Willie of a young boy back in the war. Kid had stuck to Willie like a baby duckling to his Mama. Kid liked his drink, too. Just like Lester. Got himself killed for it. Don't know whether it was the wine or his attachment to Willie. Don't matter much anymore. What matters is Willie ain't gonna let the same thing happen to Lester. Might have his issues, good Lord knows that, but he's a good kid. Willie has to re-mind himself of that fact often. Lester's no more than a kid. 'Spite his brain, 'spite his stupid actions, he is just little more than a boy. What is he, eighteen? Twenty, maybe?

Willie slaps Lester on the back and moves back to the lean-to shed cov-ering their still. He picks Pearl up off her blanket and cradles her to his chest, the dog giving a soft growl from being wakened from her nap and taken from her warm spot.

Willie makes to walk back toward his Mama's house and his waiting truck. Got to run a few errands and pick up some supplies in town before starting on the next run. Lester remains where he is and Willie turns back to regard him. "You comin'?"

Lester shakes his head. "Think I'll stay out here next to the still a bit lon-ger. Gotta check the pump and make sure everything's good to go for later." His eyes shift back to the jar dangling at his side.

Willie looks at him drawn for a moment. "All right. Well just make sure ya give Mama that bit of cash she's owed 'fore ya get too far gone in the lik-ker, ya here? Stay as sober as ya can. We got a bit of work to do yet."

Lester nods.

Willie turns back to leave. "See ya in a bit."

Lester doesn't reply and Willie doesn't look back. His head tilts down to see Pearl looking up at him with her tongue out, her little puff of breath fogging in the cold air. He pats her head and disappears into the trees.

TOMMY SITS EXACTLY where Willie knew he would be: under the cover of some brush and pine trees a few miles in between his mother's farm and his own homestead. He smiles as Willie pulls his truck to a stop next to his own and gets out with a small bag containing a few jars of his moonshine. Tommy remains in his vehicle; he waves, however, as Willie walks toward him. Tommy looks much healthier without the bumps and bruises from fighting his partner.

Willie jangles the bag as he nears the car and smiles. Tommy's smile grows wider. "How's the tailing of that criminal goin'?" he asks as he leans against the open cab of the truck.

Tommy looks around at the deserted dirt road, still grinning. "No 'spicious activity. Pretty quiet, really." He meets Willie's eyes then glances down at the bag with another mischievous grin on his face. "What 'bout you, Willie? Seen anything suspicious?"

"Nothin' particular." He slips the bag through the cab, laying it on Tommy's lap. The mason jars tinkle lightly inside. "Little something to keep ya warm this Christmas. Some in there for Jack as well."

Tommy takes a quick peek into the bag like a naughty child getting a glimpse of his presents before Christmas morning. His face goes serious again, trying to hide the smile and failing. "I don't know whatcha talkin' 'bout, Willie. Just an empty bag here."

Willie pats his arm and begins to walk back toward his own truck. "Good luck with catchin' that shiner, Tommy."

Willie gets into the cab of his truck and shuts the door behind him. Tommy's whistle catches his attention.

"You won't believe this, Willie. Just found some evidence out by that tree over there." He points to a tree, holding up a jar of shine. "Guessin' he's been 'round here. Better dispose of this 'fore some poor, unsuspectin' soul stumbles upon it." With that, Tommy unscrews the jar and tilts it back, imbibing in half of the jar in his first go. He smacks his lips. "Yeah, probably better I get rid of this."

Willie laughs, waving as he pulls back out onto the road. As he starts forward, he sees Tommy in the cab of his truck taking another good hit from the open jar. Willie can't help but laugh again, the sound cheerful in the chilly air. It begins to spit a few flakes of snow; it is a light fall but will surely build as the day progresses. Willie thinks that he wouldn't be surprised if he woke up tomorrow to see a few inches covering the rocky ground around his home. He likes snow. For some reason, it seems pure to him.

It is coming down in large lazy flakes by the time he pulls into the rutted dirt drive of his home. Dr. Monroe's black buggy sits out front. A canvas roof has been added to it for the colder months and to keep the snow from falling onto the man as he drives the horse to his patients. He is inside at the moment, the buggy sitting empty and cold in the mid-morning gloom. Every now and then, the shaggy horse twitches its body to shake off the melting snow that sticks to its coat. As Willie gets out of the truck, grabbing the heavy bag from the floorboard, Monroe exits the house and pulls on gloves against the cold. He has a black knit scarf hanging loosely from his shoulders over the large coat of the same shade that reaches past his knees. He waves cheerfully at Willie as he makes his way down the stairs: one hand on the rail and the other hand bracing his left knee with each step, presumably sore.

"Howdy, Willie!" Monroe calls, leaning heavily against his buggy, his breath coming in thick white clouds.

"Doc." Willie approaches him and shakes his gloved hand with his free one. Willie nods toward the house. "She up and about?"

Monroe laughs heartily. It's not an uncomfortable laugh, but one of mirth. Excitement. "Damn sure wants to be. She 'bout nearly had me convinced of letting her back to 'er normal routine." He grabs at his left knee and winces a bit as the snowflakes continue their peaceful descent around them. "Damn cold gets my joints every time." He smiles again despite the discomfort. "It's workin', Willie. She'll be back to her old self in no time."

Willie doesn't say anything. Only smiles. He reaches into the bag and pulls out a large jug of moonshine. He sets it on the porch for his own use and offers the bag and what remains inside to Monroe. "Little somethin' to ease the joints." Monroe takes the bag and looks inside. "Threw in an extra one. Little Christmas gift from me to you. A thank you, really."

Monroe hefts the bag and puts it into the back of the buggy under the driver's bench and out of sight from any prying eyes that may take it upon themselves to look closely into the contents of his vehicle. "And a Merry Christmas it will be, then." He laughs again.

Willie pulls out the envelope containing his share from the latest run from his coat pocket and begins counting out bills. He offers a healthy stack to Monroe. "For her treatment. This payment plus the next one, and for the visits out here, too."

Monroe waves it off with his left hand, shaking his head at the same time. "This one's on me. 'Sides, not only is that liquor good for some drinkin', makes some damn fine antiseptic as well. Ya just replenished my stock for free and gave me the strength to make it through the holidays to boot." He climbs into the buggy, wincing a little from his knee trouble, and looks back down at Willie still holding the money out toward him. "The cousins and all them coming over for Christmas Eve. Be 'round sixteen children runnin' 'round my house, not including my own. Your gift is payment 'nough for now." He grabs the reins and releases the brake lever.

Willie stuffs the money back into his coat pocket. He smiles up at Doc Monroe. "Any chance she'll be good for goin' to take the boy to see my Mama on Christmas Eve?"

Monroe scratches at his chin. "I want her restin' today and tomorrow if she can. She can start gettin' 'round a bit after that, but I don't see why she can't go over for a visit after. Just don't let her be tryin' to help Betty in the kitchen, ya hear? She probably won't listen, though. She's a tough woman, Willie." He smiles again and snaps the reins, sending the old mare high-stepping forward.

Willie waves at the back of the covered buggy as it pulls toward the road. Monroe hollers about having a Merry Christmas. Willie returns the saying heartily, and he means it. What little snow had accumulated on the canvas top of the buggy blows away as the cart rattles its way off Willie's property. Pearl yips happily in the grass, dancing back and forth and trying to catch snowflakes in her snapping jaws. Willie watches her for a minute, leaning against the post. After a while, she tires herself out and, panting, trots to where he waits by the porch steps. He rubs her head lovingly.

"You're a good girl."

He wipes at the damp spots of melting snow on her coat, and she licks at his hand in return, the slobbery wetness of her tongue making the section of hand that she licks instantly cold. He grabs the bottle resting on the porch steps and heads into the house.

It's warm inside, the woodstove burning and making the house cozy and smelling faintly of burning pine logs. The door to their bedroom is open and the glow of a lamp flickering dances on the soft shadows of the doorway. Even the shadows seem to be less foreboding now that everything seems to be taking a turn in the right direction.

"Willie?" Mabel calls from the bedroom. The voice is stronger than it had been when he had first arrived back home, getting off the train to find his world turned upside down. It was a wonderful voice again. It was *her* voice.

"Just a second, Mabel." Willie places the jug of moonshine on the counter and covers it with a rag, pushing it as far away from the edge as possible in case Fletchie were to walk in early and reach for it, mistaking it for something else.

His steps make the wood floors creak in places. Pearl leaves his side and makes a running hop to land on top of Fletchie's small bed. He thinks of telling her to get down but lets her stay where she is. She's not harming anything. He approaches the door, the caution that used to be present in his entering of their bedroom all but gone. Ever since her sickness, ever since coming home, that feeling of caution had been there. Perhaps he would have walked in and she would be lying dead in their marital bed. This had been his greatest fear. He wouldn't have been able to handle such a sight. He had had to be careful with everything. Careful not to wake her if she were sleeping, careful not to disturb her if she were awake, just careful. It isn't caution anymore but nervousness. Nervous hope, perhaps.

He peeks his head into the room, clean and without the buckets of sick and the litter that was strewn about the floor when he'd first arrived back after his long absence. The room is clean, quiet, and cozily warm with the light of the lamp on the chifforobe and a candle burning softly on a table next to the bed. Mabel sits up with her back against the headboard instead of sunken deep into the pillows as he had so often found her of late. She is smiling: a smile of welcome, and love, and absent of fear of not being able to smile at him for much longer, but instead filled with the knowledge that she will be there to smile at him every day. It is a wonderful smile. It is Mabel's smile. Willie grins in return, an awkward, boyish smile that bunches his eyes together and reveals his straight teeth with tobacco stains through the longish hairs of his mustache whiskers.

In this moment, Willie wants to tell her. Tell her everything he has done with the going back into the moonshine business, his talks with the Sheriff, everything. He wants to tell her his plan. Yes, Mabel, he has a plan. An escape from the life that he has been forced to live. An escape for them. She's the first person he wants to share this information with. He wants to tell her so bad it hurts him, fills him with guilt. He looks at her. Her features showing concern in response to the pain that stretches across his features. She picks up a glass of water and drinks the last few drops out of it and raises it toward Willie. A small smile spreads across her plush lips once more.

"How 'bout you bring the bottle in for us to share a drink?"

Willie doesn't know how to respond to this; can't think how she could have possibly known. This turn smacks him upside the head and leaves him feeling dizzy for a moment. He puts a hand on the bed to steady himself. Does he lie to her? Ask her what bottle? Chalk it up to the last remains of the sickness in her body? He doesn't do any of these things. He only stands where he is by the bedside with his mouth slightly ajar and his breathing intensifying like a child waiting to be doled out their punishment for doing something particularly naughty.

She shoos him with her free hand. "Go on. We have to talk about all of this eventually."

He, again, doesn't reply. He simply turns around in the doorway and retrieves the jug from off the counter. He is back in the bedroom and making to sit on the bed when he realizes he didn't remove the rag from the bottle. He whips it off and stares at the glass jar with the clear liquor sloshing shallowly inside, dancing with the color in the light of the flickering flame of the lamp.

Mabel reaches out her glass. He pours her a small slug from the bottle without thinking and watches as she brings the glass to her lips for a sip. Her body shivers as she swallows, the left edge of her lip curving up, not in a bad way, but in a show of pleasant warmth.

Willie can't think of how to begin, so instead he starts with a weak, "Are ya s'posed to drink that while you're sick?"

She laughs. Brings the glass to her lips a second time, taking down the remainder and holding it out for him to refill.

He does so, letting her look at him a moment before finding his words. "How long you known?"

She takes another tentative sip and offers the glass to him. He drinks and refills from the jug. "'Bout when you told me you were going to find a way to fix me. I got really suspicious when you told me how you were goin' to be doin' it." Her smile widens and she looks up into his eyes playfully. "Postman? Willie, ya know I know you better than that."

He looks at the floor sheepishly. "Seemed like the right thing to say. It's how we've been makin' our deliveries."

She nods as if this makes complete sense. "Guess I knew for sure when Doc Monroe started treatin' me. Knew we couldn't be affordin' nothing like that on wages you earned workin' on your Mama's farm. Knew you weren't runnin' mail."

Willie doesn't say anything. What can he say? She knows. He abandons the glass on the nightstand and rests the jug against his forearm, tilting it up to his lips and making the liquor bubble and sink about a half inch in the jug.

"Why'd you lie to me, baby?"

He doesn't know how to answer that question either. What can he say that would make it seem okay? All the excuses he had once thought of, thought of while he was at his still, driving to his still, spreading the word to previous buyers of his product, all of them sounding petty and poor for what he'd done. His head sinks farther into his chest and his eyes water with the shame of it all.

"I'm sorry, Mabel."

"What?"

"I'm sorry," he says, a little louder than he'd meant for it to come out.

The tears flow down his cheeks in two small streams now. The tears that he'd kept in, tried to hold in to show his strength in front of her, they let loose now. "I didn't know what else to do. I couldn't let you suffer like ya were. No matter what ya say. I couldn't do it. I wasn't strong 'nough to sit idly by and watch it happen."

She shakes her head, her hand coming out to rest on his own. For the first time since before he'd been hauled off to jail, her hands are warm. Not a feverish warm like they had been sometimes when they weren't devilishly cold, but an actual, normal warmth. *Her* warmth. He looks up at her through the mistiness of his eyes.

"I just wish you would have told me," she says, smiling at him.

Willie chuckles at this. "How was I s'posed to tell ya that? That I was back doin' the very thing that got me sent away from you in the first place. That the promise I had made to you was a promise I couldn't keep, a lie I told you to try and protect you in case something were to happen to me. In case I were to get caught again."

Her finger glides into his beard and finds his chin, lifting his eyes up to hers. "Ya just tell me the truth. I deserve that."

"I know." He is silent after this for a few moments. She continues to look at him, her hand still buried in the bushiness to touch the skin of his face. They sit like this for a while, the only sounds being their breathing, paired together to where their inhales and exhales come out at the same time, her breaths lacking much of the rattle that had been there before.

"Thank you."

He looks to her in surprise. "Thank you?"

"Yes. Thank you."

"Why?"

"Because without you doing what you did, I might not be here right now with you, with our Fletchie. I almost certainly wouldn't have lasted much longer if I was." She smiles at him and he smiles back through the foggy mist in his eyes. "Are you safe?"

"I'm safe."

"Are you lyin' again?"

"I'm safe. They're lookin' for anything they can to get me, but I'm safe for now." He almost promises her this but thinks better of it. No sense in lying again. Plus, his promises might not mean all that much to her right now. Would she even believe him?

"I do what I do for you, Mabel. I do it because I love..." Her leaning forward and planting a kiss on his lips shuts him off mid-sentence. They stay that way for a long moment before she pulls away from him.

"I love you, too. Just be careful. I can't lose you again. I really just got ya back."

He doesn't have time to reply before her lips meet his once more. After a moment, her hand gingerly makes its way down to his pants and undoes the belt holding them in place. He pulls back from her in surprise.

"No. We can't."

"Why not?" Her hand continues its work.

"Because you're sick. You're just now recovering."

"I'm not too sick anymore. Not for this. I miss my husband." She finishes undoing his belt and leans back into the bed, leaning over to the bedside table and blowing out the flame, extending the darkness through the room. It is not an unpleasant darkness as it had been in the room for so long, but a comforting absence of intruding light. An intimate space. Willie uses the darkening in the room to undress, standing before the bed awkward and naked until she flips back his side of the quilt and pats the spot next to her. He slips in beside her and they lie there for a moment, listening to each other breathing in the dark.

They roll to face each other, staring at the other's silhouette that begins to take shape as their eyes adjust to the soft lighting overtaking the bedroom. She kisses him again, this time her lips remaining as she tugs gently at his beard so that he rises and moves to where his body towers over her own, held up by his palms digging into the soft down of the mattress.

"Are you sure?" His breath is ragged, almost as bad as hers had been a month ago at the height of her sickness.

Her hand guiding him to her answers his question. They remain like this for a while, both breathing heavily, their eyes locked with each other. Mabel reaches down and brings her slip over her head, revealing her frail body. Her ribs show prominently, and her hip bones jut out from her sides, the flesh having lost the softness that had always been there. The sight of her almost brings him to tears once more—how the sickness and fever had ravished her body and had almost taken her away from him. Her hand coming up to guide his eyes back to her own keeps the tears at bay. Her neck has lost most of the swelling, and the veiny spread of blue and black bruising is gone. He plants kisses along that neck, breathing in the scent of her skin as he works methodically. Her face, though a bit more hollow, the eyes more sunken than when she was fully well, is the same. The face of the woman he fell in love with. She smiles at him and her arms against his back, showing some of her old strength, push him down toward her.

They go slowly, a steady rocking motion, their hips moving in time with each other: together and apart, together and apart. Willie is careful to keep most of his weight on his own hands, fearing that if he leans too heavily on her, he might shatter her fragile bones: his heavy, bear-like mass on top of her brittle, tired body. It lasts a while—time seems to fade for Willie at their overdue love-making. There is only her in these moments, only them together. The same. Their eyes remain locked without speaking. There is no need for words. Their bodies, their touch, does the speaking for them. When he finishes, he is looking at her, and her at him, and they stay together for some time afterward before Willie gently rolls, careful to not squash her skinny leg, and lets himself fall to the bed. Exhausted and sweaty, but content and fuller than he has felt in a long time.

Mabel scoots over on the bed and curls up against him, her small head resting on the bed of hair covering his broad chest. Her finger reaches up into the black hairs, some patches flecked with gray, and twirls them in her fingers. Willie's eyes are closed and his head rests atop her own, her long hair in a braid and curled around her shoulder, lying on the pillow where his hand lies. He picks up the braid and brings it to his nose, breathing in the sweet scent of her hair. It smells clean and of different spices, warm. She smells like her. They lie together in silence, their bodies entangled, the feeling of skin on skin. Their breathing evens out eventually to where the room falls into a blissful silence. Willie traces his finger along the contours of her stomach, tickling her sides with his soft touch. Mabel doesn't pull away, letting him continue to rub his callused finger against the smooth skin of her side until she laughs, a giggle, really. A joyful sound filled with love and tenderness. Willie joins in. They laugh until the tears stream anew and they are gripping at their sides. Mabel coughs a bit, but it is not the dry croup cough as it had been before.

She recovers quickly and leans away from him, reaching for the glass on the bedside table. She takes a drink and swallows, whistles a long, almost musical-note-of-a-breath at the burn before handing the glass to Willie. Only a few swallows remain and Willie tilts the glass up and back, drinking it down in three gulps and lets the last drops drip on this tongue before handing it back to Mabel. They are silent for a moment more, and then he talks. He is no longer afraid of her scorn or disapproval, scared that she will be angry or love him less for his actions. It is better than working in the woods logging. The likelihood of fatality is far less in what he does than in the logging industry. She mentions this at one point, encouraging him to continue. He loves her. He tells her everything.

CHAPTER IX

THE NEXT FEW DAYS PASS in the closest thing to bliss that Willie has known in a long while. Mabel's recovery continues, as do their moments of intimacy together. Willie tries to keep her confined to the bed as Doc Monroe has instructed. The trying seems futile. He goes to work, leaving her tucked comfortably in the bed with the covers tucked snugly under her arms, a book in her hand. He works for a few hours, readying the mash and getting the first run of beer started, Lester looking over his shoulder throughout the whole process and Pearl sleeping soundly at their feet as they work, waking lazily every now and then to come and rub at their pant legs in the cold air for a pat on the head or some of the venison jerky Willie and Lester gnaw on while they work then returning to her soft blanket next to the radiating heat of the furnace. Upon returning home, Willie finds Mabel up and about, either in the house working at small tasks she talks of falling behind on or sitting on the porch and reading. The day before Christmas Eve, Willie comes home to find her in the yard with Fletchie running back and forth, picking at the small patches of snow that have accumulated from the recent falls and balling them up to throw at their shrieking son. One of the snowballs smacks Willie in the chest as he emerges from the cab of his truck. He loses all sense of her ever being sick in that moment, grabbing at a pile of snow and retaliating, sending them both running toward the woods with him in hot pursuit, Pearl yipping at his side.

The weather continues its steady drop in temperature with more snow throughout the days. The sky remains cloudy, an ominous sign of more wintery weather in the near forecast, spitting flecks of snow during the day, only to unleash their loads in the quiet of the night to add to the building accumulation around Stone County. Sunshine appears briefly on the 22nd for an hour or two, making the temperatures rise briefly to a tolerable forty-five degrees before shrinking back behind approaching clouds and dropping back to the upper thirties before night fall. The rise in temperature is enough to melt away a decent bit of the slushy snowbanks that cover the ground, leaving behind a muddy mess in its wake with small patches of lingering snow staying stubbornly where it has fallen in defiance of the fickle Arkansas weather. Early morning on the 23rd, though, it is back to below freezing and snow blankets the ground nicely in a luminous mixture of crystalline ice and white powder that crunches underfoot when Willie leaves for the still after sitting with Mabel in bed most of the morning.

It has been quiet. Peaceful. Sheriff Baker hasn't found any reason to make himself seen by Willie and had honestly faded from his mind as far as he could during those days. Even the tail, under the close watch of Jack or Tommy, seems to have slacked off the last few days, Willie not having seen them in their usual spots waiting on him to pass by. Probably laid up somewhere drunk on the liquor that Willie'd slipped 'em. He had laughed at the thought on his drive, hoping in the back of his mind that if them being drunk is the case, the boys are smart enough to keep it out of Baker's sight. Despite the drink that they'd shared that night seeming so long ago, Willie didn't figure that the sight of his Deputies intoxicated would sit too well with the Sheriff. These worries and thoughts are soon gone, however, as he continues about his routine and enjoys the work he is doing. Enjoys the time with his family. Family. That's a word he'd almost forgotten the meaning of. Mabel helped him find it again. He is getting reacquainted with the concept. He remembers why he liked the idea so much, didn't want it to end. Didn't want to screw it up this time. He'll give anything to make sure that doesn't happen again.

December 24th begins with much the same feeling of peace and serenity that has encompassed Willie's life for the past little while. He'd slept in later than usual, waking with the soft glow of the sun's rays glinting through a thick layer of clouds and reflecting through the curtains with the twinkle of fresh snowfall. He opens his eyes, rubbing at the sleep in them, to discover the chilly, misty light of a cloudy morning reflecting off the pure whiteness through the frosted glass panes. He rubs at his eyes again and yawns, his left hand reaching out to touch Mabel next to him, only to find her side of the bed empty and made up nicely, her pillow standing starch and upright against the headboard. He glances around the room, neatly done up the way he remembers it before he was dragged away over a year before to serve his sentence on the farm, to find that she is not sitting in the handmade rocker he'd made for her, the quilt she kept there resting folded and draped over one of the arms.

A childish giggle from the main room of the cabin, the door to the bedroom closed and making the noise muffled, has him smiling. As he swings his long legs over the side of the bed, he can hear the faint crackle and popping of something frying in grease. He takes a big whiff. It smells of caramelized pork: bacon, pork chops, perhaps sausage of some kind. He'd been given several pounds of fresh-slaughtered pork in several different cuts—salted and cured—from George Lackey from his stock at the store in town for a couple jugs of his shine. After his repayment of the tab, which he'd paid for the same way, George was more than happy to trade out for some good meat and vittles that'd keep the Henderson homestead stocked. It was probably a good thing, too. It seems to Willie that Fletchie might have grown quite fond of the hogs in the back of their house in his father's absence. Willie doesn't think that Fletchie'd allow him anywhere near those pigs with a knife if he had anything to say 'bout it. Damn kid had a heart of gold. Big heart, so big it would probably interfere with Willie's pork consumption after he quit with the shinin'. That, though, is a sacrifice that he is more than willing to make. With Mabel getting better, and all the bills caught up, he's ready to start thinking about calling it quits. After the next few runs there will be more than plenty of money to start looking for legal work. Might even actually get into a mail-carrying gig. That sounds pretty good to him if he can't farm his own land.

Willie shuffles into the main room. It is pleasantly warm and the window's curtains are tied back to reveal the whiteness of the outside world. Willie had cut down a small tree from the woods yesterday evening. It now stands in the corner of the cabin near the window, Pearl sitting beside it, wagging her tail as Fletchie runs around it, decorating the branches with a string of popcorn in uneven passes and spaces. Pearl jumps up and tries to snatch at a few pieces as the boy makes a low pass with the string, causing popcorn to droop down low enough for the dog to feel confident enough for a try. Mabel stands before the woodstove, a smile on her pretty face—some of the weight that she'd lost coming back into her cheeks from her more-than-healthy appetite the last couple of weeks. She works in the heat of the frying pan, her long hair tied back in a braid and hanging along the back of her night dress and matching robe. She flips a large piece of ham in the skillet, and Willie's mouth begins to water at the sight and the smell of popping pork fat. He'd tried to get her to take it easy, let him worry about the household issues until she had fully recovered. That had been about as good as trying to get Pearl to stop shitting in the grass and to use the outhouse. Not well. He still tried, though, wanting her to recover fully and quickly. That's probably why she'd slipped out of bed while he was snoring to make their breakfast.

She smiles at him as he gently closes the door of their bedroom, buckling one of the straps of his suspenders to his pants, leaving the other to hang behind him and gently bang against his back as he walks behind her, wrapping his arms around her stomach and tilting his head to give her cheek a peck.

"You're not supposed to strain yourself."

Mabel reaches behind her and pops him in the side with the greasy fork she uses to maneuver the ham in the pan. He laughs and she swats at him again, Willie dancing out of the way as grease flies off the fork to splatter on the floor. Pearl yips happily, trying to dodge their feet, and goes to lap up her lucky treat off the wood flooring.

Mabel kisses him again, Fletchie grunting in mock disgust. "Coffee's on the table." Willie turns to go sit down and she swipes at his behind with the fork for good measure.

The morning continues this way: the family gathered around together eating and laughing, talking of the holiday and teasing at Fletchie about whether he'd been a good boy that year. When they settle back from their large breakfast of ham, eggs, and red-eye gravy, Fletchie reads to them from his book on the table. A Tale of Two Cities. Willie's never read it before, but he likes the duality of the language and the back and forth, almost rhythmical quality to the words. The part Fletchie reads is quite sad about Paris in turmoil. Willie thinks to himself that the French have had it rough. Turmoil just seems to follow their people throughout history.

The ride to Betty Henderson's house is a pleasant one with the fresh snow on the ground that covers the dirt road and makes their bald tires slide around turns. Fletchie squeals in delight at these curves in the road as Mabel's hand digs playfully into Willie's arm, mock terror across her face as they make a particularly sharp curve. Willie cracks his window for a moment to let in the crisp air. It takes his breath away—the shock of the icy wind in his face that soon after enters his lungs, but it relaxes him, and he takes slow, deep breaths. Mabel touches his arm and he smiles, wanting to close his eyes with the pleasure of it all, knowing he can't. Fletchie sings Christmas carols in between them and Mabel joins in. He loves to hear her sing and he rolls up his window so he might hear her better. So he can keep the sound trapped in the car with him for as long as possible.

They reach Willie's Mama's place to find smoke floating from the chimney and a couple trees in the yard decorated with wooden ornaments that Willie's father had made when he was a young boy. He'd made a few every year and his Mama's tree eventually got so full that she had nowhere else to put them. She'd started putting them on the trees outside to make the house seem more festive. Willie likes thinking about his father during this time of year. The man was a sight, for sure, and not always the friendliest of men, but he was a good father who taught Willie a lot about how to be a man. He only wishes that his father were here to see him now. He wonders if he would be proud of the man he is today. He hopes so. Perhaps he wouldn't be proud of what he does, but then again, Willie's not sure on that. He might just be proud that Willie has been able to pull it off for this long.

Betty Henderson opens the door and steps out on her porch in a hand-stitched apron, little sleigh bells hang from the corners so that she jingles when she walks. She waves happily at them as they exit the truck and make for the house, crunching in the fallen snow and frozen grass. Fletchie reaches the porch first, jumping into his grandmother's arms as she stoops to catch him. She lifts his small body up and rests him in the crook of her arm, his long legs for a boy his age dangling down past her knees. She's stronger than she likes people to know. She wouldn't have caught him as she did if there had been people there to see her. It was just her family, though. No one else around to see behind the thin façade of feebleness to match her age.

"Well, hello there, Fletchie."

"Hi, Grandma." He smiles down at her from his vantage above her head where she holds him.

OLD FIELD PINES

"You know, I was lookin' for somethin' sweet to finish off my pie. Glad ya finally got here." She fakes gnawing at his arm and the boy giggles wildly in her arms, kicking his feet to be let down. She sets him on the ground and wipes her hands on her apron as Willie and Mabel walk up the porch steps, Willie protectively keeping an arm around Mabel's waist in case she should tire. Despite her improvement, Willie can't help but be careful with her. She is still so thin. Her smile is back, though, a bit hidden behind layers of clothing and a scarf she has wrapped around her neck.

Betty Henderson turns, smiling toward her son and his bride. She goes first to Mabel, her arms open wide. "It's such a blessin' to see ya up and about, honey." They embrace, Betty patting Mabel's back gently. "Skinny, though. Gotta get you some meat back on them bones."

"Hello, Betty. We're workin' on it."

They break the embrace and Betty Henderson holds her daughter-in-law out at arm's length, appraising her with a look that Willie can't quite understand or put his finger on. She smiles knowingly at Mabel and then flicks her eyes toward Willie, patting his hand and gesturing toward the door where Fletchie already waits inside near the tree with the presents, no doubt.

"Well, come on in. Catch our death out here in this chill."

They walk into the feeling of warmth mixed with a variety of smells of different baked goods and supper in the oven. Fletchie sits beside the tree, as expected, digging through the brightly-wrapped packages stacked underneath, bringing a few of them up close to his ear and giving them a good shake. Betty scolds him teasingly about waiting for after supper to open anything. Fletchie grins and returns to the examination of his packages. The adults go into the kitchen where Betty returns to her work of cooking. Mabel makes to help with what she can.

Betty clicks her tongue. "No, ma'am. Not in your state. You just go on over to the table and sit and talk with me while I work." She stirs at a bowl balancing on her stomach, the wooden spoon working furiously at a glob of dough. "Lester's out by the old smoke shed if'n you want to go see him," she addresses Willie without looking at him. "Go on and do your work and let us talk a bit. Supper should be ready in 'round about an hour or so."

Willie nods, leans down, and kisses Mabel's cheek then makes for the door and back into the cold. Pearl sits next to Fletchie in the main room under the tree, pawing at a few packages bigger than she is. Willie whistles and she trots happily to his side. "See ya in a bit, son."

"Where ya goin'?"

"Work with Lester for a bit."

Fletchie rises from the floor, brushing a branch of the tree with his shoulder and sending a bell hanging there tinkling. "Can I come?"

"No. You just stay here and keep an eye on your mother for me. I'll be back before too long."

Fletchie doesn't reply but gloomily sinks back to the floor as his dad leaves the house, letting in a blast of cold wind with the opening of the door. He doesn't wait long. He gets up and goes to the window to watch his father trudge toward the treeline, past the barn and on toward the cliff overlooking Roastnier Creek. He stands there long enough to watch Willie's shape disappear into the shade of the evergreens laden with snow and ice, he slowly disintegrating into the shadows of the wooded area. He peeks into the kitchen where his grandmother busies herself preparing their supper and his mother sits at the table laughing politely at the jokes the old woman tells. He makes for the door and opens it just a crack, his breath once more being taken away with the cold, and slips out into the chill of the afternoon.

WILLIE REACHES THE STILL, cradled in the roofed confines of his childhood play area. Much of the structure had been useless in the rebuilding in order to house the still. The pine-thatched roof was all but nonexistent, and two of the four support beams had rotted enough so that when Willie touched them, they crumbled. They'd taken boards from his father's old smoke shack sitting about fifty yards away at the edge of the treeline to prop up the rotting structure and repair it enough so that they might work in relative safety. The leveling of the ground and the digging into the side of the hill had been a different story and another few afternoons of work for them. Now, though, the lean-to structure looked a sight better, with the still sitting cozily underneath the freshly-thatched roof. The old smoke shack, however, looked a bit more dilapidated, much of the walls having been salvaged for their new still site. His Papa wouldn't have been happy with the state of everything. Willie thinks to himself that he will rebuild the shack, even better than before, after the next couple of runs so that he can start using it himself. It would be nice to have something to do other than sit in the cold while the beer cooks. He shakes this thought away, though. It will have to *replace* the beer cooking and general shine work. It's all a means to an end.

Pearl takes her traditional spot on the blanket next to the furnace. Lester sits next to it, a wooden structure in his lap, his hand steadily going over it with a sharp pocketknife. Willie doesn't call as he approaches, Pearl's presence is warning enough. Lester looks up from his work with a crooked smile.

"Hello there, Willie."

"Lester," Willie replies, taking a seat next to the furnace and warming his hands in the heat. It was certainly mighty good of Lester to come out and get the fire going. Meant they could get started as soon as they were ready.

Willie looks to the carving in Lester's lap. Lester follows his eyes and hands it to Willie with a smile. "Wanna see?"

Willie takes it, marveling at the wonderful craftsmanship of the miniature carving of their own still, complete with an unworked knot of soft wood in front of the furnace to represent Pearl's usual spot. "This is pretty damn good, Lester. How long you been workin' on this?"

Lester rubs his neck shyly at the praise. "Ah, I don't know. 'Bout a month, prolly." Willie makes to hand it back but Lester waves him away. "Made it for ya. For Christmas and all."

Willie is speechless, staring quietly at the wonderful gift, clearly touched at the gesture. He brings it closer to his eyes to admire the smooth, steady knife strokes that brought the miniature to life in a way that makes it seem like a small version of himself might walk on the piece and begin his tiny work. "Thank you." The emotion is clear in his face and he clears his throat quickly to keep from seeming as such.

Lester smiles and rises from his seat, turning to face the still. "You ready to get to work?"

Willie sets the carving on the lip of the furnace. He looks at it for a few moments more before looking Lester's direction. "I reckon I am."

FLETCHIE SNEAKS INTO THE TREES, moving with all the stealth that his young body can muster. He doesn't particularly know why he is sneaking. It's not like his Papa can be too mad at him. It's Christmas, after all, and he is only curious, just wants to spend some time with his father and his Uncle Lester. Yet, from the moment he stepped into the woods, his mind warned him that he should tread carefully, that there might be something that he isn't supposed to be seeing out there. He shrugs these feelings off the best he can, but they persistently remain in the back of his mind as he picks his steps through the brush-littered ground, his feet crunching softly in the snow and foliage despite his best efforts to remain silent. It feels like an affront to the very nature of the woods. They do not want noise to disturb their quiet holiday.

There's a small path leading deeper into the woods, not cut but worn from use, that resembles more of a deer trail than anything else. He knows that it isn't, though. His Papa'd taught him how to recognize deer markings when they went scouting and hunting. The track looks similar, but it's too straight. Limbs aren't brushed back in the right places and the absence of any rubs helps to solidify this notion in his young mind. It's man-made, probably by his father and his Uncle Lester. It had been travelled just often enough to leave behind the small trace of their continual presence. He's never been out here with his father, but he's seen the shack a couple of times when he had been over to his Grandma's and had wandered into the woods to play. It was an old structure, apparently having been his grandfather's favorite spot on the entire property. He'd opened the door once and gone inside the last time he was out this far. It had been a little scary, like something from one of those scary stories he'd read in one of his books. It had seemed like someone was watching him as he checked out the old building. Fletchie had pretended that the feeling he felt was his grandfather, of whom he had no memory—he'd gone to be with Jesus before he had a chance to be born. It was kind of comforting when he pretended like that and made the trip out there pleasant. He's sure that's where his father has gone. There's nothing else out in the woods that Fletchie can remotely remember. One thing, though, is that the feeling of being watched, disturbing something out here, has returned, and no amount of pretending it to be a never-met grandfather is helping to soothe it.

OLD FIELD PINES

He walks for some time, his breath fogging before him. The cold of the day and the snow clouds above make the woods darker than they should be in the middle of the afternoon. It would be scary but he thinks about Sheriff Baker deputizing him. This gives him courage to continue, knowing that he is a real-life Deputy on the hunt for something. He doesn't know quite what it is, but he pretends that he is chasing bad guys through the woods, men who want to hurt his Papa and his Uncle Lester, bad men who do crimes against the state that he is charged with finding and bringing to justice. He grips an imaginary pistol in a make-believe holster at his side, holding his fingers in the form of a gun and resting his other hand around the weapon to steady his shaking hands. He's ready to perform his duty as a sworn Man of the Law. Lawmen don't run when they are scared. They pull out their pistols, knowing they may not make it back home, and go charging headlong into whatever danger awaits them.

A bit farther along, Fletchie looks around to discover the path has widened considerably, a tunnel of overhanging limbs that open to more of a highway than the deer-path track that he'd been walking along. It's big enough for someone to drive a truck through. He looks around the darkened woods to make sure that no one has discovered him before kneeling on the widened path. It continues through the woods the way he was walking. The other end stretches back in the direction that he had come, from his Grandma's house, in a round-about way it looks to him. He places his small, shaking hand in a tire track rutted into the soft earth and halfway buried by the fallen snow. He might not have noticed it except for the indention where the snow rises a bit higher than the rest of the ground around the edges of the ruts. A few feet away, parallel to the prints he feels around with his hand, is another rut made by tires ripping up the wet earth. Somebody been driving out this way but he can't imagine why. Nothing really to do out here but go to an abandoned smoke house. The barn with the tools and other farm equipment was far to the other side of the house near the fields that grow hay in the summertime. This confuses him but he shrugs it off. There must be a reason why his Daddy or whoever would drive out this way. He stands and continues down the widened path, sticking more to the edge of the woods for the cover they offer and gripping his imaginary pistol tightly for safety and courage.

Fletchie hears the fire—flames flickering and heavy breathing from men at work—long before he sees anything. The glow of the flames has been blocked by something but the sound is unmistakable. The men curse and laugh as they mill about in the afternoon cold. The structure comes into view, the boy crouching behind some bushes at a safe distance so that he can see and hear without them catching on to the new presence among them. He holds his breath and is afraid. From his vantage point in the bushes, he can see his Uncle Lester—he'd met him a few times with his Papa—holding a large bag, struggling with the heavy weight as his father measures out the small grains to place into a large vat of shiny metal. When he finishes, his Papa closes the lid and Lester walks over to a contraption with valves and a pipe leading off toward the smoke shack and beyond. He turns a few valves and his Papa takes a seat next to a makeshift furnace and rips off a chunk of his chewing tobacco with his teeth, holding his hands out toward the fire to warm them.

Fletchie wants to cry. He's never seen one before but he'd read about it plenty after his Daddy had been hauled away and was gone for so long. They were working at a moonshine still. He, being so young, knows that he shouldn't know of such things. Sheriff Baker says that moonshining is bad and that it turns people bad, too. The papers he'd read spoke similar of the process and the men who chose to make it. People in a small town are liable to talk. Kids overhear this talk and choose to repeat it to their friends. This is how he'd discovered why his Daddy had been arrested, why he began reading about what it was. He didn't know much but he knew that's what he was seeing now.

There is an awful feeling inside him as he watches the men work. Not only is this bad, and it is certainly bad, but his Papa'd promised him that he wasn't going to do nothing to get sent away again. If what he'd read was true and the folks around town were correct, this had the potential to do just that. It is not only the feeling of betrayal and sadness that he feels, but anger. He feels mad at his Papa for going back on his word, mad enough to make tears sting his eyes in the cold. He wipes them away angrily but they continue to come. He continues to stare. He can't take his eyes away.

OLD FIELD PINES

Pearl, lying by the fire, must smell him, for she stands and stretches, sniffing about the air for the familiar scent that has approached her. She spots the bushes where he is hiding and makes for them. Fletchie panics. He'll be caught for sure if she comes running up to him. He gingerly reaches his hand out of the bushes, watching his Papa carefully to make sure he doesn't turn around to see him reaching out, and gives Pearl a stopping motion with his hand. The dog looks at the small hand in a funny way, stopping her approach. He waves his hand gently at her and the dog sits where she is, staring intently at the bushes.

His Papa looks up to where Pearl has gotten to and sees her staring at the bush. Luckily, Fletchie'd taken his hand back into the confines of the dense shrubbery already.

"What is it, Pearl?" Willie asks, rising from his seat, his eyes scanning over where Pearl is looking.

The dog growls and makes for the bush. Fletchie is terrified. The dog is sure to give him away now. He watches his Papa in horror as he pulls something from his waistband, watching Pearl approach the bush and making to follow her. The boy's stomach feels sick as he glimpses the pistol, real as anything, that his father brandishes. The look from behind the bushy beard is one that he isn't familiar with. It is much darker and more suspicious than the kind face that reads to him and helps him with his homework. The face he sees is not something that he can recognize with his young age but it scares him nonetheless. It is the face of a man who is ready to kill to protect himself.

"What's it, Willie?" Lester asks, sitting up from his spot near the fire.

"Pearl. She's…" He stops as the dog approaches the bush. Fletchie holds his breath and squeezes his eyes tightly shut. This is it. He's for sure in for it. His Papa'll wear his behind out if not something worse. What if he doesn't recognize him and just lets loose with his six-shooter?

Pearl reaches the bush and sniffs. Her growling stops, smelling Fletchie's familiar scent. She peeks her head into the bush a bit, her tongue hanging out happily. Fletchie motions for her to back away. The dog's head turns up in confusion for a moment but does as the boy's hand commands. Despite her obeying, she squats and pees near the bush, turning the snow yellow before kicking at her bathroom spot with her hind legs and trotting back toward the flames.

Fletchie opens his eyes to see his father standing over his hiding spot. Thankfully, he doesn't look down, his eyes too busy scanning the surrounding area.

He grunts. "Musta smelled a squirrel or somethin'." Willie walks back over and takes a seat by the fire, rubbing at the dog's head. "You're just curious, ain't ya, girl?"

The dog pants happily in the warmth of the furnace and continues looking confusedly toward Fletchie's bush. The boy breathes a sigh of relief, grateful that his position wasn't given up by the dog's keen sense of smell. He breathes out again to settle himself and continues his watching. He has a responsibility to shake off the moment of fear and to perform what he was tasked with. This is the kind of thing that Sheriff Baker had wanted him to keep an eye out for; he's sure of that, if nothing else. His heart still aches for discovering such ills being performed by his Papa, the man who has always taken care of him. There's nothing to be done of it, though. His duty is not yet over. Not by a long shot.

BETTY HENDERSON WORKS IN HER KITCHEN, putting the top crust onto an apple pie for the oven. The smell of spices and cinnamon fill the air of the house and coffee boils on the stove about ready to be taken off and served. Mabel sits at the table watching, a bit fidgety, wanting to do something other than sit. Her mother-in-law has strictly forbidden this, however, giving her a throw blanket to spread on her lap with a mug sitting before her for when the coffee is ready.

"So he told ya, then?" Betty asks with a nonchalant air about her. She doesn't turn when she asks, just keeps to her task of cooking and making things ready for them to eat.

Mabel nods from her chair. "Yes."

"Are ya angry at us?" Again, her tone seems less concerned about how Mabel feels about the situation if it is to be negative. Besides, they are making money. This is what she cares about: the liquor keeps flowing out and the cash keeps flowing in.

"Not angry, no. I just wish I would have been a bit more informed is all." She says this with a bit of hurt coming through in her tone. Betty Henderson turns and pats at the air as if it were her shoulder in a soothing manner. "I've had my suspicions for a while, though. That he'd gotten back into it. The farm here is good enough, but it wouldn't have given him the kind of income he needed to pay for the medication." She laughs. "And deliverin' mail? That was a long shot, and no mistake."

Betty turns and smiles at her. "I had told him that was a long shot. Don't sound like him one bit." She turns and puts the pie in the oven and takes the coffee from the stove. "It's not that he wanted to keep it from ya, honey. I didn't either, for that matter, but I figured it would be for the best with your condition and all to not have to worry about your husband in that way." She pauses while she pours the coffee, her eyes never leaving Mabel's. "He did it for you, love."

Mabel nods at her from her seat, taking the steaming mug and blowing on it from the rim. It smells divine. "You're keepin' him safe?"

Betty smiles. "Of course, dear. With my life if need be. If he gets caught, though, I'll probably go down with him, the still being on my land and all. We're careful, though." She gives her daughter-in-law a knowing smile. "'Sides, can't have the boy goin' back off. Not when ya got a little one on the way."

Mabel is taken off guard by this comment. "Little one? We aren't expec-tin' right now."

Betty gives another knowing grin and her eyebrows shoot up toward her gray hair. Mabel unconsciously lays her hand on her thin belly. Betty pours herself a cup of coffee. "Might not know it yet, but I have a feelin'." Her eyebrows wrinkle mischievously. "It's a Mama thing, darlin'."

"Think your feelin's might be off this time?"

Betty sips at her coffee tentatively. "Never have been before. Your flow come yet?"

Mabel shakes her head, her hand still on her stomach. "No. S'posed to been here yesterday. But that's normal. I didn't bleed for two months with the sickness. Doc Monroe said that was normal with the fever and all. I just figured it would come on its own time."

Betty gently pats Mabel's hand, the one holding the stomach. She takes another sip of her coffee, cradling the mug in her hand and letting the warmth spread through her fingers. "I wouldn't count on it, dear. Mother's intuition. It's hardly ever wrong."

WILLIE AND LESTER FINISH THEIR WORK as the sun begins to set behind the trees, unbeknownst to Fletchie crouching and shivering underneath the brush, watching them. Willie packs the yeast and a few other items into a sack. He doesn't stick the model of the still in there, instead leaving it next to the crackling furnace and admiring it.

"Really is a nice piece of work, Lester."

The young man smiles shyly, looking up from his task of setting the water pump for the running of the beer while they are asleep. He shrugs, "It's really nothing, Willie. I's happy to do it."

Willie looks at him as he hefts his pack filled with their equipment that they bring in and out every time they come to and leave the still. "It means a lot." He turns back to the furnace and the small model. "Looks mighty nice there. Think that's where it should stay."

Lester comes and joins him, looking at his present to his cousin. "Then there's where it will stay."

Willie gives the still a quick once over, making sure everything is good for the beer to sit overnight and for them to return to work after Christmas. "Should be all good for the next day. Don't figure there's much reason for us to really come out here tomorrow. We'll take the day and enjoy ourselves with the rest. Be ready for us when the holiday's over and we can get everything goin' to finish this run and start the next."

Lester nods, hefting his own pack and doing his own lookover of the still. "Sounds good."

"You're joining us for supper, ain't ya?"

Lester smiles. "'Course."

Willie nods. "Good. Somethin' you need to hear just as much as the rest of them."

Lester looks at him concerned. "Somethin' wrong, Willie?"

He gives the younger man a smile. "Not at all. Just have some business to discuss with everybody. It'd be good to just get it done in one go."

Lester nods, looking in Willie's face to try and get a hint of what news is to come when they reach the house. "Okay, Willie. Ready to hear it."

OLD FIELD PINES

The two men turn toward the house, Willie putting his arm around Lester's shoulder as they go. He gives a quick whistle and Pearl rises from her place next to the furnace and makes to follow.

THEIR BOOTS PASS CLOSE BY to where Fletchie hunkers, shivering with the cold, the discomfort, the fear of them stepping a few inches to the left and stepping on him to discover his hiding spot. They don't, however, and their footsteps begin to fade with the crunching of snow and leaves and twigs. When Pearl passes, he has another moment of panic as the dog makes her way to the bush with a familiar friendliness. He waves her off gently. The dog stares at him confusedly for a moment before giving a soft whimper for being rejected by him. It soon passes, though, as his Papa gives another whistle and Pearl dutifully bounds off after him and his Uncle Lester. The boy, for the first time in some hours, miserable hours, can breathe a sigh of relief for finally being able to move from his hiding place.

His young body is stiff with cold and having to lie still for so long. His entire front side of his pants and coat are soaked through with the snow that he had been lying in, melting into his clothes with the warmth of his body. He is cold and wet, miserably so. Most of all, though, Fletchie feels hurt at his father having lied to him about what he had been doing. He'd promised to stop, after all. That was a lie. The evidence is in front of him as he crawls stiffly from his bush and he brushes what he can of the snow and muck and twigs from his clothes and hair. His teeth are chattering with the cold as his eyes leak the tears he had suppressed with his hiding. He lets them come, now that he is alone and the threat of being caught is fully gone. He sits in front of the still and cries for what seems like a long while to him.

When the poor child has cried what he feels to be all the tears he has in his body, he is left with nothing but the hurt and the anger. He wants very much to smash the still to pieces. It would put an end to everything, for certain. All it would take would be a big stick and some effort and he could put an end to all this lying and sneaking about. But that won't do. He knows this. The act, while satisfying, would certainly get him caught. Who else would have come out here and found the still to only smash it in anger? No. There must be another way to get his father to stop. He wants very much to figure this out if he can, but the cold and his general miserable disposition prevent him from coming up with anything that would work.

Instead he turns, his teeth still chattering and his arms wrapped around his chest to try and ward off as much of the chill as he can, and trudges back in the direction that his Papa and Lester have gone, back toward the house where there will be a fire and food and presents to open. The thought of presents, now, seems to only fill him with more sadness and dread. Not even the thought of Christmas can make the hurt he feels go away.

WILLIE AND LESTER EMERGE FROM THE WOODS to the view of the house with its chimney leaking pinewood smoke. They are tired and hungry as they reach the porch and open the door to let a blast of pleasant warmth hit their faces. They are grateful for such luxury of heat as they shed their coats and gloves, stomping their boots in the doorway before removing them and placing them in the house to dry from the wet and cold. Pearl trots in before them and makes directly for the kitchen and the delicious smell of cooking food and coffee. Willie peeks into the living room where he had left Fletchie to find it empty. This seems a bit curious but he shrugs it off with the delectable scents coming to meet him from the kitchen.

Betty Henderson and Mabel sit at the table when they enter. Betty rises from her chair and goes to the cupboard to take down two more mugs to pour them some coffee. Lester takes a seat on the far side of the table. Willie goes first to Mabel, sitting in her chair, and kisses the top of her head. Her hand rises from her lap to reach for his, and their fingers intertwine as he takes his seat.

"Where's Fletchie?"

Mabel looks about from her chair. "He's not in the sitting room?"

Willie shakes his head and he turns to his Mama, who comes bearing more mugs and begins pouring out the coffee.

She shakes her head as well and shrugs as she pours. "Probably just out exploring near the barn. That boy always did like to play in them fields."

Willie nods. This is perfectly reasonable and the boy's absence is soon put to the back of his mind as the simple nature of a child at play. He sips the toothsome coffee from his mug. It's just as he likes: black and hot. The warmth and the conversation start like a light, them asking about their work and the men politely talking away about their process and their plans for the current "big" run.

Willie takes another sip of his coffee and gives Mabel's hand a squeeze at a lull in the conversation. This is his moment to talk and Lester and Mama are already looking at him expectantly. It must be the look on his face that gives him away.

His Mama smiles at him, holding her steaming mug in front of her face. "You got something on your mind, baby?"

Willie looks to Mabel next to him. She smiles at him warmly and gives his hand that rests on her leg a squeeze. He notices now that she keeps her other hand on her stomach protectively. He thinks this strange but shrugs it away. Perhaps she's cold. He clears his throat and looks around the table at his family. They will surely understand. It was always going to come to this, one way or another. He takes another sip of coffee to stall for a moment while he thinks of where to start before he begins. "Y'all know this run's gonna be big. Biggest run that I've ever had completed since I started shinin'."

Everyone around the table nods in turn except for Mabel, who smiles sadly at this. Lester waits patiently, but Mama nods her head in a greedy manner as if she can already hold the money rolling in once this liquor is distributed.

"Well, I've been thinkin'."

Mama chuckles a bit, good-heartedly. "Well that's never good, son."

Willie smiles along with her joke but his eyes shift to find Mabel's. She gives his hand another squeeze, encouraging him to continue. "I've been thinking that after we get this run finished and sold off that it's time to start lookin' for other means of income."

Everyone is silent for a time. Willie looks around the table. Mabel smiles at him with a look of relief showing clearly in her features. Lester seems a bit sad at the prospect of it all coming to an end, but his head nods in affirmation and he gives Willie a comforting grin. Betty Henderson is a different story. She sits staring off at nothing, her wrinkled hands gripping her mug tight enough that Willie is afraid it might shatter. He reaches out his free hand toward her arm, giving it a loving squeeze. She looks at him finally and laughs.

"You've been hittin' the product, ain't ya, son?"

"No, Mama. I ain't been drinkin'."

She laughs again and sets her mug on the table. "Then ya just plum stupid, then. Stopping now? That's ridiculous."

Willie gives her a look. He is hurt by her response but he is also adamant. This is for the best. "You knew it wasn't gonna go on forever, Mama."

She rises from the table and turns back to the kitchen. Her hands search for something to do but everything is either in the oven, on the stove, or sitting ready for them to start their Christmas supper. Finding nothing to busy herself with, she turns back to the table incredulously.

"Have you lost it, boy?"

"No'm. Believe I'm thinkin' clearer than I have in some time." Mabel gives his hand another loving squeeze at this. He looks to her and she gives him a smile of thanks and relief.

Betty Henderson returns, placing her hands on the table and leaning heavily on it. "You really think it's a good idea to just walk away now? We're just startin' to make the kind of money that could really set us up for good. This could get Fletchie money for his education. Could give you money for the new—"

"I think it's for the best," Mabel cuts her off sharply. She gives her a look that tells the older woman to let it drop. She turns to her husband, having seen the looks that passed between the two women of his life. "I want my husband safe." She looks over to Lester sitting next to her. "I want both of you safe. It's only a matter of time before something happens and they get caught. Stopping while we're ahead is the best option."

Betty lets out a long huff of a breath, shaking her head so that her curled hair bobs on her head. "This is foolish. We're just comin' into the money."

"This run is gonna give us plenty for now, Mama." He gives her his own look, pleading with her to see his way of looking at the situation. "It was a means to an end. We started because Mabel needed treatment. She got her treatment and she's doin' better, praise the Lord. The treatment's paid, the bills are caught up, this run will give us a nice cushion to get us through winter and beyond." He turns to Lester, who looks at him from across the table with his coffee mug raised in salute to his cousin. "This spring, Lester and

OLD FIELD PINES

I'll start farming this land for real. We'll get his water pump modified to start bringing fresh, cold water up here for the hay and other crops. We'll have the best-runnin' farm in the county that way. No need to pray for rain. We can bring the rain to us."

Lester nods his approval at this plan. "Think I might be able to get that pump workin' toward these fields. It'll take some tinkerin', but it could be done."

Willie turns back to his Mama triumphantly. "See. We can do this. Do this right and proper. No worries about the law breathing down our necks with this plan."

Betty sinks back into her chair. She looks tired but she isn't ready to give in yet. Willie can see it in her face. She opens her mouth to reply but then the front door opens and closes quickly. They all turn to see Fletchie enter the house. He shivers and is wet and dirty. They all rise in concern and make for the poor shivering child, asking him what had happened and where he'd been to get so dirty.

Fletchie, through the chattering of his teeth, simply mutters that he fell playing before allowing himself to be led toward the stove to thaw his freezing bones. Betty Henderson gives Willie a look as they help the boy shed his clothes and dry him off. "We'll talk about this later."

Willie rubs a towel along the boy to get his blood working through his arms. "It's done, Mama."

Betty has her doubts about this, but she turns her attention to putting her grandson to rights. After a time, they have him warm, with fresh pajamas and a cup of steaming apple cider, and clean enough to begin their Christmas celebrations. The conversation of quitting shining seems to have been put to rest for the time being as the family gathers together to celebrate the holiday. Food is plentiful and mouthwatering. The mood is light. The house is warm. Presents come and are opened and played with. All of them seem to be in good spirits with smiles on their faces. Despite his gratefulness at being warm once more and the excitement of opening his Christmas gifts, the smile on Fletchie's face is but something that he paints on to hide his hurt and pain. He sneaks glances at his father every now and then, and throughout the evening, wonders as to how he could be so cheery after having told such lies. So many, at that.

CHAPTER X

THE WEATHER HAD WARMED to above-average temperatures for January. The amounts of snow that had accumulated were melting away to make the unpaved streets around and surrounding Mountain View a muddy, rutted mess with the passing of foot traffic and wheels alike. Vehicles and buggies were bogged down by the 3rd, and the work to pull them out was nearly made impossible by the slickness of the sticky mud left behind in the wake of the rising temperatures. Teams of horses sequestered by Sheriff Baker were used throughout town on a rotating basis to help rid the streets of the pile-ups that blocked the main drags across town. Folks were pulled out in the morning and then stuck again in the evening. Old timers in the future would sit around the fire in the spring runoffs to discuss the floods and mud only to say, "You ain't seen nothing. You should have been here in the winter of '26. That was a true mudhole."

On the 5th day of the year, a logging truck—a full load in tow—jack-knifed in the muddy mess and turned over outside of town toward Timbo, littering the roadway and knocking over three trees in the tumbling logs. Two houses were damaged in the fiasco. Thankfully, no one was injured during the event.

As a result of the terrible road conditions, Clyde had been unable to make it to Willie's Mama's by the 2nd as they had planned. Instead he came on the 5th. Willie hadn't minded the change of plans. He and Lester were already well on their way to getting the new run going. His last run, hopefully. The quickness of the turnaround would only mean more money sooner than expected; besides, it had already been some time since Clyde had last delivered. Before the holidays as it was. People would be ready for their liquor. And the extra load would appease some of his Mama's anger at his abrupt stopping of the production. It would all work out for the best. Might even be some extra for Willie to distribute among the rest of his cohorts. Clyde is rather fond of this idea.

OLD FIELD PINES

The extra loads of jars—packed safely into mailbags—made the truck seem as if Clyde was carrying an unprecedented haul of mail for the sparsely-populated rural areas of its usual route. Clyde pays this no mind. He was a government man, after all.

Clyde thinks about how well everything is going as he drives through Mountain View township on the morning of January 5th. He's heading back toward Leslie to make the mail drops and the liquor runs on his return route. It's not his normal means of delivery. Usually he'd have been making the mail drops along the way, starting on the far side of Leslie almost to Marshall before doubling back and working his way through the communities and hamlets outside of Mountain View before reaching the city for his last drop at the Mountain View Post Office; he'd adjusted his normal delivery methods for days like today: leaving early to pick up the mail from Leslie's post office, heading toward Willie's Mama's to load the liquor into his deliveries, and then working backward toward home. It was a much longer day this way, but the pay had been worth it in the end. 'Sides, Clyde had grown fond of Willie and Lester. They were good folks just trying to make them a living. He respects that and is happy to help them along for the substantial cut he is taking for it.

The roads are bad, but not as bad as they could be. Clyde drives too fast for them to really matter in his old tank of a truck, tires spinning so fast that the mud just can't stick to 'em. He'd liked to drive since he was a young buck. He'd learned how, mostly, on the wagon his Mama had used to get back and forth from town when he was a child, sitting on her lap and turning the reins to steer the horse along the rough roads surrounding their property, leading to the town of Leslie. His Mama—having raised him on her own after his Pappy passed, killed himself after the War of the States, living with the atrocities that he'd witnessed for nearly thirty years after the conflict was ended—brought home their first car when he was around twenty years old. He'd driven the vehicle into the ground within a year, receiving a whipping from his Mama like none he'd ever experienced growing up. He'd told her that he would pay her back for the loss and had gone out hunting for jobs that same day with his backside tanned and sore.

He'd stumbled upon the postman job soon after, delighted at the opportunity to be able to drive a car for a living. It had taken him several days to convince his Mama to let him keep the job. Having lived through the hardships of Reconstruction, she'd developed a bitter taste for the federal government and had mistrusted anyone working for them ever since. It was his convincing her that it was the best place for him, an inside job to keep an eye on the Yankee bureaucrats that had done the trick. He'd worked at the post ever since and had driven every day of his working life to his great internal fulfillment.

He laughs at the memory of this as he barrels out of Mountain View's township toward Leslie. Thinking on times past and how good he has it now is more than likely what distracted him. Before he knows it, he is ripped out of his revelry at the sight of a blockage in the road, cutting the wheel hard to the left to avoid one of the volunteers helping to clean up the logging accident from the roadway. He makes it through the thick of the mess and the cursing of the startled volunteers without killing anyone. He passes where Sheriff Michael Baker leans against his patrol truck, smoking a hand-rolled cigarette. His staring at the Sheriff nervously causes him to bump a log, having yet to be cleared, with his front left tire. The car jolts upward for a brief instant, rattling the cargo and himself alike. He curses, getting back control of the vehicle before continuing on his way. He thinks nothing more of the situation. He slips easily back into his care-free thoughts, ignoring the yells of Sheriff Baker behind him, chalking them up to more of the angry calls of outrage at his driving. It is a good day and he will be making some good money soon.

Sheriff Michael Baker throws out his cigarette into the cold mud and stops hollering at the mail truck. The large mail sack lying in the wake of the vehicle is almost black from the gunk sticking to it, but seems unscathed with the contents tucked safely inside and secured by a drawstring running around the opening and tied securely shut. Baker hefts the bag out of the mud, surprised at the weight. But it's not the weight that catches his suspicions, it's the smell: a strong, antiseptic sort of stench that mixes with the coolness of the air and burns the nostrils. He looks down at the bag and sees the dripping coming from the bottom. The sound of broken glass rattles as he sets the bag back in the mud to examine its contents.

OLD FIELD PINES

SHERIFF MICHAEL BAKER CROUCHES IN THE BRUSH, looking toward the residence of Billy Clyde Davis, a mail carrier for Searcy County who delivers the larger quantities of mail to post offices throughout Stone County. Baker had asked around about the man. From what he could gather, Billy Clyde Davis was a quiet man, very private, who did his job and went home. He was seldom seen in Leslie unless coming or going from work. He lives with his mother in the house that Baker now crouches in front of—the mail truck in clear sight with the bags of mail, possibly loaded with jars of bootlegged liquor, still in the bed—with Sheriff Alfred Hitchinson of Searcy County and three of his Deputies. Sheriff Hitchinson had allowed him to tag along for the arrest due to the influx of illegal liquor being distributed throughout Stone County and because it had been Baker who put in the word to the Searcy County Sheriff's Department about the liquor in the mail sack dumped on the side of the highway in Baker's territory. Also, Hitchinson had been one of Baker's Deputies when he was Sheriff of Searcy County, so when asked if Baker could join in on the arrest, Hitchinson had been apt to oblige him.

The house is still quiet in the early morning hours. The sun has not yet fully risen behind the treeline. Hitchinson had wanted to just walk up on the front door and knock, but Baker had been able to talk him out of that. There was no reason to alert Billy Clyde Davis of their presence just yet. He might run. He might do something stupid and Baker wants him alive and well so that he can talk. He must talk. Baker will make sure that he does. Surprise is their best option. Hitchinson hadn't liked it but had begrudgingly conceded to Baker's judgment of the situation.

Across the narrow dirt drive, a cow stands staring at them behind a fragile-looking barbed wire fence. It stomps its hooved feet into the ground a few times, snorting in the early morning chill. The warm front that had moved in is slowly dissipating once more, and the cow's breath fogs hot in the cool air. It doesn't like their presence, clearly. Baker thinks about shooting it but that would defeat the purpose of their stealth. If it begins throwing a fit and ruins this arrest for him, Baker decides that he will save a bullet special to place between the sow's round eyes.

A flame flickers to life in one of the windows. Baker clutches at his gun in anticipation. Hitchinson sees this but doesn't say anything. He'd worked with Baker in his early days as a Deputy and trusted that he wouldn't do anything brash, wouldn't do anything disturbing. He pulls his own pistol from the holster at his waist.

"All right," Baker whispers, his breath fogging in the early morning glow. "Prolly gonna come out to take a piss in that there outhouse."

"And if it's the mother?" Hitchinson asks.

"I say take her, too."

Hitchinson glances over at the man who was once his superior, a respected lawman, in surprise. "She's not part of this."

"How we know that? Could be in on it, too. The sooner we take everyone into custody, the sooner the situation defuses, and we can start sortin' things out with some questions."

Hitchinson doesn't like this but he nods anyway. "All right." He looks to his Deputies kneeling behind them. "Wait till the door to the house is closed and whoever comes out is in the yard before we make a move. Quiet as possible, now."

Baker doesn't pay much attention. He fingers the pistol in his hand and bounces lightly on the balls of his feet. He hasn't felt so young in a long time. It's finally happening for him. This is how Willie Henderson has been doing it, his distribution system. There's no real evidence to prove this, not yet, but he knows it in his bones. The sooner they get Billy Clyde Davis, the sooner he can get Henderson.

The front door of the house opens and a sleepy man, Clyde Davis surely, steps out shivering in the early morning chill. He wears long johns stained from years of wear that Baker can see even from where he crouches down in the brush. Clyde stretches on the porch, scratching absently at his crotch before taking the rickety steps and making his way to the outhouse. Baker looks to Hitchinson, who gives him a nod and they rise from the bushes, their guns leveled at Clyde.

Hitchinson emerges first with Baker hot on his trail, the Deputies spanning out on the sides and behind them. "I'm gonna have to ask ya to put your hands in the air, Mr. Davis!"

OLD FIELD PINES

Clyde jumps nearly out of his unlaced boots, giving a small shout of surprise at the disturbance of his morning piss. His eyes light with fear and his hands shoot skyward when he sees the men with their guns leveled at him. He squints at Hitchinson a moment in the early morning glow. "Sheriff? I don't know what this is all 'bout, but I…" His eyes shift to meet Michael Baker's. The smile on the Stone County Sheriff's face is one of a pure, sick joy. Clyde loses his train of thought, can't finish what he was about to say. There's only one thing now on his mind. They know. For God's sakes, they know. His eyes dart to the mail truck standing a few yards away. Too far to run. They'd shoot him dead. Baker would, for sure.

"Don't make any decisions yer goin' to regret, Mr. Davis," Hitchinson says, approaching with his gun hand pointing low. He raises the weapon along with his free hand, trying to disarm the frightened Clyde. "Just go ahead and kneel on down where ya stand. See," he raises the gun to point skyward before slowly placing it back in his holster. "We just wanna talk to ya, Mr. Davis. Sheriff Baker here has some disturbin' allegations brought forward involvin' ya."

Clyde sinks to his knees as Hitchinson reaches him, Michael Baker close behind. He wants to cry, almost can't help it, but crying would make him look even more guilty than they already believe him to be. Hell, what is he thinkin'? He is guilty. They got him, for sure. Baker's gun is still drawn and pointed at Clyde's head as he kneels and involuntarily lets a sob escape his lips.

"Put it down!" a Deputy yells from behind Baker.

Clyde's face looks to the porch in shock, his eyes growing wide with fear and warning. "Ma, don't—"

The crack of the rifle startles all of them. Sheriff Baker's head flinches as a Deputy falls directly behind him clutching at his lower leg, blood coming from between his fingers. Baker doesn't hear his screams, his ears still ringing from the blast, blood pumping between his ears in a rush. He pivots toward the porch, his revolver swinging up as he turns. As soon as the nightgown comes in front of his barrel, he lets off two rounds rapidly, striking the elderly woman clutching the rifle in her stomach and chest. The shots knock her off her feet. Hitchinson shoves a screaming Clyde into the cold dirt. The shot Deputy rolls around on the ground hollering as the other kneels before him to check his wound. The woman falls onto the porch, almost in slow motion as Baker watches her with utter fascination. His gun barrel follows her fall, smoking in the cold air. He does not see the movement of his companions, hear the screams of the wounded or the heartbroken, the yells of Sheriff Hitchinson. He only hears a loud buzzing in his ears, like static from a long-distance phone call, as the rifle clatters to the porch.

MICHAEL BAKER SITS IN THE OFFICE of Sheriff Hitchinson at the Searcy County Sheriff's Department. He is alone in the room, his feet propped up on the desk that was once his. Hitchinson had been hard at work on Clyde Davis for some time now. Baker is patient, though. He can wait for his turn at Clyde once Hitchinson has had his fill. They'd brought the body of the woman in as quickly as possible so as not to alert the townspeople of Marshall of any kind of disturbance. Baker had asked for the incidents to be kept out of the press for as long as possible, giving him time to gather information for the bigger arrest of the manufacturer of the illegal liquor. Hitchinson had agreed to this, not so much to help Michael Baker in his investigation, but to keep the shooting out of public knowledge for as long as it would take for him to put a more positive spin on this. He was unsure as to what he would tell his constituents as to why an elderly woman had been shot outside her home by a neighboring county's Sheriff. It probably wasn't going to sit well with the people. Making an arrest was one thing, but shooting someone, an old woman no less, on her own front steps was an entirely different matter.

Bringing in Clyde Davis without drawing much attention had had its obstacles. People knew their mail carriers quite well in small towns. Besides, the man had been distraught to the point of hysteria when they'd hauled him from the back of the vehicle. He hadn't stopped his caterwauling the entire ride. He screamed and cried himself nearly hoarse in a cell until he'd gotten calm enough for Hitchinson to begin questioning him about the liquor. That hadn't been much of a challenge to keep hidden from the public eye. Each of the jars of moonshine had been tucked snugly in the large mail sacks with different letters and parcels stuffed between them to keep the jars from rattling and breaking. Baker had watched the Deputies—two now with the other being looked after by a physician for the rifle slug that nearly tore his leg off below the knee, probably have to cut the damned thing off before it was said and done—unloading the sacks of mail and liquor, separating the envelopes from the jars, and stacking them on the desks of the main office space. It was a big haul, the largest that Baker had seen in his career. They'd run out of room on the desks and had started stacking on the floor when Baker went into the office to sit and smoke in peace.

Baker reclines in the chair, his muddy boots resting comfortably on the desktop, lighting his third cigarette when Hitchinson enters the office. He doesn't ask Baker for his chair but instead sits on the opposite side where visitors would sit and puts his head in his hands, exhausted. "Well," he says with a sigh, "that was a hell of a mess."

Baker passes a rolled cigarette across the desk at his former Deputy. "A victory. For me and for you, Sheriff." Hitchinson accepts the cigarette and leans forward for Baker to light it. He reclines once more and allows his weary body to sink deeper into the chair and sucks at a long drag, holding in the smoke for some time with his eyes shut, head tilting toward the ceiling. "You should be proud of yourself and your department for this."

Hitchinson's eyes remain closed. "An innocent woman was shot today, Sheriff." He doesn't understand why he still refers to Michael Baker as his superior. They are of equal positions now. He wants to think it is out of respect to an old mentor and friend, but knows better. Old habits die hard and Michael Baker's shadow is a dark, tough son of a bitch to climb out from under.

"She shot at us. Hit one of your men. I did what was necessary."

"I don't know what I'll tell the town."

"You tell them the truth. A win for justice, and a harrowing one at that, for two departments working together." He takes another drag on his cigarette casually. "After the investigation is complete, of course."

Hitchinson nods. He is tired. Just wants to get everything over with and Sheriff Baker back across the county line. "I'll keep it quiet for as long as I can. Day or two maybe, but then I'll have to come out with the full news, try and spin this, as you said. As a win." He spits the last part out with disgust.

Baker rises from the chair behind Hitchinson's desk. "Speaking of news, he talkin' any?"

The weary Hitchinson shakes his head. "Not a damn word."

"Mind if I have a few minutes with him? Gotta get what I can for my investigation."

Hitchinson is suspicious. He no longer believes he can trust Sheriff Baker's judgment. It hadn't been the shooting of the woman. It had been his eyes afterward. They showed no remorse. He hadn't even gone over to check on the body or the wounded Deputy, for that matter. After the shots were fired, Baker had just lit a cigarette and smiled, going to the back of the mail truck and slicing open a sack to pull out a jar of liquor. There was no remorse, only triumph. Hitchinson had agreed to Baker interviewing Clyde Davis. He figured he had to let him. Keep his word and all. He didn't know what Baker would do if he told him no at this point. He passes the keys to the cell to Baker. "Few minutes. I want details when you're done."

Baker doesn't answer. Only crushes out his cigarette and makes for the door and the hallway that goes to another door, locked tight and separating the office spaces from the cells. He doesn't look back as he inserts the key, opening the door and firmly shutting it behind him, the click of the lock resounding in the silence of the room he has left. He never notices Hitchinson standing in his office door watching him go, worry plastered across his too-tired face and what might have been a prayer falling silently from his lips. The layout is different compared to the cell block of the Stone County Sheriff's Department, but all too familiar as Baker walks the halls, his boots tapping out the sound of a recent memory when he had clipped them down last as Sheriff of Searcy County. The sound of his boot heels resonates loudly through the hall and the concrete floor, echoing off the brick walls *click, click, clicking* toward the cell he wants. Baker takes his time. He is in no rush. Hitchinson won't disturb him. He wants answers almost as bad as Baker himself. Except Baker doesn't want answers, he needs them: a deep, burning fire of a need that makes his eyes dance and the temperature of his body rise to the point of a low-grade fever. He's within reach of those answers. So close. *Click, click, click.*

His boots stop in front of the cell. Billy Clyde Davis sits on the cot pushed against the left wall. His head is in his hands, gripping his hair in a way that makes it seem like he might rip patches out at the root if he's not careful. Baker smiles at the thought of witnessing such a thing.

"Mr. Davis."

Clyde doesn't answer. Doesn't even look up from the tucked position he is in.

Baker slips the key into the lock with an audible click and slides the door open, stepping into the cell and letting it slide back into place with a *bang* behind him. "Do you prefer Billy or Clyde?"

Still no answer from the man on the cot.

Baker smiles. "No matter, Mr. Davis. I prefer addressing people with their family name as it is. Seems much more civilized that way, don't you think?" There is a chair against the far wall that Baker grabs and slides over in front of Clyde. "May I sit a spell?"

No response. Not even a twitch.

Baker sits anyway, crossing his legs in a relaxed posture. "You wanna tell me where all that liquor came from, Mr. Davis?"

Clyde sighs, the first sound he's made since Baker came into the cell, the first notion that the poor grieving man is even alive. He refuses to look at Baker, still. He is in the handcuffs that they had placed on him at the scene.

"No," Baker sighs as he says it, letting out a resounding breath. "You've been through hell and back today. I can sympathize with that. Arrested and losing your mother all in a single day—"

"Go to hell." It comes out as a mumble from between his hands, still refusing to look Baker in the eye.

"What was that, Mr. Davis? 'Fraid I can't hear ya too well."

Clyde looks up now. His face is dirty and wet from being pressed into the dirt at the house and the tears that have flowed since the shooting of his Mama. His eyes are red, nose dripping snot into his mustache and across his trembling upper lip. It leers into a snarl. "I said, go to hell."

"It was a terrible shame that it had to happen like it did. Poor woman probably couldn't help herself."

Clyde's eyes water once more with fresh tears, but they have lost the sadness. They are cold, angry now. He glares at Sheriff Baker with a hatred that is clear without his speaking of it.

"If she'd have just stayed in the house and kept quiet—"

"That's 'nough!" Clyde shouts, his breaths coming in heavy and quick.

"Wish I could say that I didn't wanna shoot her, but ya know, using the pistol's the fun part of the—"

Clyde makes to lunge at Baker but he is too slow, the Sheriff rising to his feet and drawing back his arm quicker than Clyde thought possible. He was ready for it. Baker hits Clyde with an open palm across the cheek—not a slap, but more of a club—sending him reeling to the floor in a clatter of cuff chains. Clyde makes to rise and Baker drives the toe of his boot into his stomach, knocking the wind from him and making him feel like he might vomit. There wouldn't be much left to vomit up anyway. He'd done that twice from crying on the way to Marshall. He spits a wad of blood from his cut cheek instead.

Sheriff Baker smiles at the sight of the man on the floor and rears back his foot for another go, feeling the toe of his boot sink into Clyde's middle with speed and then stopping in the squishy flesh of his stomach. Clyde dry heaves while gasping for air at the same time. Baker's smile grows wider. He enjoys this part, has always enjoyed this part of the job. They never want to talk at first, which angers him, but the anger comes in handy here. It lends power to his swings and kicks. Then Clyde'll talk. He'll tell what he knows just to make the beating stop so he might be able to catch a painful breath.

"Now, Mr. Davis, no need for that. Just tryin' to have a conversation, express my sympathies for what happened." Clyde makes to rise again and Baker drives the heel of his hand down hard between Clyde's shoulder blades, sending him back onto the concrete floor, his head knocking hard. "How 'bout ya just stay down there, Mr. Davis?"

Clyde only gasps, his mouth wide open with blood running from the corner of his lips onto the floor.

"Let's start with where you are getting your supply. I have a hunch, you see." Baker pulls the chair forward and retakes his seat, resting his elbows on his knees and bending low to talk to the prone, wheezing Clyde. "I believe I know exactly where you're gettin' it from, but I want to hear it. No, I *have* to."

Clyde only lies still, trying to get his breath back into his lungs.

Baker leans down and lightly slaps at Clyde's back. "Come on, Mr. Davis. Speak up, now. I ain't got all day. I could really use your help."

Clyde looks up from the floor, his lips spreading into a bloody smile. "Why don't ya just eat shit, Sheriff?"

Baker's hand comes down to smack his cheek again, sending his head careening back down to slam against the concrete. Clyde lets out a groan as Baker rises from his seat and walks behind his chair. "Better yet, help yourself, Mr. Davis. Let me help you."

"I said, eat shit."

"You know how long you're lookin' at, Mr. Davis? I'd reckon this is the biggest bootleg operation in the history of both Stone and Searcy Counties. Hell, probably biggest one in the *state*, for that matter. Public opinion in favor or against, this is not just gonna be local news. This'll attract the attention of the feds. They'll wanna make an example out of someone like you."

"Don't know what yer talkin' 'bout."

"Sure ya do, Mr. Davis," Baker says with a laugh. The laugh makes Clyde more nervous. "Never see freedom again, I'd bet. Just workin' on a farm, chains 'round your ankles, day in and day out. Till you drop. Then they'll throw you in a grave, just like the grave they's 'bout to throw yer Mama in."

"Fuck you."

"'Cept your grave won't be nothin' fancy," Baker continues, as if he hadn't noticed Clyde's outburst. "Just have a little board with to mark it surrounded by other boards in a field within the state facility. Might carve your name in it if you're lucky. I'd suspect not, though." He regains his seat, pulling a silver container from his pocket that holds his cigarettes he'd rolled the night before so he could smoke without the interruption of rolling them today. There are initials engraved upon the silver container that he slips into his pocket. They are not his own, just another trophy.

He slips the cigarette between his lips and lights up. "I don't think you want that, do you, Mr. Davis?"

Clyde only stares up at him, his face a blank, bloody mess.

"I could help you out of this, Mr. Davis."

"What do you mean?" Clyde says, spitting more blood onto the floor.

His face screws up in a grimace of pain from talking or breathing, Baker isn't quite sure. Probably a bit of both. He's almost certain he'd felt a rib crack on the last kick.

"Exactly what I say, Mr. Davis. We both know that you weren't the one behind all of this. You were just helpin' out someone. Runnin' distribution of the product." Baker takes a long drag on his cigarette, blowing smoke down onto the floor to swirl around Clyde before floating back up to hang in the cell, a glowing haze in the dim light. "I don't really want the man deliverin' the shine. I want the source. I want you to say his name. Just say Willie Henderson's name, out loud, and I'll see what I can do for you to get you out of some of this mess. Reduced sentence, maybe. What do ya say, Mr. Davis?"

Clyde looks up at him, the look of pain vanishing for a moment as he paints on a mock look of confusion. He smiles. "Henderson? I don't believe I know that name. Ya wanna describe him? Maybe something'll come to me."

Baker considers hitting him some more. He wants to. But what real good would that do? It would only make himself feel a bit better. It wouldn't get him any closer to Willie. Instead he straightens the collar of his shirt and notices a fleck of Clyde's blood that had made its way onto it during the beating. Baker wipes at it absently with his hand before giving up hope of getting rid of the stain. Blood doesn't come out easily. He'd have to throw the shirt out, more than likely. He runs a hand through his gray hair, smoothing down some of the rogue strands having gone wild in the excitement.

"Last chance, Mr. Davis."

Another bloody smile stretches Clyde's ruined face. He laughs and his eyes wince with the pain of it, the smile remaining. "Ya know. It's just not comin' to me. 'Sides, Sheriff, what's in those mail sacks ain't my business. I just deliver." He starts laughing again, harder this time, tears forming in the corners of his eyes with the pain of it.

Baker rises, stifling the urge to let loose more kicks to the man's body. Kick him in the face with his boot until it's a bloody mess, unrecognizable; kick him until his insides start to squish and bubble up from his smiling face. He doesn't, though. Sheriff Baker restrains himself, returning the smile that Clyde gives him. He makes for the door. "Have it your way, Mr. Davis." The Sheriff's boots make a *click, click, click* on the concrete to the exit with the sound of laughter ringing in his ears. He doesn't turn back, no matter how bad he wants to. The court will deal with scum like Clyde Davis. Sheriff Baker has more pressing concerns.

Hitchinson sits in a chair in the main office as Baker emerges from the cell hall. He rises when Baker comes through the door and heads for the office. "Get anything?"

"Nothin'," Baker says, heading into Hitchinson's office. The Sheriff of Searcy County makes to follow but is stopped by Baker reemerging into the main office, pulling on his coat as he walks. "He's useless at this point."

"You leavin'?"

"Got work to do. Keep all this out the papers as long as you can, Alfred." Baker reaches the door and makes to open it.

"Wait a minute," Hitchinson says, Baker stopping mid-stride. "What happened in there, Michael? You look a mess."

Baker turns back to him with a wicked smile. It scares Hitchinson for a moment. As soon as Baker leaves, he thinks, he'll have to make sure Clyde Davis is still alive in that cell. Baker's teeth shine a yellowish-white through the bushiness of his mustache. "Really? 'Cause I feel quite wonderful. You just tend to our friend in there and keep everything quiet for me." With that, he turns and exits the building.

His truck sits near the front door. He climbs into the cab and fires it up, backing into the street and pointing the vehicle toward Mountain View. He is not angry at Clyde for not talking. No one ever wants to talk when in that same situation. It's all right. He doesn't need Clyde's statement or confession. There's more than one way to get the information he needs. He just needs a little bit, enough to justify his taking action. He knows exactly where to get it, too. The Sheriff pulls another cigarette from his shirt and lights up, the tires kicking up dust and dirt as they head easterly toward the Stone County line. His county now.

CHAPTER XI

WILLIE AND MABEL UNTANGLE THEIR NAKED FLESH from each other with the pleasant stickiness of passionate sweat in the soft morning glow coming through the curtained window. They giggle together as they lie apart, their hands clasped between them, both panting softly from their exertions. The night had grown cold, an ever-changing enigma in the Ozarks. The cold had woken them early in the morning with their breath visible in the chilly cabin. Willie had gotten up to stoke a fire in the stove. Fletchie was in his small bed fast asleep. His nose was a bright pink hue from the cold. When the fire was stoked and slowly warming the house, Willie gently laid an extra blanket over his son, careful not to wake him. The boy had sleepily shifted in the bed with a shiver and a small smile for the extra warmth. Willie had kissed his forehead with a smile and went back into the separate bedroom. The cold had woken them both enough to thaw a morning stirring in them that resulted in the rigorous tumble between the quilt. Lying together now, Willie sends up a silent prayer of thanks for her recovery and health, for her love.

Mabel rolls onto her side, facing her husband. Her breast slips free of the covers. She makes no move to cover herself in front of her husband. She stares at him with a smile crossing her sultry lips. Willie lets a glance fall back to her breast. He sees a small bruising mark from his kissing her there that will surely get darker as the day goes on. She is beaming at him when he looks back toward her eyes.

"Sorry," Willie says shyly, casting his eyes back down to his own hands. She pays this no mind. "Did you really mean it?"

"Mean what?"

"What you said at Christmas. This really the last run?"

Willie's eyes move back up her body, taking in her neck, her chin, before settling back on her eyes. He runs a gentle hand back and forth over the smooth, bare skin of her arm. His hand slides off to her hip as his thumb traces small circles there. He smiles. "If everything goes to plan, yes. I'm done. It's time to start thinking about a future that doesn't involve someone coming up to find me with a gun drawn."

Mabel says nothing in reply. She quickly leans in and gives him another kiss, firmly planted on his lips. He kisses her back and they hold it for some time before Mabel comes back up, breathless and radiant. "That's the best news I've heard since you told me."

Willie shrugs, looking around at their small room. It is small and sparse, but it is comfortable. He's never been much one for fancy material possessions. He decides that he has all he needs at reach in their cabin. It's not much, not by many standards of success, but it is enough. It is enough for him. He begins to speak as he stares off at the wall and at nothing, looking beyond to his own thoughts deep within him. "It was always a means to an end, Mabel. It was never meant to continue forever."

She sighs and rolls back into her pillows, staring up at the ceiling. Her breath no longer comes in puffs of visible clouds. "Your Mama didn't seem so happy 'bout that resolution."

Willie laughs. "Ain't Mama's decision. She'll get over it. I've got plans, Mabel. Actual plans. I think I can really make something out of that land she got."

He speaks of his plans for a while. Dreams really, and dreams are a wonderful thing. He talks for longer than he truly means to. Never really having been one for long conversations, how all of it just pours out of him surprises him. Mabel sits and listens, back on her elbow and looking at him now, as he describes the wonderful fields that will be popping up with produce and hay, how Lester will rig the water pump system to deliver enough fresh water for everything to grow healthily. She can't help but smile as she watches him. He is wrapped in his descriptions, clearly passionate about the future possibilities that lie ahead. This makes her truly happy.

After a time of contented conversation, Willie rises from the bed, slips on a thick shirt and pants, buckling suspenders to the waist, and heads into the kitchen to cook breakfast for his family. Fletchie isn't in his bed when he enters. He finds this strange. The boy is nowhere in the main room of the cabin. Pearl is missing as well. He shrugs this off, though. The boy probably rose early to complete some of his chores before heading off to school. Soon, strips of bacon sizzle and pop in an iron skillet atop the stove and biscuits in the oven—a pleasant warmth spreading throughout the cabin—give off an inviting scent that has Mabel coming out of the bedroom in her robe.

"Where's Fletchie?" she asks, looking about the room.

"I s'pect he's out doing some chores 'fore school. You mind runnin' out to fetch him in? Breakfast is about done."

She pecks him on the cheek as she passes him heading toward the door. She opens it and gives a small start to find Fletchie sitting on the porch steps with his back leaning against the railing. He is reading a book and doesn't look up at her as she stands in the doorway.

"Fletchie, what are you doin' out here?" she asks with a laugh.

He slowly comes to the end of the line he is on and marks his page. He looks up at her now with eyes distraught. "Just readin'."

"Well, is everything all right?"

He nods, rises from his seat, and makes for her in the doorway. He brushes past her and heads for the table where Willie is dealing out bacon and biscuits onto plates.

"Mornin', son," Willie says cheerfully, and he means it. He is in a good mood with everything and can't seem to contain his excitement for the day, hopefully one of his last working the still.

Fletchie doesn't sit. He grabs his book bag on his bed and slings it over his shoulder. He takes a biscuit from a plate in front of his chair, peels it apart, and stuffs it with crispy, hot pieces of bacon before making back for the door.

Willie and Mabel both look at their young son in surprise. They are speechless at first as Fletchie silently makes back for the door with his shoulders slumped and his books slung over one of them.

Willie finds his voice first. "Where are ya off to?"

Fletchie turns. His eyes still contain that sadness, the hurt, that he has felt since the betrayal of his father's word. "School."

Willie smiles and takes a seat at the table. "Well, take a seat and let's have breakfast. I'm headin' out to the farm in a bit anyway. I'll give ya a ride." Willie pats the boy's chair next to him.

Fletchie ignores this, gives a small, meek smile. "I think I'd rather walk if that's okay."

OLD FIELD PINES

Willie is certainly confused. He looks to Mabel to see if she knows anything, but she only shakes her head. Willie turns back to his son. "Everything all right, son?"

Fletchie gives a slight nod. "It's good. Just kinda sad. I'll be okay." He turns and heads for the door. Pearl follows him out, panting and happy. She catches up with him at the steps to the porch and looks up to him. He ignores her want of petting, telling her to stay instead and making for the road.

Mabel seems to find herself once more and hollers out, "Be careful, sweetie, and have a good day!"

Fletchie gives a wave over his shoulder but continues on his way. They watch him until he is at the end of the drive and out of their sight. Mabel turns back to Willie, who only stares off after the way Fletchie had gone.

"What do you think was gettin' him?" she asks concerned.

Willie shrugs. "I've no idea. Boy hasn't been quite himself since Christmas time. Didn't even seem like he had much in him then."

"You think he's gettin' sick with something?"

Willie grunts, picking up another biscuit and putting in some bacon. "I don't know. Maybe he's gettin' picked on in the schoolyard. Need to teach him to stick up for himself. Maybe if he'd smack some of them around, they wouldn't be botherin' him no more." He closes the biscuit and gives a small whistle. Pearl trots up and nabs her prize from his fingers. She hauls it over to a corner near the stove to eat her breakfast. Mabel and Willie eat in silence, their conversation halting with Fletchie's odd behavior and their meal. Willie eats four bacon biscuits before it is all finished. He is happy to see that Mabel consumes two, to see some of her appetite returning. She looks much healthier now with her eating and the sickness driven from her body. They sit in silence, sipping coffee in the warmth of the stove.

Willie checks his pocket watch hanging from a chain in the front pocket of his trousers. He sighs contentedly, looking at his wife sitting next to him. He gives her hand a pat and a squeeze before rising and taking the plates to the sink. Pearl has finished her own breakfast and trots over to Willie's feet, rubbing her sides against him in a cat-like fashion before turning around three times and settling there before him. "Probably goin' to be at it all night. 'Bout done with this last batch, and I aim to see it finished tonight."

Mabel's smile twitches on her face briefly, too quick to notice. Her hand goes to her flat stomach at a bit of sickness coming over her. She breathes deeply for a moment and it passes quickly. Willie doesn't notice this either, looking down at where Pearl lounges beneath him.

"Lester'll be with you?"

Willie nods. "Should already be gettin' everything set for tonight."

She rises from the table and begins packing the leftover biscuits into a bag, wrapped in a towel, and slips a large hunk of uncooked bacon into the pack beside them in its paper covering. "Well, take these so you both'll have something to eat. You two don't go gettin' too drunk neither. I know what y'all do out there in them woods while you're waitin'."

Willie laughs at this. He sees his fiddle sitting on the counter on the other side of the stove. It rests in its black bag that he uses for a case. Why not? He picks it up and slings the string over his shoulder. It will be a cold evening. Some music might help to keep them warm. Lester has a decent voice from what Willie can remember.

Mabel looks up to him and rises from her chair. She folds into his arms easily and remains there for a time, stroking the muscles of his back through his shirt. "You be careful, okay?"

Willie rests his bearded chin on her head, breathing in the scent of her hair. "I always am." He leans down and plants a kiss on her puckered lips. He pulls back and stares into her eyes for several moments, lost in their love and beauty. His face darkens with worry. "You two gonna be okay here tonight?"

She leans in and kisses his whiskered cheek. "We'll manage fine. I can take care of us."

"I know you can," Willie replies with a sigh. His eyes are concerned as they look at her. "I'm just 'fraid that damn Sheriff might try somethin' stupid."

Mabel gives a small laugh. "I wouldn't worry too much 'bout us. Ya just go do what ya gotta do. I got the rifle here." She points to the corner where his old hunting rifle sits unloaded against the wall. "You just be safe."

Willie nods. "All right." He kisses her again. "I love you. Both of you. Make sure to tell Fletchie that before bed tonight." Willie puts an arm around her waist and pulls her in for one more kiss. A sadness and urgency befalls him then to where he doesn't want to stop, as if he has to make it last. It is a strange feeling, but a fleeting one, and it soon passes him by. Willie breaks the embrace and heads toward the door. He pulls on a coat hanging from a hook and opens the door, letting in a blast of cold air into the house. He whistles. Pearl jumps to her feet and sprints through the door after him.

He is in the cab of his truck and looking back at his home. Pearl curls up on the bench seat next to him. Mabel stands waving on the porch for a moment, shivering in the cold, before going back into the house. When he is alone, Willie reaches underneath the seat and grabs his pistol. He flips open the chamber to make sure it is loaded and slams it back shut, satisfied. He puts the weapon on the seat between his legs and starts off toward his mother's land.

FLETCHIE WALKS ALONG THE WAY toward town, sadder than he's felt in a long while. He feels awful for being angry, but how could he not be? His father had lied to him. He'd lied and then he tried to make it seem like nothing was wrong. That doesn't sit right with Fletchie. Doesn't sit right with him in the slightest. Papas ain't s'posed to lie to their sons. The child can't explain it himself, but the anger is only present falsely to hide his hurt. It is hurt, the previously unfelt sting of someone he trusted going back on his word, that truly brings him down, has brought him down these past couple weeks. It hadn't been a very merry Christmas season for him, and, not hearing his Papa's plan to get out, he hadn't been truly happy since.

He picks up a stick from the side of the road and beats at a bush in frustration. He continues on his way to school, a place that seems more a constant in his life than anything at this point. He wonders as he walks and beats at the shrubbery with his stick if his mother knows about Papa's heartbreaking betrayal of his word. He can't imagine this in the slightest as his Mama doesn't abide by lies. She's whipped him pretty good before for bending the truth. Tanned 'em pretty good a few times to where he now understands that honesty is certainly the best policy.

Despite all his pain, what he wants is to help his father. He doesn't want to see him go away again. Even with the hurt that he is feeling now, he only wants his father to be there for him when he needs him. A little boy needs his

Papa. He only wishes that there were some way to help him.

SHERIFF MICHAEL BAKER WAITS IN HIS TRUCK on the side of the narrow dirt road. He's been waiting here since early morning, knowing that eventually the boy would have to pass through on his way to school. This is his chance. There's too much riding on it, he just needs some confirmation from the child to be able to make his move. How delicious it is, using the man's own son against him. Children are special. They are innocent and loved by God and man alike. The best thing, though, is that children are honest. They will tell you anything you ask without any semblance of guilt because the truth is just easy for children. That childish sense of the truth is lost somewhere between childhood and adolescence when they learn to understand a lie and how effective the twisting of the truth can be used to their advantage. Willie Henderson is a product of sin and dishonesty; of that, Baker is certain. His son, however, is still under that Godly influence possessed by youth. Michael Baker likes to think that he himself still possesses much of that virtue despite his age. Sure, he has lied and been false in his life. More times than he can count, honestly. But he knows this: every misrepresentation of truth was in furtherance of good, for the good of the law. Those kinds of lies aren't sins. The Lord will look upon him and smile when he arrives at Heaven's gates. He will tell him that he understands; his lies were necessary for the good of all whom he protects.

Baker doesn't wait long, at least it doesn't seem like it to him before he sees Fletchie Henderson trundling through the cold morning toward his truck sitting on the side of the road. The boy has his books slung over his shoulder and a stick in the other hand, beating at the roadside shrubbery as he walks. Sheriff Baker smiles at this image. There is something pure about a child at play that seems to melt his heart. It gives him hope for the future. Baker waits until the boy is near before letting his siren give a shrill yelp, startling the boy and the quiet of the morning alike. Fletchie jumps a bit at the sound, a quick sidestep that almost sends him reeling into the brush that he was beating at with his stick. Baker sticks his hand out the open window in a wave. Fletchie sees him, his eyes going bright for a moment and his own small hand shooting up in vigorous greeting.

OLD FIELD PINES

The hand only remains at its frantic waving for a moment before sinking back to the boy's side, unsure of the situation. The stick is left on the roadside, forgotten. Baker can see the change in the boy. He's been talking to his father, no doubt. Willie Henderson has planted ideas about Baker into the boy's head that give him pause. How dare he pollute the mind of an innocent. Michael Baker would do no harm to this child or any other. The thought nearly sends a shiver of revulsion through his spine. He loves them like the Father loves them. Yet, here is Fletchie, a boy he has befriended and made to feel important, looking to him like he would a snake: filled with curiosity, but leery of the lethal fangs that he knows to be inside the reptilian head.

This will not deter him. The boy is important and will warm back up to the Sheriff. It is vital that he does, and quick. Baker puts on an even bigger smile. It is genuine. It must be. "Howdy there, Deputy Henderson."

The boy beams once more at the mention of his imaginary title. He stops where he is, near the driver's side door of the truck, and gives a stiff salute that Baker returns heartily.

"At ease, Deputy." The boy has more discipline than either of his rotten Deputies. They're probably off waking from a drunk. He knows they get some of Henderson's liquor from somewhere, the traitors. He can deal with them another time. It's time to focus on Henderson. "Off to do ya some learnin'?"

The boy nods. "Yessir. Headin' ta school."

Baker slides over and opens the passenger side door of his truck. "Well, hop on in. I'll give ya a ride so we can debrief a bit together."

The boy hesitates, looking back down the road the way he'd come. He's thinking about his father for sure, Baker thinks to himself. This angers him. But it's not the boy's fault. That devil of a man has gotten into his brain. Baker can fix this. He smiles again. "That's an order, Deputy. Can't have one of my own freezin' on his way to the schoolhouse, now can I?"

The boy shivers a bit at the mention of the cold, but smiles and gets in. Easy enough. Baker pulls back out onto the road, going slow. There's no hurry here, and it might just take him some time to get back into the boy's trust, breaking the horrible lies that his father had told him. Baker's got a secret weapon, though. Something that will surely have the boy nearly bouncing in his seat with the excitement of it.

"You know, son, I was thinkin' the other day."

"Whatcha thinkin'?"

"Well, I was thinkin' that while we got you all deputized and everything, we never really made a proper show of it. How's folks s'posed to know you're a man of the law?"

"Thought I wasn't s'posed to tell no one?"

"That's right, Deputy. And you've done good with that so far, I'm sure of it. But, with everything going on right now, I could really use some extra help." With this, Baker reaches into his pocket, his left hand resting comfortably on the steering wheel, and pulls out the brass star he'd put there that morning. It was a plain piece, nothing special, an antique really, but Fletchie's eyes light up all the same at the sight of the badge.

Baker pulls the truck to the side of the road for a moment and leans over, unclasping the pin on the back of the badge. "Here. Let's get this pinned on to see how it looks."

Fletchie puffs out his chest as big as it will go while Baker pins the star over his left breast. He lets out a whistle, the boy continuing to stare at his chest where the star now rests as Baker pulls back onto the road. "Wow. Fits like a charm on there. Now you're officially on active duty for Stone County."

"Thank you," Fletchie breathes out in awe, fingering the star with shaking, delicate fingers. The boy looks near to tears he is so excited. This fills Baker with a pride that he hasn't known before. It was like pinning the star onto his own son. His very own boy, the one whom he never got the chance to have.

"You're welcome, Deputy. Thank you for your service."

Fletchie continues to stare at it and then lets out another giggle of excitement. "It's heavy."

"S'posed to be heavy. The weight'll remind you of the responsibility that you carry as a deputized servant of the law." Here it is. This is his moment. "That's what I wanted to talk to you about, son."

"What's that, Sheriff?"

"We've had a really big problem in our county, Deputy. One that truly pains me, as a man of God and the law, to see besiege the people, God-fearin' people, of Mountain View."

"What problem?" the boy asks, his attention fully on Sheriff Baker now, the star on his chest forgotten for a moment.

"Liquor, son. Illegal moonshine. It's being made and delivered to people in our county at a rate so fast that the sin is spreadin' quicker than I can stop it."

The mention of the bootlegged liquor gives Fletchie a visible twitch. The innocence of a child. Their bodies almost can't lie. Not at that age. He remains silent, however.

Baker sneaks a glance over at the boy, flicking his eyes back and forth between him and the road. "I need your help, Deputy Henderson. I can't do it all on my own."

The boy's face looks as though he might cry. Not from the happiness that had clearly been present moments before, but a sad, nervous sort of crying. He knows. Damn it, he knows about everything.

"I've heard some disturbing rumors, Fletchie. Disturbin' things about your Papa."

"Papa told me I ain't s'posed to talk to ya."

"Why would he tell you not to talk to me? We're friends. You're my Deputy."

"Papa don't know that. I kept the secret. Honest. I'm just not s'posed ta."

"Ya know, Fletchie, as a sworn Deputy of the law, it's your duty to report back to me. Report back about a crime that you might know about or have witnessed. You take your oath seriously, don't ya?"

The boy looks hurt. Tears begin rolling down his cheeks. "Yessir. 'Course."

"And you know that I'm just tryin' to uphold the law. Just as you're supposed to do."

The boy looks down at his feet. Guilt. This is what washes over his small features. Perfect guilt.

"You know anything about what I'm talking about, Deputy?"

Fletchie doesn't answer at first. He continues to stare at his feet with the hurt, guilt-ridden look on his face. He weighs his options back and forth. It is a hard thing to ask: do a duty that he believes is his sworn responsibility or protect his father, the man who shows him love and plays with him and teaches him things. "I-I d-don't know a-a-anything," he stutters out. His voice wavers as the small tears fleck down his cheeks.

The sight of this almost breaks Michael Baker's heart. He doesn't want to make the young boy cry, but the fire to get to Willie Henderson is buried too deep inside him. Come on, boy. Come on. So close.

"Ya sure about that?"

The response, again, takes some time to come out. "I d-don't know n-n-nothin'." More tears stream down his face, leaving streaks on his smooth skin and falling onto his jacket.

Baker slows the truck and pulls to the side of the road once more. He can see some of the buildings of Mountain View's downtown through the windshield. Smoke billows out from various chimneys, warmth to keep the cold of the morning at bay.

Baker sighs, his eyes remaining on the horizon. "I'm sorry to hear that, Fletchie." And he means it. "I wish I could say I wasn't disappointed." He really is disappointed. It is a real feeling, a real hurt, for him—a feeling that despite his best efforts, the boy is too far gone, so polluted by his father's influence, that he would choose wrong over right. Evil over justice. "Well, I guess that's all we have, then." He leans over and opens the boy's door, letting in a brisk winter's wind into the cab of the truck. "Not a far walk from here. You go on about your day."

The boy's tears flow freely now. His breath comes in sobs. "I-I-I pr-pr…"

"You can leave the badge on the seat. I just don't think you're quite ready to bear the responsibility wearing that badge entails."

Fletchie gasps, out of breath from his crying and in disbelief for what is happening. He clutches the badge to his chest. It shines with a coppery finish in the morning sun, reflecting the gleam back into the windshield.

Baker pats the boy's shoulder in melancholy, a gesture that their conversation is at an end.

The weight of the hand gently guiding him out into the cold sends another wave of sobbing wracking through Fletchie's small frame. "W-wait."

"You gotta get on to school, son."

"I-I c-c-can be 's-s-s-ponsible."

"I just think it's best that we part ways here…"

"I know some things!" Fletchie doesn't mean to say it so loud, but it comes out as a scream of desperation.

Yes. Yes, you do. This is it, at last. "You do?"

The boy nods. "I… I just want to help my Papa."

Baker nods. He puts out his hand and rests it on Fletchie's shoulder, leaning in to look the boy full in the face. "I want to help him, too, son." He pulls a handkerchief out of his pocket and dabs at the boy's face. He wipes away tears and snot alike. When his face is relatively dry, Baker reaches down and straightens the star on Fletchie's chest. "Well, tell me what you can, Deputy. We'll see if we can't help your Papa." It is a lie, yes, but a lie to help the common good. Baker can forgive himself for that. God will forgive him. Perhaps, one day, Fletchie might forgive him as well.

CHAPTER XII

WILLIE KNOWS SOMETHING IS WRONG as he pulls off the main road and onto his Mama's land to find her standing outside her house, pacing back and forth in the yard. He pulls to a stop and gets out, Pearl jumping to the ground behind him. He slips the pistol into the waist of his trousers as he walks toward his frazzled Mama. She looks older, tired. Like she hadn't slept the night before. She continues her pacing as he approaches, Pearl at his feet, almost oblivious to his arrival.

"Mama?"

She pays him no mind, continuing her frantic back and forth.

"Mama, what is it?"

She rounds on him quickly. Her eyes are worried, yet furrowed as well. Willie shrinks back a step at that look as if he were only a child again. "I'll tell ya. It's over. We're good as done."

"Whatcha mean, Mama?"

"They got 'im."

"Got who, Mama? Whatcha sayin'?"

She points a bony finger at him, her eyes alight. "That damned postman. I told ya he was 'bout as good as tits on a boar. The careless, stupid man you brought on."

"I'm not—"

"Got himself caught," she interrupts him. "Gone and got himself caught with all that liquor. They got him out in Searcy County. Raided his house and everythin'. Found it all. Brought him into the jail."

Willie feels his heart plummet into his chest. There's not a lot that he feels he can say, yet a thousand questions, all fighting to be voiced, catch in his throat, trying to be asked at once. "Shit." It's all he can manage.

"Shit. Shit is right. Kept it out of the papers so far. Tryin' to keep it all under wraps. God knows what he's told them, though."

Willie shakes his head, clear for the moment. "No. He wouldn't say nothin'."

"Sure he would."

"No, Mama. Not Clyde. He'd sooner die than talk, I'd figure."

"Well, we'll find out soon enough. I sent Lester off to find out what he can. No one really knows much from what I'm gatherin'. Just questions around that area, mostly. Half the damn town of Marshall saw them bring him in and unload all those mail sacks into the Sheriff's Office there. They just ain't tellin' nothin' yet."

"I can go see what this is all 'bout. Maybe talk to Clyde and explain…"

"No you ain't. You're a'gonna go into them woods and go 'bout your day as normal. Run's almost finished, right?"

He nods in affirmation.

The old woman looks to the sky, calculating. "Finish it. Last one for now, as planned. We can figure out the next move after all this settles. Have to figure out a way to get this load to customers on our own. That's if Sheriff Baker don't come huntin' us down. If that Clyde confessed to anything—"

"Clyde ain't gonna talk. I know him well 'nough to know that." Willie had heard her comment about the last run *for now* but decides to ignore it. The moment is stressful enough as it is.

She smiles meekly, nods her head, and steeples her fingers in front of her lips as if in prayer. "All right, son. You go on and get to work. I'll send Lester out when he gets back tonight."

Willie remains where he stands for a minute, lost in the new developments, watching everything they'd worked for crashing down around him.

His Mama spies him still standing in his spot. "Go on. Get to it. Sooner we get everything finished, sooner we can tear it all down and figure out what's next."

WILLIE WORKS THROUGHOUT THE DAY, busying himself in his tasks and trying not to think of the situation they now find themselves in. The work helps, making liquor, but it is also a cause for great sorrow. With the loss of their big shipment, he can't help but think about the hardships they will now face and the money they will sorely miss out on. It makes for the calling a halt to their business seem less and less likely. As he watches the embers of hope of getting out fade before him, he continues his processes through the day and into the night, watching the sun fade below the ridgeline and disappear altogether. He sees the moon rise above the trees to the opposite side back toward his Mama's house. The wind picks up in the growing night and the temperatures continue to drop. It would more than likely be snowing if the skies weren't clear of cloud cover. Instead, above him, the heavens look black as pitch with the stars vying for a hold in the darkness where they twinkle in their fixed positions in the sky. Thoughts of a vast host, perhaps heavenly, come to Willie's mind as he looks up at the specks of light against the onyx expanse of sky. The moon continues its arc as time passes and Willie can see the craters that his father had thought looked like a face. Willie doesn't think so, gazing up at the glowing orb in the sky. Those craters have always, and still do, seemed to be in the shape of a rabbit for him. He used to leave carrots out at night on the porch as a child, hoping maybe the moon bunny would hop down from its perch for a snack in the middle of the night. He would have liked to be able to catch a moon rabbit. The carrots were mostly always in the same place come those mornings, though, and his Mama would get mad at him for wasting food, setting it out to spoil or get dragged off by raccoons in the night.

He lights a lantern and sits near the furnace of the still next to Pearl to fight off the night's chill. Eventually, he gets tired of trying to stay warm and lights another fire near the small lean-to where his equipment rests underneath to give warmth from both sides. The light doesn't worry him like it normally would have. He's tired of being cold and would rather risk the chance of being spotted and be warm than die a cold, shivering death in the night. The thought of death surprises him. Not the concept so much as his acceptance that fills him at the thought. He'd always known there was a possibility, the life he'd lived, the war and bootlegging and all the rest, but he'd always been able to face it with a snarl on his lips and his arms swinging, trying to ward off the inevitable. Not now, though. He's too damn cold for such thoughts of fighting it. He just wants to get warm, come whatever may. He accepts this. It is not an admittance of defeat. More like a welcoming of something new. He thinks of his family then, of Mabel and Fletchie, and feels shame. How could he accept something like that while having his family to think of? That's just his thinking, though. Maybe they'd be better off if he was gone. Maybe they wouldn't have to keep any more secrets and lie to protect him. That, of its own, is a nice thought.

A couple jars from the last run of shine sit next to him. He was trying to wait for Lester to get there before opening them, but the thought of that warmth running down his gullet, that burning sensation spreading through him, filling him up, just seems too good to pass up. He unscrews the lid and takes a few glugs of the clear liquor. A smile crosses his bearded face at the burn as he stares into the fire in front of him. His hand pats absently at the shape of Pearl sitting next to him, snuggled against his leg. Willie is grateful for her companionship. A loyal friend, through and through. That's hard to come by in these times.

The liquor warms him but does nothing for the jumpiness that seems to have taken over his body, the feeling that someone is out there—in the shadows of the trees, watching him—sends shivers through him. Every whip of a branch in the wind, every snap of a twig on the ground, turns into Sheriff Michael Baker making his way toward the glow of the fire with his gun pointed at Willie. He reaches comfortingly for the pistol next to him. Perhaps he's not as accepting of what fate might have for him after all. But the thought remains in his head. If those snaps of twigs were to in fact be the Sheriff stalking toward him, at least he'll be warm. The fire is inviting, lighting up the night with its flickering crack of dried pine logs. Come on over, Sheriff. Might be cold out, but the fire is nice and the liquor is mighty stout.

Pearl stands up from her ratty blanket next to Willie in the flickering light of the fire. She growls toward the darkness of the woods and the hills surrounding them. She is on edge, too, it would seem, her back bristling at the coming threat. Willie stands with her, cocking the hammer of his pistol back as he does. He's ready for him. Just come on out of there, Sheriff. I'm right here waitin' on ya. It's quiet on the family land at night; an owl hoots in the distance making Willie jump with the noise, sounding more like an auto horn in his heightened state. The dog continues to growl.

"Pearl," Willie whispers, pointing the gun toward the darkness surrounding them. "Whatsit, girl?" The crackle of dried leaves and footfalls makes its way faintly through the holler and into the dim lighting. Willie swivels the gun toward the sound, his finger sliding down to rest on the trigger. He'll shoot. He's sure of that now. Anything to make Baker fire his pistol as well. Death must be better than going back to that damned farm, working in chains for the rest of his days. It must be. Bible talks about a paradise waiting for the Christians to enter upon hearing the final trumpet. Either that or damnation. Willie wonders at to which he will be sent. Also, he hopes that Mabel and Fletchie will understand. He can't go back to prison.

A silhouette stumbles toward the small circle of light. Pearl ceases her growling and returns to the blanket next to Willie; the weapon remains pointed at the figure. "I'm right here," he says into the darkness. "Come on, then."

The arms of the approaching figure rise over its head in a sign of surrender. "Now, hold it there, Willie. It's jus' me."

Willie lowers the pistol as the man comes toward the light. "Goddammit, Lester. Liketa blowed ya out from your hat."

"Yeppers. Lookin' like you's 'bout to cut cha galluses and go straight up."

Willie spits a glob of tobacco juice in the dirt. Some splashes on the toe of his dirty boots. He sits on the log where he'd been working. "Reckon I was. Figured I'd be spectin' company here before too late. 'Sides, you never showed up."

"I'm here now."

"You are."

Lester sits down next to the fire. Pearl walks over and gives his hand a lick and lets him pet her head a moment before settling back down next to Willie. "I wouldn't be s'sure 'bout all that company business."

"Whatcha mean?"

"Mean," Lester says, warming his hands over the flames of the fire, "that, from what I gathered, Clyde ain't said nothin'."

Willie spits in the dirt. "How ya figure?"

"Well, folks saw our friend Sheriff Baker leavin' that day. Said he looked mighty ornery when he was a gettin' in his truck."

Willie nods.

"'Sides, I don't think Clyde's the kind to sell us up creek."

"Didn't think so neither. You tell Mama?"

"Yeppers. She wasn't so sure 'bout it all, but I think it eased her mind a bit."

Willie reaches behind him and grabs one of the jars of liquor. He tosses it over the flames to Lester who catches it deftly in one hand. Willie grabs the other jar and unscrews the lid. He raises it up, the flickering flames dancing in the sloshing clarity of the alcohol. "To Clyde, then. God keep him durin' all this."

Lester raises his own jar. "He sure as shit didn't deserve it."

"Nope."

They both take a long drink. Willie screws the lid back onto his own jar and rummages in his sack for a moment as Lester takes a second drink to catch up. Realizing he hasn't had the thought of eating all day, Willie produces the wrapped biscuits and bacon, grabbing a skillet from behind him and resting it on the flames. "Want some breakfast?"

Lester nods in reply. Willie tears open the wrapped bacon and sets it in strips on the skillet. Then he splits the biscuits in half and sets these in the warm ashes near the coals to heat. When this is done, the bacon pops and sizzles in the pan. Willie reaches in and flips the strips with his bare fingers.

"You mind gettin' that there swab stick and givin' the mash a good turn?"

Lester rises from his sitting position and walks toward the still. He ducks his slender frame down underneath the low overhang of the lean-to and opens the cap of the heater box, dipping in the carved wooden handle of the swab stick. They both work in silence for a few minutes, the sound of bacon blackening the only disturbance in the night. Willie flips the bacon a final time and checks the biscuits in the coals.

"Ready. Come on over and eat."

Lester returns as Willie breaks crispy bacon in two and places a few pieces on one of the biscuit halves. He closes it together with the other half of the biscuit and passes one to Lester. He makes two more from what remains, taking one for himself and setting the other in front of Pearl. She gets up and takes a tentative bite of the biscuit.

Willie pats the dog's head. "Good girl."

Lester chuckles at the sight of it. "Don't bet I'll ever understand you wastin' a good biscuit on that there dog of yours." He takes a bite of his food and sucks air in through his open mouth. The bacon is hot and some of the grease from the pan still clings to the strips. He swallows after a moment. "Just don't seem all that right ta me. Dogs eat scraps."

"Pearl don't." Willie pats the dog's head once more. "Saved my skin once."

Lester laughs again. "Whatcha mean?"

"Well," Willie takes a bite of his biscuit and chews at the crunchy bacon. A few flecks crumble down to lodge in his thick whiskers. "Back when I was still learnin' my way 'round shinin', back before all this mess got complicated, I was workin' off some land deep in the woods away from the house. It was a long walk back there, and I was gettin' ready to make it. Pearl was puttin' up a fuss as I was leavin', thought she'd wake up Mabel and Fletchie, so I took her with me. 'Round the time I made to go into the trees, she starts barkin' and hell raisin' all over again, just starin' at them woods with a mean look. She wouldn't keep going so I's just gonna leave her. Before I could step into the treeline, she jumps in front of me and won't let me walk around her. This went on for some time 'fore I just gave up and went back toward the house. Turns out they'd been searchin' that night for shiners. Fire from the furnace mighta brought 'em down on me. She warned me away from it."

"Bullshit," Lester says with a laugh. "That dog didn't know all that."

"Sure she did. That's the same night they got John Henry the first time."

"No shit?"

"No shit," Willie says with a nod, patting at Pearl's head again. She looks up at him with her tongue hanging out, her big eyes shining in the firelight. The fur around her muzzle is matted down with the grease from her biscuit. "Ever since then I've always got 'er with me and she always gets her a good breakfast."

"Wish she'd been with Clyde the other night. Maybe he'd of gotten out okay if he had Pearl there to warn 'im."

Willie nods sadly at this, finishing his biscuit and taking up his jar of shine. He swallows the remains of his meal down with a gulp of the clear liquor, sighing at the warming feeling it brings. The silence of the night reigns once more, the two men taking the occasional sip from their jars and staring at the fire.

OLD FIELD PINES

Lester looks up at last. "What we gonna do about this load?" he asks, nodding toward the still.

"Don't know. Get rid of it the ole fashion way, I suppose. Not much else we can do. Mama says she wants us to tear down the still when we are finished with it, though. Better be safe right now."

Lester nods. "Yep. Betty told me. Prolly have to break the pump's line just to get it mobile quick 'nough. Don't reckon we have time to fiddle with it." He looks toward his contraption that delivers water for the still with a nature that only comes from things you make with your own two hands. "You still plannin' on gettin' out after this?"

Willie sees the look Lester gives to the pump. Willie has given similar looks to his still before. It's a pride in ownership, being good at something. "I...yeah, I guess. Don't have much a choice now anyway. Got to get out 'fore we get caught. With the loss of that last load, though, I don't know how we'll make it."

Lester nods meekly in reply.

Willie can't blame Lester for being a bit downtrodden about having to stop and tear down all their hard work. They'd had it damn near perfect right where they were sitting. Willie also knows that the entire operation would have more than likely failed if it hadn't been for Lester's ingenuity. The man was damn near a genius and not half so blown out as Willie had once believed. "Mind if I ask ya something?"

"What's that?" Lester asks.

"How come ya didn't go off a few years ago? Go get some schoolin'? Ya surely got the brains for it."

Lester shrugs. "Not like I didn't think about it. Came close once."

"When was that?"

"Few years back, I s'pose." He grins. Willie remembers how young Lester actually is. Almost a decade his junior. The smile brings out more of his youth.

"What happened?"

"Don't know. Got scared, I guess. Didn't know where I'd even go. The war wasn't quite over, and I saw some of the folks comin' back after what they'd seen. Guess it made me think the rest of the world was like that. Cruel and hard." He sighs. "Mountain View seemed safe. Safer than goin' out there."

Willie nods. He can understand. The world is a rough place. The world at war was even worse. He'd been there. He'd been one of those men coming home with the look in his eyes that Lester had no doubt seen. A look that said they'd been there in it and they never wanted to go back.

"Then I started drinkin'. Got kinda lost in that for a while. Hadn't been for your Mama takin' me in like she did, hell, probably be dead by now."

Willie nods. That's about the time he remembers beginning to think less of the kid. By the time Willie got back from the war and started shining, Lester was about where he described: a drunk who couldn't do much other than drink, sleep it off, and wake up to do it all over again. He'd changed, for sure. There was no doubting that. The man before Willie was someone that he would trust his life with, knew that he could. Lester would go above and beyond anything Willie ever asked of him just to prove himself.

"I'm sorry, Lester."

Lester smirks in the darkness. "Sorry for what?"

Willie scratches his neck uncomfortably. "Never really gave you a fair shake at first. I figured you was about a lost cause, didn't figure ya'd amount to much. That ain't fair of me."

Lester smiles, his eyes watering a bit in the firelight. He sniffles. "Thank ya, Willie."

"Ya got some kind of smarts 'bout ya, though. I couldn't have done all this," Willie gestures to the still, the pump, "without ya here. This entire thing would've gone to pot before long if it hadn't been for that brain of yours. Without all this, I don't know if I'd ever been able to get Mabel the medicine she needed in time. You probably saved her life." Willie raises his jar to his cousin across the fire. "Thank ya."

Lester raises his jar, saluting Willie. They both drink deeply, the liquor bubbling up with their swallows. With each jar around halfway drunk, both men feel the cozy fuzziness that comes with drinking a good amount of the powerful liquor. Willie reaches around behind him and grabs the black bag that contains his fiddle. He unties the various knots keeping the bag together and takes it out. Lester watches from across the fire. Willie lays his chin in the rest and strikes at the strings with the bow, testing its tune. He twiddles with one of the keys and then draws the bow once more. He nods, satisfied with the sound and puts his fingers up to the strings and begins to play. The bow glides up and down along the strings, his left hand moving along the neck to press where they need to make the tune he has in mind.

Lester listens to this, nodding his head as the opening to the old tune peals through the cold night air. It is a mournful melody. One that almost brings tears to drunken eyes. He stares into the fire and begins to sing as the opening strokes round into the first verse.

I'm just a poor wayfarin' stranger
Travelin' through this world of woe.
But there's no sickness, toil, nor danger
In that fair land to which I go.

Come the chorus Willie joins in, still making the fiddle cry its mournful sound into the night. Pearl looks up at the noise and even she seems to be filled with the melancholy of the music.

I'm goin' there to see my father.
I'm goin' there no more to roam.
I am just goin' over Jordan.
I am just goin' over home.

SHERIFF MICHAEL BAKER PULLS ONTO THE DRIVE that leads to Betty Henderson's house and farm. He doesn't worry about hiding any longer or trying to keep his presence a secret. He'd been hiding in the damn woods all day, his truck parked far enough off and down the road that no one coming to or from the house could see him. He's through waiting around for something to happen. He'd given Henderson all the time in the world to leave. He was clearly not going to be going anywhere tonight. He's making a new batch; Baker just knows it. That's why he's out here all on his own in the wee hours of the night. That's why he never pulled out of the farm heading for his own home. He is working, and Sheriff Baker is going to be able to catch him in the act. He's got him now. Besides, everyone else on the property will long be asleep by now. It is nearly three in the morning. He pulls next to Willie's truck in the yard. No one sits in the car and the house in front of him is completely dark. Ms. Betty Henderson will be fast asleep, completely unaware of what is happening on her own land. What a betrayal. There's no need to bother the poor woman. Surely, she can't know what her son is doing in the late hours of the night.

He shuts his vehicle off and gets out into the cold of the night. His breath fogs before his face. He turns back around and grabs the rifle that he'd put into the cab, checks it for bullets once more. It's a lever-action Winchester repeater. Good gun for close confines and quick fire. He also checks the pistol at his hip, opening the chamber to count the six shots and then flicking it back into position. He slips the pistol back in the holster, shoulders the rifle, and slams the door of his vehicle shut.

The flickering light of the lamp on the porch startles him enough to reach for the pistol at his hip. He stops himself, seeing the elderly woman standing there, blinking out at him from the comfort of her porch.

Sheriff Baker raises his hand in greeting. "Hello, there. Ms. Betty Henderson, I presume."

"Yes?"

"Sorry to disturb your evening, ma'am. Just heard some troubling sounds off in your woods when I was driving by and I thought I'd—"

"It's late, Sheriff Baker," the woman interrupts.

Baker nods his head. "Yes, ma'am. I know it. Just need to check out what's goin' on out in those woods. Don't want ya to be unsafe."

"I'm plenty safe, Sheriff. I'll take care of it."

This surprises Baker. The poor woman has no idea what is going on. She should be spared everything that's about to happen. "Ma'am. Just go on back in your house and get some sleep. It's no trouble, really." He hears the click audibly through the night air. It almost screams in the silence of the night. He takes a good look at the woman, studying her for the first time. He'd been too excited to notice much of anything. He was ready to get on his way to Willie. He was surely waiting for him out there. But he sees now. Betty Henderson is fully dressed, not in nightclothes of any kind, but dressed for the day, as if she hadn't been to bed yet and was just getting ready to go out for some chores. Her right hand holds the lantern aloft over her head to reflect the light a bit better and to keep it out of her eyes. Her left hand, no doubt the hand that cocked the pistol, is behind her back. She knows. She knows exactly what's been going on. She knows about everything.

"I'm 'fraid I must insist, Sheriff. Go on and get back in your truck and drive away."

Baker smiles. Plans to spare her have flown from his mind. The idea of all this excites him greatly. He wonders what trophy she might have for him to take. "Can't do that, Ms. Henderson. I'm goin' in them woods to find him."

The woman smiles back at him in the light of the lamp. It is not an unpleasant smile. It reminds Sheriff Baker of what a normal grandmother would smile like. There was plenty of the old bitties about town, had been in Marshall, too. They all had a similar smile to the one that was beaming at him from the porch, it just seems grossly out of context in their current situation.

"Ya know, Sheriff. Don't believe ya will be."

Baker's smile widens. He enjoys the game. Cat and mouse. Cat and cat. It doesn't matter. It is all like a dream to him, this sort of play. He wants to play. Just pull the gun, Ms. Henderson. I'll send your boy along to you shortly. "Last chance, Ms. Henderson."

The woman laughs, a sweet sounding tiddle in the back of her throat. She says nothing. Her hand holding the lantern opens to let it fall from her fingers, her left hand moving around her body quickly to reveal the pistol with the cocked hammer. The lamp hits the wooden boards of the porch and the glass shatters, a musical tinkling sound in the night.

THE CRACK OF GUNFIRE was only barely audible with the distance and the wailing drone of the fiddle. Willie hears it, however faintly. Lester looks up at the dying groan of the fiddle music, his mouth still open to sing the next line of the song. He'd heard it, too. To confirm their suspicions, Pearl, who'd been curled cozily next to Willie and the warmth of the fire, stands rigidly to her feet. The dog looks off into the night toward the house, and a soft growl rumbles low in her throat. The growl grows in volume until she lets her small lip snarl back over her teeth, letting out a shrill bark into the night air. She barks again. Willie pats her head and she looks up at him for a moment. The moment passes quickly and she turns back to the direction of the gunshots and growls once more.

Lester looks to the dog and then to Willie. His mouth has gone dry. He reaches for his jar of liquor and drinks down the last few swallows to clear up the blockage that has formed in his throat. "That a—"

"Yep."

Willie would know. He's heard plenty of gunfire in his time. Some of that fire was aimed at him. The same sound often visits him in his dreams at night, accompanied by the haunting screams of men dying cold and alone in the mud and the muck.

"We need to get gone," Lester says, rising from his seat on the ground and moving to gather what little he can carry with him. He continues his work for some time, not noticing Willie hasn't moved for a few moments. Instead Willie remains seated, his fiddle still clutched in his left hand and the bow in his right. Pearl continues her growling next to him, looking up at her owner every few seconds to make sure that he approves of her making the noise. She takes his lack of interest as approval.

"Willie," Lester tugs at Willie's shoulder. He looks up at Lester for the first time since hearing the shots. "We gotta move."

Willie looks back toward where the gunshots came from, the crack of a revolver for sure, where his mother's house sits. He looks back to Lester with his eyes drawn downward. The look of a man supremely exhausted. "No. *You* gotta get goin'."

Lester ignores the you and tugs at Willie's shoulder again. "Come on. We need to get movin' quick. Sheriff'll be here 'fore too long. The fire will help lead him here and we can be gone in the other direction."

"I'm not leavin'."

"'Course you are," Lester insists, tugging some more on Willie's shirt.

Willie catches the hand and shoves it off of him, knocking Lester, already unsteady on his feet from the drink, on his ass and away from him. Willie looks at him again, oblivious to having shoved him down. There's an apologetic look on his face spread over the resolve that Lester had been trying to ignore. "He ain't gonna stop, Lester."

"'Course he ain't. That's why—"

"Gotta finish it. Only one way to do that." Willie rises from his place in the dirt and walks over to where Lester lies sprawled on the ground. His hand comes down to help his cousin back to his feet. When Lester is back up, Willie clasps his shoulders in both hands, giving them a hearty squeeze. "Go on. Get out of here before ya can't anymore."

Lester is now near to tears. He looks at Willie's bearded face in the fire-light, his eyes reflecting the light back. "I ain't leavin' ya."

"Sure ya are. You watch after them, my family. Fletchie'll need some-body to check on him. You go on, now." He lets go of Lester's shoulders and bends down to Pearl standing at his feet. The dog looks nervously up at Willie and licks the hands that wrap around her furry body. Willie hugs the dog to his chest for a moment and Pearl pants happily. After a few seconds, Willie hands his dog to Lester. "Take Pearl." He looks to the dog. "Ya watch after him, girl."

The dog lets out a whine at having been handed to someone else. She'd never been fond of anyone picking her up in the first place, especially people who weren't Willie. She gives another yip to show her disapproval, her big eyes bugging out and looking back and forth from Willie to Lester holding her gently.

Willie points off away from the house along the ridgeline. "Go on. Get out of here."

Tears do fall into Lester's small wiry beard now. Pearl rears up and licks at the salty droplets falling down his chin. "But Willie…"

"None of that. Go on. I'll be all right." He nods away once more. "Go on, Lester. Don't worry 'bout me. You just make sure my family's taken care of, ya hear?"

Lester nods without realizing it. Before he can truly understand what is happening, he wipes at his eyes with the sleeve of his coat. His legs turn of their own accord and begin to walk away from the dancing light of the fire, from the glow of the still's furnace. He wants to stop but his legs won't let him. They carry him forward, his arms cradling around the dog held to his chest. Pearl looks back toward Willie over Lester's shoulder. She yips once more as Lester's gait widens into a jog. Willie watches them go, fading into the blackness of the night, away from the light of the fire.

IT IS THE UNIQUE SMELL OF BURNING LIQUOR that hits Sheriff Michael Baker first. The wind lifts and snakes its way in just the right direction for him to smell it ahead. There is no glow from a fire yet, and, as he'd been too excited to bring a lantern with him, he picks his way through the evergreens and leafless shrubbery in the dark. He doesn't mind the dark. It allows him to move unnoticed. Part of him wants to call out to Willie Henderson, just to let him know, if he doesn't already, that he is on his way. It's not his mother picking her way through the trees in victory—poor bitch was lying on the porch with a hole in her chest and one in her head—but him. I'm coming for you, Mr. Henderson. That would spoil the fun, though. Making yourself known wasn't part of the rules, and Michael Baker plays by the rules. He lives by them. Loves them.

The shot that Betty Henderson had gotten off went a little too far right and had merely grazed his arm. There was a nasty burning sensation coming from the torn ruin of his shirtsleeve, but nothing that couldn't be patched up. He can manage. Too close to turn back now. The smell comes through the pines again. A warm, almost inviting smell. Baker takes a large whiff into his nostrils, breathing it past his palate and into his lungs, holding it there for several moments to relish the scent. The smell is intoxicating. The sweet smell of the hunt coming to a close. And what a hunt it had been. He knows that he will look back on his time with Willie Henderson in fondness and respect. He had almost beaten him, just so close. But no one beats Sheriff Michael Baker. No one can match him.

As he continues ahead, trying to make his footfalls as light as possible, he fingers the lighter in his pocket. He'd wanted to smoke a cigarette after shooting the woman on her porch, craved it, but there had been no time. Willie Henderson was out here waiting on him. Baker knows that Willie will be there, despite whether or not he heard the shots fired, despite whether or not he had suspicions. Willie Henderson is not a runner. It isn't in his nature. Michael Baker, of all people, can respect—envy—such an attribute in people. The trees and brush around him seem a little less dark as he passes over a hill and down into a lower holler, a grove of natural clear cut surrounded by pines with the occasional hickory tree in the mix, their trunks a pale color in the dim moonlight. The glow, almost ghostlike in its movement—a fire—dances ahead of him. He is almost there. The urge to scream at the top of his lungs comes to him once more. Instead he stops long enough to pull a cigarette from the pocket of his coat and stick it in his teeth, the flicker of his lighter illuminating his eyes in an eerie, mad light. I'm here, Mr. Henderson. Check mate.

WILLIE HAD MOVED AWAY FROM THE STILL after standing there a few moments. Part of him wanted to kick it over, break what he could while he still had the chance, not give Sheriff Baker the satisfaction of tearing it apart himself, but he'd thought better of it. Instead he looked lovingly at the still before him, still churning out the firewater he had slaved over to make as quality as possible, patted the copper cap lovingly, and walked out past the broken shell of his father's smoke shack and beyond to the edge of the ravine towering at least one-hundred feet above the banks of Roastnier Creek.

Someone had once told him the actual name of the creek was 'Roasting Ear,' that the people around its parts had just been pronouncing it wrong all these years. It was in the accent, he'd been told. He remembers having laughed at such a notion. Sure, people 'round here had an accent, himself included, but there weren't no way that they'd been sayin' it wrong all this time. They should know; it was the ancestors of these people who named the creek in the first place. It had been Fletchie who had confirmed to him the mispronunciation. Showed him in one of his books. I'll be damned, he'd thought, and he thought this now, laughing at the memory. Roasting Ear. Roastnier. Roastnier still sounds better to him. When he leaves this world tonight, he wants to remember it as Roastnier, simply for the fact that it's what he's called it his entire life, what it would always be to him.

He stands over the ledge for a moment, the wind whipping at his coat, separating his long beard in two on his face and blasting the split sides up to tickle his ears. He leans over and looks down at the drop. The night is quite dark but the January moon gives off just enough light to see the black snaking of the clear-water creek below him. If he were to fall, it would surely kill him. Even if he were to hit water, it's shallow and the force of smacking onto the water would be enough. He thinks about it, taking the satisfaction away from Baker. If he took his own life, the Sheriff couldn't say *he* took it. He could go out on his own terms. The thought weighs heavy on him for a moment, and it is this that makes him remember his pistol tucked in the waistband of his trousers. He reaches behind his back and pulls it out, admiring the revolver in the moonlight. This is another way to do it. Just the barrel to his head, in his mouth, and goodnight.

His thoughts then drift back to Mabel. To Fletchie. This settles the matter immediately. He'd taken the easy way out of things before, let his family down in the process, and he wasn't about to do it again. He fingers the gun one final time, twisting it this way and that. He could fight, but that won't do either. Any sort of struggle would surely only stoke Baker's fire further. He might even get angrier than he already was. He might take it out on Willie's family. With this thought, he tosses the gun over the edge to plummet toward the creek bed. He looks to the stars above him, hoping to see one shooting across the sky, something he'd never seen before, some kind of final good-bye—but nothing comes. He thinks of God. Thinks about how many times he had cursed that name lying face down in the muck and the blood and the dirt overseas and in prison.

"I'm sorry," he says. "I hope that's worth somethin'."

A stick cracks behind him. He doesn't turn. He only waits and continues staring out into the nothingness. "You want to tell me what makes you not like talkin' of the war, Sheriff?"

The footsteps stop. Everything is silent for a while. "Does it matter?"

"Humor me."

There is a sigh behind him, heavy breathing trying to calm rushing nerves. "I ran. Krauts comin' for me while I's deliverin' messages, and I ran."

Willie nods at this, looking down on the trees below him.

"That satisfy you?"

Willie shrugs. "Just a matter of curiosity."

"It changes nothing."

Willie nods again. "I know." He sighs. His last thoughts are of his wife and son as he hears the distinct sound of a rifle cocking behind him. Willie ignores it, ignores Sheriff Baker stepping closer to him, and pulls his plug of chewing tobacco from his coat. He rips off a large piece, chomping down and savoring the flavor. This is good. He spits a glob of dark spit over the edge of his world.

OLD FIELD PINES

"All right, Sheriff." He turns around to face the man bearing down on him with the rifle leveled at his middle. With the glow of the fire behind him, Sheriff Baker looks like he might have flaming wings attached to his back. The thought seems fitting to Willie. "I'm ready for ya," he says, spitting out another glob.

The Stone County Democrat

15 January 1926

Local Bootlegger Takes Own Life to Evade Capture

The body of William F. Henderson, native of Stone County, was discovered Thursday morning by Sheriff Michael Baker of the Stone County Sheriff's Department. Henderson, after having murdered his mother, Betty D. Henderson, committed suicide by jumping from a nearby cliff into the waters of Roasting Ear Creek.

Sheriff Michael Baker had been on the hunt for Mr. Henderson for some time. After the capture of Henderson's accomplice, Billy Clyde Davis of Searcy County, and receiving an anonymous tip of Henderson's involvement, Sheriff Baker went out to the Henderson homestead to investigate.

"It was horrific," Baker stated, describing the scene. "To become so desperate as to take your own life and the life of your mother. Well, I just can't comprehend such depravity."

The illegal still site found at the top of the ravine from where Henderson's body was recovered has Sheriff Baker confident that Henderson was responsible for the majority of the illegal liquor production that had been sweeping Stone and the surrounding counties.

"Henderson's operation was extensive," Baker said. "In my years as a public servant, I have never once seen a still site able to produce the magnitude of liquor that Henderson's was capable of. I am proud to chalk this up as a win, a sad one, but a win against the nefarious blight that has been seeking a hold of our county. I promise you now, that as long as I am your Sheriff, I will not suffer for the fine folks of Stone County to endure such sinful nature."

William Henderson is survived by his wife and son. It is with...

EPILOGUE

LESTER REACHES DOWN TO PICK AT THE WEEDS growing up around the block of stone that marks Willie's grave. It is nice weather for March and the cemetery is high up on the hilly expanse in between Onia and Mountain View. Many of their family is buried in this very cemetery, and Mabel had thought it a fitting place for Willie to find rest. Lester looks over to his right to see the graves of both Willie's father and mother side by side. He is in good company here. As he pulls the stubborn crabgrass up at the roots, he notices something shine in the sunlight at the base of the headstone. He picks it up and wonders at the old-style badge with its blank, coppery surface. No name is engraved along the front, no place of origin either. He thinks about throwing it aside but then decides against it, placing it at the base of the headstone once more. He reaches into the canvas pack he carries over one shoulder and brings out a mason jar of clear liquid. He unscrews the cap and pours a heavy portion onto the ground in front of the stone.

"Drink up, Willie."

He takes a healthy three-gulp drink himself, letting the whiskey burn down his throat and spread warmth through the pit of his stomach. He screws the lid to the jar back in place and stoops to set it next to the badge. They are an interesting combination leaning on the stone, and it makes him smile at the irony. He pats the stone, letting his hand rest along its rough surface for a minute before giving an awkward wave and walking toward Willie's—now his—truck idling at the gates to the cemetery. A warmish breeze blows across the hilltop and he looks back toward the stone, half expecting to see Willie sitting there and raising the jar up toward him in a toast. He is not there. Just a yard of stones. He gets in the truck and pulls off the narrow dirt track, twisting and switch-backing around the hill to reach the main road.

When he gets back onto the packed dirt, he revs the engine and tears along the curvy mountain roads leading toward Mountain View. He gains speed on a straight stretch a few miles outside of town, pushing the truck for the fun of it, shifting gears and grinding them into submission until he roars along, kicking up dust in his wake. A mile or so outside of the downtown square, Lester passes a couple cars parked side by side along the edge of the highway. He doesn't slow any, blasting by the figure of Sheriff Michael Baker and his Deputies.

The swift blast of wind from the moving truck nearly sweeps the burning cigarette from Baker's lips.

"Holy shit," Jack remarks, looking after Lester as he barrels toward town. "I'll get him, sir." He makes to get into his vehicle, hollering for Tommy to hop in and head off with him.

"No need," Sheriff Baker says, waving his Deputies down. He watches the truck disappear from sight like a mere apparition. Like it'd never been there at all. He looks into his own truck behind the seats. The thump brush with the carved wooden handle and "THUMPER" etched along the smooth shaft sits in the floor of the backseat. In front of this, on the dash of his pickup, sits the beautifully-carved miniature of Henderson's moonshine still. It looks exactly like the real thing had been before Baker tore it down, piece by metal piece. He smiles at this memory and from looking at his trophies. He pulls another cigarette out, dropping the butt of the one in his lips, and lights up once more. "Don't bother. The one in that clan we had to worry about was taken care of."

Lester has half a mind—as he does at almost every encounter—to turn back around and run Sheriff Baker over. The sound of his head smacking onto the metal hood of the truck would be a pleasant sound indeed. He doesn't, just as always, though. Instead he continues into the downtown area of Mountain View, slowing down to allow for the possibility of foot traffic, passing the courthouse and turning down the road that leads to Willie's old farm. He thinks about him a lot these days, especially when making the drive. It was precisely this constant thinking of his friend and kin that had led him to drive out to the old cemetery once more. He needed to be close to him every now and then.

The woods along the road thicken as he leaves Mountain View township behind, the growing town fading into the lush expanse of wilderness and mountainous overgrowth that make the Ozarks a place of true beauty. He can't imagine there being a more perfect spot on God's green earth and is sure to thank the Lord of that and his luck thus far every day. Mostly, however, he thanks Him for having brought Willie into his life. That is what truly matters to him.

He cranks down the windows of the truck for the last few miles so that he can smell the clean air filled with the scent of the pines. He loves this smell. Tries not to let it pass him by without him taking advantage. The narrow dirt drive looms before him and he pulls into it naturally, almost by instinct now. The cabin is near the same as it has always been. A pleasant smoke drifts from the chimney, signaling that Mabel was at the stove more than likely working at something for supper. His stomach rumbles as he pulls to a stop and gets out of the truck, stretching his gangly limbs in the soft breeze.

Fletchie Henderson sits on the porch steps reading a book as he approaches. The boy gives a hearty wave at the sight of Lester. He'd taken Willie's death hard. Who wouldn't? A boy loses his father, it'd be normal to expect a deep sadness to set in. He tries to talk to the boy as much as he can. He looks to have grown three inches every time he comes back by, which is often. The door of the cabin opens as he reaches the steps and Mabel, her belly growing bigger each day, steps out onto the porch to greet him.

She smiles at him as he doffs his hat to her, holding out an envelope for her to take. She used to not want to take the money that he'd offer her, but it only seemed fitting with him having set up in the hills around her property in the first place. Besides, he'd made a promise, and Lester meant to keep such a promise.

"How is he?" she asks, taking the parcel from him and rubbing her swollen belly.

Lester nods. "Right as rain, far as I could tell. How ya feelin', Mabel?"

She smiles again. "Sick most mornin's. But it's gettin' better each day. Doc Monroe came by today to check on everything. Way it's sitting in the stomach, he thinks it might be a girl."

Lester smiles at the thought of a little girl running around. "Like the sound of that." He turns and takes the two steps down from the porch and back onto the grass. He rustles Fletchie's hair as he passes him. The boy laughs and swipes at Lester's hand. Lester smiles back at him and turns toward the trees.

"Be havin' supper ready 'fore too late this evenin'. Stop on in and get ya a plate when you're finished."

Lester waves toward her on the porch, still proceeding toward the edge of the woods, past the shed and pig pen and on. "Will do. See y'all in a bit, then." Both Mabel and Fletchie give another wave as Lester walks on, away from the cabin to the treeline.

As he gets closer, he lets out a long, loud whistle from his lips. Pearl, having been half-asleep on the porch, springs to her feet and runs at the sound. She leaps from the porch and lands with her legs already pumping when they touch the grass, sprinting toward Lester. He waits for a moment at the edge of the woods while the dog catches up. He bends down to scratch her hairy ears, pulling a bit of biscuit wrapped in a handkerchief from his pocket. He breaks off a chunk and lets her eat for a moment, continuing his petting as she gobbles down the treat. He then stands and lets her look toward the expanse of hilly woods, making sure she doesn't give any kind of sign that there might be something out there waiting for them before he continues, her trailing next to him all the while. Together they fade into the thick brush and towering pine trees that cast shadows before them in the soft light shining through the branches until the brush swallows them up and out of sight.

THE END

AUTHOR BIO

C.F. LINDSEY IS A FULL-TIME WRITER and 9th grade English teacher in Northwest Arkansas. After shirking a promising law career, C.F. donned his trusty Resistol and hopped a train before landing on a riverbank where he began writing fiction. His works of short fiction and literary criticism have been featured in *Failbetter Magazine, The Wilderness House Literary Review, The Wagon Magazine, Heavy Feather Review, Nebo: A Literary Journal*, and other online and print publications. An avid fly fisherman and former trout fishing guide, C.F. draws a great deal of inspiration for his fictional characters and stories from the profound, natural interest instilled in him through countless hours on a riverbank or in a tree stand with his father as a boy. When not writing, teaching, or daydreaming about living in the Old West, he enjoys spending time in the natural beauty of his Arkansas home with his loving wife, Alyssa.

ACKNOWLEDGMENTS

THERE ARE COUNTLESS PEOPLE who deserve mention here. If I miss anyone, I am truly sorry. Let me see now, though, thank you for everyone's support, guidance, and love through the process of making this novel possible.

None of this would have been possible without the love and support of my beautiful wife, Alyssa. Thank you, honey, for all that you do.

To my father. You've been a supporter of me through thick and thin. I have never known a truer friend. It has finally happened. Thank you.

To my aunt, Terri White. The countless hours of research you completed on my behalf for this novel made the writing of this book a smooth process.

To my little brother, Conner. Thank you for your support, love, and friendship.

To my mother and father-in-law. Thank you both for accepting me into your lives and showing me support and love. It's more than I could have asked for.

To Dr. John Vanderslice. If it wasn't for your Novel Writing class at UCA, I'm not sure this novel would have made it out of my head and onto paper.

To Jon Billman. A reader. A friend. A mentor. Thank you.

To Hayden Tweedy. Thank you for all that you have done to support me throughout the years. I'm grateful to have a friend like you to tell me when my writing is crap and to go do it again. Thank you for your friendship and honesty.

To Brett Baker. Thank you for your friendship. Also, thank you for the use of your name and general rugged demeanor that helped take Sheriff Michael Baker from a flat character to a full-blown outlaw to be reckoned with.

To my family for your love and support. Thank you.

To the folks at April Gloaming Publishing. Thank you for believing in my work and helping to bring this story of the South, and of Arkansas, to life. I am truly grateful.

To anyone I missed mentioning, let me thank you here. I am truly blessed with a loving group of family and friends that support me and want to see me succeed. Thank you all for everything.

ISBN 978-1-953932-00-6

90000

9 781953 932006